Breaking Rules

S.B. ALEXANDER

Chapter 1

Montana

I RAN DOWN THE EMPTY HALL of the brick building that I now called my school. *Argh!* Another new school. Another new town. More strange people to ignore. More teachers to yell at me. More classes to fail. I wanted to scream holy hell at my mother. Actually, I had done just that before I stormed out of the house like a hurricane about to hit this coastal Southern town.

I hated my mom at the moment. We had one of those tense mother-daughter relationships. She was constantly complaining about something I'd done, and I was constantly complaining about her many boyfriends. Granted, it was partly my fault we were on our second move in the last year. I'd gotten expelled from my last school for defacing the walls of the gym with my beautiful artwork. Not only that, I ran with a wild crowd that, according to Mom, was only going to get me in more trouble.

"New York City is full of opportunities for teenagers to get into trouble," she'd said during an argument.

My response had been, "Then you should've thought about that before you decided to live close to your publisher."

With my tardy note in hand, I skidded to a halt outside my computer science class, when a five-foot girl barreled out, dancing on one foot then the other.

The edge of the door hit me square in the forehead. The sudden excruciating pain made me wince. "Fuck." I had a mouth on me, thanks to a couple of my mom's former boyfriends. Nevertheless, I narrowed my gaze down at the bouncing brown-haired girl.

"Oh, I'm so sorry. I have to pee. I have a small bladder." With a painful expression on her rosy face, she ran down an empty hall, spewing the word "yikes" several times until a door creaked and she was gone.

I held my forehead. No doubt a bruise would be forming. *Great!* I was officially the new girl with a third eye on her head. I dared anyone to bully me on the subject.

A bald-headed man holding a dry-erase marker greeted me at the door. "May I help you?" he asked in a curt tone.

Jeepers. I didn't even get, "Are you all right?" Yep, my senior year should be one crazy ride. I mean, if my first day was starting off with a painful bang, I couldn't imagine how the rest of the day or entire year would even go. All I knew—I was the new kid on the block, and that sucked the big one.

I handed my late slip to the bald-headed man, whose name—Mr. Salvatore—was scripted on my note. He glanced at it then back at me with lines creasing around his dark eyes. "Name?"

"Montana Smith."

"Well, Ms. Smith, you're extremely late. Take a seat." He balled up the note then tossed it in the trash can.

I stifled a yawn as I strode into the room with my hand still attached to my forehead. It was useless to tell the teacher I'd overslept, as did my mom. We'd been up all night, unpacking boxes. Regardless, late was late, and nothing I did or said would correct that.

Beady eyes flickered my way. While other students took my arrival to check their cell phones underneath their desks, I searched for an empty seat and found two. One was in the front row, which wasn't happening. The other seat was tucked away in the back next to a window. *Wow! Pay dirt!* At my last school, that seat would have gone for high dollar.

I crossed the room then down the aisle until I reached the empty desk. I was about to drop my backpack at my feet, when the boy in the seat next to mine peered up at me with brooding sea-green eyes and the longest lashes on the planet. I wasn't exaggerating. His lashes fell to the tip of his strong patrician nose. Maybe I was stretching the truth a bit. I didn't give a shit. All I saw was a boy with eyes that dampened my panties.

I shuddered, the act snapping me out of the lustful world I lived in.

I didn't ogle guys too much, and I wasn't a slut, but a girl had needs. Mine were stronger than most, at least among my friends at my last school—the same friends I'd had to say good-bye to. A growl zipped around in my head.

"Ms. Smith." Mr. Salvatore said my name as though it was a swear word.

I snarled over my shoulder.

He dipped his bald head. "Seat. We're all waiting on you."

Well, keep waiting while I admire.

The corner of Gorgeous Brooder's mouth turned up. Bingo! He liked me. *Who wouldn't like me?* I had long, wavy blond hair, the kind that boys liked to run their fingers through. I was sassy. Okay, the spunkiness in me could fill up a high-rise building in New York City. I had no shame. Oh, and I didn't give two cents about what people thought of me.

"You should sit down," a girl with a mousy voice said to me from the desk in front of mine. "The teacher will send you to the principal's office."

I laughed. Then my mom's words ran through my head. "Remember, no trouble." My reply to her had been, "Remember, you promised we would spend time together."

The teacher cleared his throat.

Gorgeous Brooder Boy, who wore a black T-shirt with the words "Funk You" spray-painted in red, raised a thick eyebrow then lowered it as he sized me up.

Goose bumps bloomed to life over my entire body. I knitted my eyebrows more at myself than at Funk You. Goose bumps were for those girls who got all mushy over a boy. I wasn't one of those girls. Sure, I loved boys and sex and having a good time, but mushiness and love didn't fit into my life or vocabulary, not after I'd gotten my heart ripped out of my chest by the only boy I ever loved. Not to mention, I'd seen my mom get hurt too many times when one of her dates dumped her.

Mousy Girl dug her fingers into my arm, breaking me out of my stupor. Instead of snarling at her, I planted my ass in the hard wooden chair.

Mr. Salvatore glared at me one last time before he resumed writing on the dry-erase board.

I stole a look at Funk You to find he was piercing those sea-green eyes of his right through me. What I wouldn't have given to have his long lashes tickle every part of my body.

I shivered. "What?" I asked in a low voice.

He shook his head, grinning.

I leaned over my desk until my boobs were pressed onto the top. His gaze flew to my cleavage.

"Any parties in this town? Or do you know any taggers?" My fingers itched to show this clean town my colorful graffiti work. However, from the confusion on his face, he clearly didn't know what a tagger was, or maybe he'd just never seen a set of size C cups before.

I scratched that last thought. As mouthwatering as he was, I would bet he'd had those strong hands or even his thick lips on a set of ta tas. I held back a snort at that last word. I'd always found the boob slang funny, especially when a former beau of my mom's used the word constantly.

Mousy Girl whipped her blond head around, her ponytail swaying. "Shhh."

"That bruise on your head is growing," Funk You said in a Southern drawl.

Automatically, I touched it as I squeezed my thighs together at the sound of his Southern accent, deep and smooth. I would have to thank Small-Bladder Girl for making her mark on me. "It's nothing." It hurt like a pisser. I also learned that phrase from one of my mother's boyfriends. "Back to my question. Parties. Taggers. Music. Dance. Booze. Or is this a dry town like in the movie *Footloose*?"

Mousy Girl sneered at me with her wide hazel eyes.

"Seriously," I said to her in a hushed whisper.

At the moment, Mr. Salvatore was oblivious to the class as he wrote the syllabus on the board. It was the start of the school year, and the class already looked bored. Hardly anyone was writing. Bladder Girl came back in with a smile that wrapped around her head. I had to laugh. I knew how it felt when my back teeth were floating and my stomach hurt in pain from a full bladder.

Funk You chuckled. "You always this forward?"

"Do you always brood?"

He lost the gorgeous smile as his light-brown hair fell over his forehead, and his eyes darkened. Or at least I thought they did. *Scratch that.* Fire burned in their depths.

"Hey, I'm sorry. I tend to be…" I had to think of the word.

"Rude?" he asked.

I shrugged. "I wouldn't say I was rude as much as I would say I call it like it is."

Mr. Salvatore turned around. "In this class, we'll discuss theory and coding. I will also assign a senior project that you'll learn more about tomorrow. In addition, we'll spend one day per week in the computer lab either applying what you learn or working on your project."

Funk You began doodling in his notebook.

I sat back and crossed my arms over my chest. With my low grade point average, I should have been paying more attention if I wanted to graduate, which I did. My goal for the year was to bury myself in books and study my ass off. At least that was the plan.

"Pouting?" Funk You asked.

I splayed my fingers on my cheek then lowered each one, leaving my middle finger showing.

He chuckled.

While Mr. Salvatore droned on about quizzes and grading, I rubbed my fingers lightly over the growing lump on my forehead.

"Maybe you have a concussion," Funk You said.

"And maybe you have a stick up your ass."

"You know what happens to girls with feisty attitudes around these parts, Hannah Montana?"

Heat squeezed the life out of my cheeks, thinking of all the naughty things he could do to punish me. But calling me Hannah Montana was enough to flare my nostrils like a bull in a ring. Everyone always thought they were hilarious when they blurted out "Hannah Montana."

He gave me a wry grin. "I hit a nerve."

"You know, I thought you were a badass when I first laid eyes on you. I was wrong." My voice rose. "You're a dick like the rest of the men on this planet."

Surprise, surprise. Thirty pairs of eyes, including the teacher's, were now staring at me.

"Ms. Smith." Mr. Salvatore's tone was icy. "I suggest you watch your language, and not another word for the rest of the class. This is your final warning."

He didn't need to say "or else." I knew the next step was heigh-ho, heigh-ho, off to the principal's office I would go. At my last school, I'd lived in the principal's office, mostly for mouthing off. Physical fights weren't my thing. Then again, many students over the years had been afraid of me. Some girl I'd befriended once told me it was my confidence. Maybe so. Or maybe it was my height. I was about five foot eight, slender, big boobs, with a face that got the attention of a modeling agent, if that said anything about my beauty.

As pathetic as it sounds, I was saved by the bell.

Students pounded out of the classroom as though they were headed for a Black Friday sale. Funk You pushed to his feet, watching me the whole time.

"You got a name?" I asked. "It's not fair you know mine."

His thick lips split into an amazing smile that practically knocked me out of my chair. "Train Everly."

I thought about asking him why his parents had named him Train, but I had my own issues with my name. Besides, his name was super cool.

I rose, trying to shake off the aftereffects of the explosion that had rocked my body from the minute I laid eyes on him. Then I began yelling in my head. *Guys never affect me the way this dude does.*

"Well, Hannah Montana. We have beach parties. We don't dance. We do drink. And if you don't like music, then you're not welcome at our parties."

I clenched my fist as I headed for the door, wanting desperately to go all Muhammad Ali on him even though he had me soaked to my core, but Mr. Salvatore held up his hand when I reached his desk.

I puffed out air as I frowned at Mr. Salvatore. "I know. My mouth. I talk too much. I have to pay attention. And if I don't, you'll send me packing."

Pressing his lips into a thin line, he smoothed his fingers over his mustache. "I give students two chances. You've used one today."

Yippee. I loved rules... not.

I saluted him like a sailor, thanks in part to a military dude who dated my mother. Oh yeah, I had a closet full of male stereotypes that I'd learned a habit or two from. That was how many men my mom had dated.

I dashed out and ran smack into Small Bladder Girl.

Her big brown eyes danced with excitement. "Hi. I'm Elvira. You're new here."

I nodded. "Well, Elvira, do you have to pee again?"

She was swaying back and forth as she held her backpack. "I just wanted to say I'm sorry about your head. It looks like it hurts."

"Nah. I'll live." My gaze traveled down the hallway as though imaginary hands had guided my head that way. Train was talking, or more like arguing, with Brad Pitt's twin. *Yum.*

Elvira tracked my line of sight. "Which one? Train or my cousin, Austin?"

"Do all the boys in this school look like they belong in Hollywood?"

Elvira busted out laughing.

"I'm Montana, by the way, and don't you dare make a reference to that Miley Cyrus show."

She snorted. "I wouldn't dream of it. I hate when people start singing that Elvira song. My mom loved the Oak Ridge Boys, so I'm stuck with the aftermath of her desires."

It was my turn to snort. "My mom decided to name me after the state I was born in."

"It seems we'll get along just fine, then. Come on. I'll introduce you to Austin, and you can call Train a dick again. Austin will love to hear that."

"I'm not so sure Train will," I said more to myself than to her.

When I skirted around a Gothic boy, I spied a blonde rushing up to Austin as though she was eager to talk to him. "Who's the blonde who just walked up to Austin?"

"That's Reagan. She was sitting in front of you in computer class. She has a thing for Austin."

I didn't recognize Mousy Girl. Then again, I'd had a front row seat to the back of her head.

"Train," a deep male voice shouted from behind us.

I tossed a look over my shoulder and was met with a football soaring through the air with my name on it. Elvira grabbed my wrist and pulled me toward the lockers just as a whirring noise clipped by my ear.

Jeez. This school was more dangerous than the halls of my last high school in New York.

Train caught the ball like an NFL player.

"Good thing he plays football," Elvira muttered.

I touched my racing heart, letting out a deep breath. "Good thing you have quick reflexes."

She giggled. "I couldn't let you get hurt a second time."

The bulky dude who had thrown the football sped past, and Elvira punched him in the arm. "Derek, you're not supposed to throw in the halls."

He glared down at her from his six-foot height. "I can do what I want. Besides, I was throwing the ball to my quarterback."

I rolled my eyes upon learning that Train was a quarterback. I shouldn't be stereotyping, but the girls at my last school had been all giddy over the quarterback, Deacon Shale. He didn't have the drooling good looks Train had, but I would bet the girls in this school were gaga over the hunky football player. "Isn't football reserved for the field?"

Derek raised a thick dark eyebrow. "You must be new in this school."

Train stalked up with Austin, beaming at me. "Don't pick on the new girl."

I blushed. *I never blush at a boy.* I was mentally searching my body for the lust that should have been making me squeeze my thighs together rather than that mushy, swoony, heart-stopping feeling.

Austin's brown gaze swept over my entire body. "Hey, cousin. Who's your gorgeous friend?"

I mentally raised an eyebrow. No goose bumps, no butterflies, no lust with Austin, and he was gorgeous. *Weird.* Then my attention shifted to Train, whose gaze licked every part of my body. In my head, I broke out in hysterics as my damn skin tingled.

"This is Montana." Train said my name with a heavier Southern drawl than before, and again, my body was leaning toward him, wanting him to read bedtime stories to me while his fingers did naughty things to my body.

Austin slapped his denim-covered leg. "Like Hannah Montana?"

The heat flushing through my body turned to a raging fire. I scratched my nose with my middle finger.

Austin lifted one white-blond eyebrow as Elvira swatted at him. "Leave my new friend alone."

I could certainly handle my own battles, but I stuck out my chin a bit more, happy as my former cat when I'd scratched his ear that a person I barely knew had my back. Regardless, it was time for me to skedaddle. Bonding was great, but I wasn't worried so much about Austin or anyone making the Hannah Montana reference as I was about Train and the urges I had to give him a sexual test-drive. I couldn't risk any sip out of his fountain. With my luck, he would snag my heart and probably rip it out like Nikko had.

Just as I went to take a step, a loud bang tore through the hall, sounding as if a bomb had detonated. Chaos erupted. Girls screamed. Boys shouted. Doors slammed. Kids pushed one another. Teachers darted out of nearby classrooms, waving kids in. Like everyone else, I rushed to the nearest room, but I tripped over someone or something. I scurried to my feet only to be pushed down again by people running to get away. *For fuck's sake.* I crawled in between people running in all directions, when a muscled arm, smelling like the ocean, wrapped around me, a hand clasping onto my boob. But I didn't care where anyone touched me as long as I got out of harm's way.

"In here," Train said in my ear when I was upright.

Before I could protest or react, he was pushing me into the boys' bathroom. As soon as we rushed in, the fire alarm trilled, jolting me back to life. Then a man's voice blared from the overhead speakers in the hall. "This is not a drill. Head to the nearest exit in an orderly fashion."

"Come on." Train held out his hand. "It must be a fire."

I hoped to hell it was just a fire and not some crazed kid who wanted to blow up the school. I slid my hand into his large, rugged, and protective one. When we emerged from the restroom, a faint smell of smoke made its way into my nostrils.

A sea of students paraded down the hall, their voices droning on as though nothing had happened. Then again, I shouldn't have been freaking out. I attended a school in New York, where we'd had a few scares of students getting through security with guns and knives. One boy had even threatened a teacher with his gun.

"Something happened in the chemistry lab," a girl in front of us said.

"You know the drill, people," a deep male voice shouted ahead of us. "File out to the front lawn."

I didn't know the drill, and neither did my heart.

Students began to whisper. Others were texting and shuffling along with the group.

"Um, Montana." Train's syrupy Southern voice was medicine for my frayed nerves. "You don't have to cut off my blood circulation. I kind of need my fingers to throw a football. Otherwise, Coach will have a coronary if I can't play."

"Aren't you shitting your pants?" I asked.

"Not really. I'm a lifeguard. I can't be scared when I'm saving lives."

I let go of his hand. No one else seemed scared. So I shouldn't be, either. "So a quarterback and a lifeguard?" I wouldn't mind seeing him in swim trunks.

"Do you have a problem with that?" He sounded hurt.

"I bet you get all the girls."

He leaned in. "Jealous?"

"You're not my type." *Liar, liar, pants on fire.*

He shook his head as we stepped out in the fresh humid air. I couldn't tell what his reaction was. All I knew was my life wasn't in danger... or maybe it was. Maybe Train would be the end of me.

Chapter 2

Train

PEOPLE LITTERED THE SCHOOL GROUNDS everywhere. Police cruisers, fire trucks, EMS rigs, and cars began to line the street beyond the parking lot. No doubt parents who had gotten wind of the possibility of a bomb had raced to the school, which wasn't surprising since one text could go viral in the blink of an eye. Not only that, but tons of kids lived close by. So parents could be at the school in no time.

Teachers and police officers directed us away from the building. Montana and I followed the crowd to the far edge of the lawn where it met the sidewalk. We piled up side by side as though we were in a lineup at a police station. Montana kept searching the waiting parents as though she was looking for a place to run, or maybe she was looking for her parents. I knew mine wouldn't rush down to the school. My mom would have if her arthritis didn't keep her in a wheelchair most of the day. My dad, though—highly unlikely he would ditch work. We didn't have the tight father-and-son relationship that my best friend, Austin, had with his dad.

Since my parents had divorced, I hardly saw my dad. Sure, we talked or he bailed me out of jail when needed, but we didn't hang out or watch football games together. Although he did make a point to show up for my football games and the occasional practice. He loved telling me how to play the game. More importantly, he didn't want me to fuck up my chances with the University of South Carolina football scouts watching me this year.

Out of nowhere Austin planted himself in between Montana and me. "Hey, man."

I almost high-fived him. When I thought about my old man, my brain went on a downward spiral. Plus my libido was in overdrive with Montana's coconut-scented shampoo wafting under my nose. But I would take having Montana next to me over my dad. Or maybe not. Girls weren't good for me, and I wasn't good for them, even though I itched to run my fingers through Montana's long, wavy golden-blond hair.

The funny thing was I had a hard-on for chicks with auburn hair. Maybe I was delirious from her scent. Or maybe my delirium stemmed from the fact that I'd grabbed her dick-squeezing tit, by accident of course, although I wasn't a breast man. That hunger was reserved for Austin. I got fired up over a woman with long legs that went on forever, and that bill fit Montana.

"Wow. First day of school and boom," Austin said. "Word is Drew Morris is responsible."

I shook my head. Drew Morris was a grade A klutz. I only knew that quality about him because he was my ex-girlfriend's cousin. But he wasn't a kid who would do anything destructive intentionally.

Montana's big blue eyes sparkled in the sunlight. "Is he a relation of yours?"

Austin snorted. "Fuck no. The dude shops at a different mall, if you know what I mean. He always has since grammar school."

I drilled my gaze into Montana more, trying to figure her out. She seemed so reserved compared to how she'd acted when she blew into computer class as though her shit didn't stink. I imagined it didn't. Then again, she had been shaken. To me, the loud bang had sounded more like a firecracker. Whether it was a bomb or a firecracker, my instinct had been to rescue like I had done several times when swimmers had been in distress. Although the torment I was suffering from as the hot morning sun beat down was because of how her soft tit had felt in my hand. I wanted to feel more of her. She was beautiful, and my fucking jeans were taut to the point that sweat was sliding down the side of my face.

Drew emerged from the school with a paramedic on each side of him. His carrottopped mass of hair was covered in white flecks. His freckled arms didn't show any signs that he had hurt himself.

The students around us clapped.

"Glad you're okay, Drew," a girl shouted.

Montana sighed heavily. "Yeah. It's nice to see he didn't get hurt."

"I agree, Hannah Montana," Austin said.

She spit fire on my best friend. "Look, moron. My name is Montana. Not Hannah or Hannah Montana. You got that?" She pushed her chest almost into his.

Austin held up his hands as his white-blond eyebrows disappeared into his hairline. "Chill, girl. Jeez. You're a feisty one, aren't you?"

Feisty, moody, pouty, gorgeous, bold—I could go on and on.

She huffed as she stepped away.

"Maybe we'll get the day off," Austin said as though he hadn't just gotten his ass handed to him by a girl. "Who's up for the beach?"

The tension was gone. The day was looking brighter.

I ran a hand through my sweaty hair. "We've got football practice."

It was only nine a.m., and the Southern heat was unbearable. I should be accustomed to it. *Hey, asshole, you're sweating like a pig because of the girl next to Austin.* Whatever. The ocean sounded good right about now.

"At three this afternoon, numbnuts," Austin said. "It's surfing time. We can party at your beach house."

I could work off some frustration. "I'm in."

"Han—I mean Montana. Do you want to come with?" Austin asked.

"I can't," Montana said.

Thank God. My body couldn't take seeing her in a bikini. "I could also use a drink," I mumbled.

Austin pulled out his phone. "Sounds good to me. Just don't break anyone's collarbone."

Principal Flynn walked out, straightening his tie over his large gut, then wiped sweat off his head with one of the handkerchiefs he kept on him at all times.

"Have you seen Derek, Elvira, and Reagan?" I asked Austin. I'd been so caught up in Montana that I hadn't seen what happened to the others.

Austin tapped out a text. "They're fine."

Principal Flynn cleared his throat through a bullhorn. "Okay, students. We've had an accident in the chemistry lab that I'm afraid will take all day to clean up and make sure the school is safe for your return tomorrow. If anything changes, we'll have updated information on the school's website tonight."

Montana grumbled.

I leaned forward slightly, angling my head around Austin, then pinned Montana with a glare. "Did the principal say something that bothers you?"

Her nose wrinkled, then a fucking smile broke out on her luscious lips. "None of your business."

Rein in your dick, asshole.

Our little banter ended when students hummed their praises over Principal Flynn's announcement. Kids dispersed in all directions. So surfing, beach time, and drinking would ensue, or one or two beers at most. I couldn't drink that much with football practice later that afternoon. Sun, beer, and heat weren't a good trio. Not to mention, I'd been cutting back on drinking since I landed at the police station back in June. Any trouble from me would ruin my chances of a scholarship with USC. They'd heard that I'd broken the Clemson quarterback's collarbone at a party, and even though Clemson was a huge USC rival, they weren't pleased with me. Neither were my old man and Coach Holmes.

Elvira's squeaky voice brought me out of my reminiscence. "So a beach day?" Her heavily mascaraed eyes flashed with excitement. "Montana, come with us."

Montana hurried away, faster than the speed of light. "Sorry, I can't. I have to help my mom unpack."

Elvira chased her. "Come on. It will be fun. We'll watch the guys surf, and we can get to know one another."

Their voices faded, and I admired Montana's fine ass before Austin stepped into my view. "You want her, don't you? Need I remind you that you don't do blondes."

"You know I've sworn off girls."

"Man, what about sex?" Austin's voice rose.

"Dude, once you have sex with a girl, they want more. And by more,

I mean they want a steady relationship. They want status, a football player to marry, and money. Besides, Nina fucked up my mind. I'm not ready for steady."

"Who said you had to give your dying love to a girl for a one-night stand?"

"Man, I got football to think about, not girlfriends." Besides, one ride in Montana's honey hole would surely lead to something I wasn't ready for.

His lips quirked up. "You keep telling yourself you don't want a piece of that ass." He flicked his thumb over his shoulder at Montana.

I started for my Hummer. "Let's go. The waves are calling our name." Besides, the more we kept talking about Montana, the harder my dick would get.

Chapter 3

Montana

I WALKED PAST COPS, AMBULANCES, AND kids excited about a day off from school as I trudged home. I should be excited too. I had a day to explore my new town and help Mom unpack. Part of me was elated that I didn't have to sit in school on such a beautiful day. But I had been having fun trading barbs with Train fucking Everly, although I knew I should stay far away from him. The last time I'd been drawn to a guy, the fallout had been heart wrenching. Fast forward two years later, and I hadn't fully recovered.

"Are you going to talk to me?" Elvira asked, running up to me. "Is everything okay? Did the incident with Drew freak you out, or are you running from something?"

I was always running. I tried not to make many friends because why bother when I would only move again. It was hard, though, when the kids in this new school were open, nice, and fun. At my last school, everyone kept to themselves, so it had been super easy for me not to get attached. Plus, my former high school was much larger in size, with hundreds more students than Palmetto High.

I pounded my feet against the pavement as I passed houses and moss trees.

Elvira ran in front of me then held up her hand. "Montana?"

With trash cans on my left and the street on my right, I came to an abrupt halt. "What?" Immediately, I felt bad for acting like a ninny. "I'm sorry. I didn't mean to bark." My nerves were still sizzling from the whirlwind morning I was having. The chemistry blunder paled in comparison to the way Train affected me. Or maybe the heat was getting to me.

"No worries." She studied me. "Did my cousin try to get in your pants already? Or did Train say something to make you mad? Train can be a dick sometimes."

He seemed to know how to push my buttons. Not only that, this girl had me pegged, which was both odd and scary. The only person who could read me well was my mom, and only because I didn't let anyone else get close to me.

I briefly glanced at a passing car.

Wrinkles formed on Elvira's smooth forehead. "Oh my God. That's it. Train has gotten under your skin."

"It's been a crazy morning," I said. "I should get home. My mom has probably heard about the lab explosion and is panicking." I was surprised she hadn't shown up at school or called me.

"So the morning didn't go well. Come with us to the beach. You can give Train a piece of your mind."

That didn't sound like a bad idea. "You seem like a fun person, but I can't be your friend." With the street quiet, I hopped off the curb and went around her. "I don't stay in one place very long."

She rushed to my side. "Are you and your parents gypsies or something?"

"Nah. I've gotten expelled from schools and, in some cases, not allowed to return."

"Seriously? What in the world do you do to get expelled?"

I lifted a shoulder. "At my last school, I painted a wall in the gym." I'd painted a great scene with boys playing basketball. That wall had needed some character to liven up the place.

Flecks of sparkles around Elvira's eyes glimmered in the sunlight. "Like graffiti?"

My antenna went up. I could be in more trouble than I thought if she tagged. I'd always had a hard time saying no to anyone who wanted to tag. "Yeah. Are you into graffiti?"

"Pfft. I couldn't paint a nail if you asked me to."

I giggled.

"Ah. I got you to laugh. See. We can be friends. So what if you leave town. I'll come visit you."

My heart burst open. "That's the nicest thing anyone has ever said to me."

"Really? If that's all it takes, then I won't tell anyone you're easy."

Please tell Train that I am. "So what do you do for fun other than the beach?"

We crossed the street of the dense neighborhood where houses sat amid trees, shrubs, and flowerbeds.

"Mainly parties, movies, and football games. Oh, and sometimes we head into the city to the Music Farm."

"I like music of all kinds. Is that a place for concerts?"

"They showcase newer bands that are coming on the scene. My mom loves that place. She used to live there when she was dating my dad. Anyway, I live over two streets from here. And you?"

I pointed ahead of us. "My mom found this beautiful plantation-type house that we're renting."

"No dad?"

I'd never had a dad. "He died in Iraq." According to my mom, she'd had a one-night stand when she was twenty with a boy who had taken up a summer job at her father's feed store in Montana. Then the boy joined the military, and one year later, she found out through a friend that a roadside bomb had killed the guy.

Elvira touched my arm. "I'm sorry."

I shrugged. "I never knew him." My mom hardly had, either. Sometimes I thought that his death was the reason my mom didn't want to settle down with any man. She was afraid she would lose him like she had my dad, even though her relationship with him had hardly been what anyone would have called serious.

"So, beach?" Elvira angled her face up to the sun. "The heat is oppressive, and the ocean sounds great. Plus, there are hot guys who'll be in nothing but board shorts while surfing."

I considered her a moment as I thought of Train in swim trunks. The heat was getting to me, and the beach did sound amazing, although I wasn't a good swimmer. The farthest I'd gone into the ocean was knee-deep to cool off. I had a phobia. If I couldn't see what was under the water, then swimming wasn't my gig. "I don't own a bathing suit."

She sized me up. "Mmm. I'm shorter than you, but we look about the same size." She glanced at the cleavage poking out of her V-neck blouse. "I think I'm a little bigger in the breast area. But I do have a dresser full of bathing suits. Give me your address." She whipped out her phone. "And your number. I'll be over in thirty minutes."

I gave her my info, then she left. As I walked the rest of the way home, I wanted to cringe. I wasn't ashamed of myself in a swimsuit. Far from it. What I was afraid of was Train. *It's not like you're going to fall for the guy today. Besides, you're here in this town to complete your senior year, maybe get into an art school, or maybe work at an art gallery, or both. For now, enjoy the sun, the new friend you have, and make it a blowout year. Fun doesn't equal trouble.* That was my problem. Fun for me was tagging buildings, putting my mark on something, or hanging with a guy who didn't want anything in return. Maybe Train didn't want anything in return. And I had promised my mom I wouldn't tag.

I ambled up the path that led to our wraparound porch, wiping the sweat from my upper lip. As soon as I trudged through the front door, a rank odor hit me.

"Mom," I called out. "What's that smell?"

"I'm back here in the guest bathroom," she said.

I dropped my backpack at the base of the stairs. Pinching my nose, I padded down the hall that jutted off from the open living area. I found Mom mopping the floors.

"What happened?"

She lifted her blond head. "Toilet broke. Wait. What are you doing home from school? What happened to your head?"

Automatically, my hand went to my bump. "First, I had a small run-in with a door. I'm fine. And school's out for the day because of an accident in the chemistry lab. And you thought this town was going to be quiet."

She dropped the mop and pulled me in for hug. "Are you okay?"

I flinched slightly at the sound of the mop hitting the floor. Gently, I pushed her away. It was definitely too hot to be touching anyone. "I'm good. Plus, I think I'm going to vomit with that smell."

She laughed—a sound I hadn't heard in a while. She'd been stressed because of me, her book deadlines, and life in general. Sometimes I hated that I was a stress marker for her, but she'd kept blowing me off in New York. Anytime we'd had plans to spend time together, something came up with one of her new books, or she had a publicity tour, or a new guy garnered her attention away from me. I got that her books brought in the loot for us to survive and even live in a beautiful house with some luxuries, but she had to take time for her daughter.

"Hot isn't the word. The air conditioner doesn't work, either." She smoothed a hand over her wavy hair, showing her sweat-soaked underarms. "It's a beautiful house, although I see why we got the rent so cheap."

No air. Rancid smell. The ocean was calling my name. "Do you mind if I head to the beach?"

She picked up the mop and resumed dragging it across the floor. "Homework?"

"Mom, I didn't make it to my second class. And my first class didn't give us any."

"You don't have a swimsuit."

"Elvira is letting me borrow one of hers. She'll be here soon."

Her blue eyes lit up. "You've made a friend? That's not like you, at least not on the first day. I thought you'd sworn off friends."

I liked Elvira. She seemed as though she could be not only a friend, but also a sister I never had. "I have to cool off. What better way than to throw myself in the ocean." Or at Train.

Mom gave me one of her award-winning *New York Times* best-selling author smiles. "I'm glad you're at least trying to fit in."

"You mean not tagging."

"Montana, this is your senior year. You shouldn't be spending it painting buildings or yelling at teachers or, dare I say, getting expelled. I know that I haven't been there for you. I also know that we didn't have to move again. But this quiet place with the ocean only ten minutes from us might inspire new ideas for future books, give us some quality time together, and keep you out of trouble."

"So we didn't move solely because of me?"

"In part, no. I've been researching coastal towns for my next novel, and I thought someplace hot, sunny, and relaxing would help both of us."

I scrunched up my nose. "Then why did you want me to take all the heat for us moving? That's not nice, Mom." As soon as I'd gotten expelled, she started mumbling about moving.

"Honey, I never blamed this move on you. I said a quieter town would be best so you wouldn't be tempted to get into trouble. You were running with a bad crowd in New York. I'm sorry I yelled at you this morning too. But need I remind you that graffiti is illegal here just as it is in New York."

I refrained from rolling my eyes. Otherwise, she would start yelling, and I wasn't in the mood to fight. I was hot, frustrated, and I kind of dug the plantation-style living. When I'd done some research on Charleston and the surrounding area, I found that plantations were developments that not only had houses, but schools, grocery stores, parks, a community pool, and other amenities. The best part was the quiet nights when I could hear the crickets that lulled me to sleep rather than sirens and the loud noises of a big city, which surprised me. I'd gotten used to the horns, people screaming for a taxi, and the energy.

"We've had this discussion, Mom."

"I've been thinking. Why don't you find a local art class that will tame that wild side of yours? Better yet, with all the local shops in the city, I would bet you could get a job at an art studio. I'm sure they would have classes too."

All I ever wanted was to show off my artwork, although I loved the large empty murals that buildings provided. Graffiti was freedom for me. Drawing in a sketchbook was confining and claustrophobic. Still, Mom was right. With all the local art galleries and shops within a ten-minute drive over the bridge, I could find a legal venue for my talent. "I would need a car."

Again, she gave me one of her brilliant smiles as sweat dripped down her neck. "You can use mine. I'm home, writing, anyway."

Now it was my turn to hug her. "Thank you."

She tightened her arms around me. "I want to turn over a new leaf together. I want to settle down for more than six months or a year."

I did too. I wanted to call someplace home. I wanted to call someone my best friend for once and maybe have a boyfriend. *Nah*. I scratched that idea. I wasn't ready to go that far. *Baby steps. A friend first.*

The doorbell rang.

"I look like hell," Mom said.

"It's okay. Elvira is cool."

When I answered the door, I found Elvira decked out in short shorts and a red bikini top peeking through a sheer pullover. She was holding up a white bikini in one hand and a baby-blue one in the other.

"The blue one," Mom said behind me. "It brings out your eyes."

I moved out of the way. Elvira came in and handed me the swimsuits then waved at Mom. "Mrs. Smith, I'm Elvira."

"Please, call me Georgia. And I apologize for the smell. We're having plumbing issues."

The smell didn't seem to bother Elvira. Instead, she broke out in a fit of giggles. "Are you for real? Did your daddy name you after a state too?"

"Nah, my daddy was a farmer, and Georgia means to till the soil," my mom said. "And my mom loved the name."

"I'll go change." I darted up to my room.

"It does kind of stink in here," Elvira said to Mom. "Anyway, you look very familiar."

I froze on the landing. My mom was a *New York Times* best-selling author, but she wrote under a pen name. Although she attended book events and did the occasional interview under her pen name, readers and authors in the publishing world knew my mom by her real name as well. She hardly liked flaunting her status to people, especially my friends, since she wrote erotica books. She wrote the kind that would make any shy girl blush and any parent either sneer or cheer. Mom didn't like the bad attention when it came to me. I really didn't care. I could handle myself, but I understood where she was coming from.

We'd encountered a parent or two in the last three years who had thought my mom was horrible for writing romance books with sex. I mean, come on. I hated when people judged without getting all the facts. All they had to do was read her books, which were the bomb. She'd given me permission to read them when we started talking about sex two years ago. My mom always said that an informed person was a better person to make the right decisions. Not that her books had instructions in them when it came to sex. But she knew how to take a story and characters and shape them in a way that by the end of her books, a reader would be cheering, crying, or yelling for the next book. And the sex scenes were done very graphically, but tastefully.

Elvira's voice hitched. "You're not from Hollywood, are you?"

"I get that a lot," Mom said. "Let's get something cold to drink while Montana gets ready."

If Elvira were going to be my friend, then I would eventually have to tell her about my mom. But it was too soon. We needed to build trust. But my mom's career wasn't important at the moment. I couldn't remember the last time I had worn a bathing suit, and that scared me to hell. Train would be at the beach. Train would see me in a bikini. I hit the side of my temple. *Get a grip, girl. You're Montana Smith. You don't care what people think.*

But I might care what Train thinks.

Chapter 4

Train

THE WATER WAS JUST THE right temperature to cool my heated body, although the waves sucked. "Not much in the form of waves today."

Austin straddled his board. "No, but this beats school."

He had a point. Now that I was dangling my legs in the water, I wasn't as tense, although a certain girl had my head in the wrong place. I couldn't stop thinking about how her soft tit had felt in my hand or how she'd leaned over her desk in computer class and all but showed me what she had under her tight-fitting band T-shirt. I was so dumbfounded at her boldness that I couldn't even remember what her T-shirt had said.

Austin splashed me, bringing me out of my haze. "So are you considering asking Montana out?"

"I told you. No girls this year."

"Man, you're going to have blue balls by graduation."

I chuckled. "You've heard of jacking off."

"Dude, there's nothing better than being tangled with a sexy naked girl."

"No shit. But we talked about this. The girls in this town don't want me. They want to be seen on the arm of a big-time quarterback. Look at Nina. The first chance she had, she ran to the Clemson quarterback and cheated on me with him."

"I know one girl whose name rhymes with Hannah who probably couldn't give a shit about you becoming a big-time football player for USC."

"She's trouble, and I don't need more trouble." I had no idea if she was or not, but I'd gotten an intense vibe that she could give me a run for my money. "My old man is still trying to smooth things over with the USC sports director."

"Fuck, dude. Your dad has power with USC. He's an alumnus and pays a lot of dues. Surely, he can do something."

My fingers were crossed that he could. "Whether he can or can't, I have to be the model player this year."

"Doesn't mean you can't date. Jeez, dude. Have you seen Montana?"

I'd more than seen her. I couldn't stop thinking about her, and the sad part was I'd just met her not three hours ago. "So when are you going to ask Reagan out?"

"Not sure. Maybe I'm like you. Maybe I don't want to get hurt."

"Dude, you've been salivating over her for a year now. She's sweet, has a rack that you like, and is feisty—just how you like your women. Hell, she told Montana to all but shut up in computer class." Reagan was the perfect match for my best friend.

"Enough about girls," he said.

We checked behind us for a wave. No luck. Not even a faint breeze to stir up the water. Ahead of us on the beach, rows of houses sat up on stilts, and kids from school started to filter in, spreading out their blankets. This area of the beach was normally quiet since it was private property, but my dad owned one of the houses, so we had access at any time.

"Wouldn't it be funny if I applied to Clemson? My old man would have a coronary." I chuckled, imagining my dad turning a thousand shades of red if I spilled that news to him.

Austin splashed me. "Where the fuck did that come from?"

I'd been thinking about a backup plan in the event USC didn't offer me a scholarship. "You said you didn't want to talk about girls."

"First, Clemson would never consider you since you broke their quarterback's collarbone. Second, your old man would never let you wear orange. And third"—he splashed me again—"we agreed that we would go to USC together. They're the Gamecocks, for fuck's sake. Girls love Gamecocks."

I rolled my eyes. "Chill. I'm only thinking."

He clucked his tongue. "Think about girls and not about Clemson, because if you so much as decide not to go to USC, then I'll be the one to cut off your head."

"Ah, you love me."

"Damn straight. Dude or not, we've been best friends since the second grade. We *will* do college together. It'll be our last hoorah of freedom before real life hits us."

I couldn't argue with him. College wouldn't be the same without Austin.

"We're not getting married," I said as seriously as I could.

He slapped a hand over his heart. "You know how to hurt a guy."

We both broke out laughing.

"Let's get a beer." He lay down on his board and paddled.

"I'll race you."

He had a head start, but it didn't matter. I always beat him. As we were reaching shore, I was about to pass him, when I glanced up and spotted Montana setting up a blanket not far from mine in front of my house. *Holy mother of the ocean. Kill me now.* Her breasts were practically spilling out of her baby-blue bikini top. I didn't get to linger on her amazing body because a wave pushed me, causing me to fall off my board. Not a wave in sight for the last hour, and suddenly nature decided to make me look as though I couldn't surf.

Austin was laughing at the shoreline when I got up. "Sucker."

I threw him the finger as I waded through the surf to get my board, which was caught in yet another wave. As I did, I checked to see if Montana had been watching me make an idiot out of myself. But she was absorbed in something Elvira was saying as she shimmied her hips out of her shorts, exposing more of her curves and those long-ass legs that I was picturing wrapped around me.

"You better get your board before that wave comes in," Austin shouted.

Before I could react, another fucking wave knocked me over. Once I resurfaced, I snarled at the sky or the sun gods for making me look as if I couldn't swim. I was a lifeguard, for fuck's sake. Good thing I wasn't trying to save someone. Then I dove in and swam a ways before I got my hands on my board. With another wave on my tail, I hopped on my board and surfed in.

I tucked my board under my arm as I met Austin on shore. "I need a beer." I had to get rid of the salt water invading my mouth, and I also needed to soothe my ego.

With our surfboards in hand, Austin and I trampled through the hot sand to our blanket, which was oh so close to Elvira and Montana.

"You want Montana so bad," Austin said.

I glanced down at my crotch to make sure the semi-boner I'd had in the water was gone. "How do you know that?"

He belted out a laugh. "Did you just check your dick? See. You want her."

"So what. I can look. Eye candy." I wasn't looking at Montana right now, though. If I did, I would have a permanent boner the rest of the day with my luck.

"Eye candy, my ass," Austin retorted. "You need to lick that candy."

Images of me licking Montana burned brighter than the sun. Before I had a chance to discard my board or grab a beer, Derek, one of our tight ends, trudged through the sand with a football in hand.

Derek tore off his T-shirt. "Let's throw. We can warm up before practice."

Fine by me. Anything to keep my gaze from wandering—or my mind, for that matter. I stuck my surfboard in the sand and barely eyed Montana. She was wearing big movie-star-like sunglasses with dark lenses, so I couldn't tell if she was looking at me. I hoped she wasn't since I was trying to calm my dick down.

I opened my hands. "Ball."

Derek tossed the football to me. Within a second, other guys spilled onto the beach—some with their girlfriends, others with coolers and chairs. I jogged down to the water's edge as Derek and our center, Lou, went long. Well, Derek went long. Lou, on the other hand, couldn't run all that fast. He was all neck and gut, and rightly so for the position of center. I reared my arm back and threw a perfect spiral as the ball sailed down the beach and into Derek's arms.

As I waited for him to return the ball, I caught a glimpse of auburn hair out of the corner of my eye.

"Heads up," Derek shouted.

Before I could react and take my focus away from the girl with snow-white skin, the football hit me in the side of the head. I stumbled backward, not feeling an ounce of pain. Instead, a sudden coldness blanketed me even though the hot sun bore down.

Nina, the girl who'd cheated on me, was there. The girl was supposed to be living in Florida. The same girl who'd sliced and diced my heart into a million fucking pieces sauntered down from the private beach access along the side of my house. She was dressed in a yellow halter top and bikini bottoms. Her hips swung, and her average-sized boobs bounced with every step. She had curves, but not as defined as Montana's.

What the fuck? I was analyzing the difference between a girl I'd just met and my ex. Maybe that was a good sign. Good sign or not, a haze settled over my brain. I hadn't seen Nina since the beginning of our summer vacation when she'd tried to apologize for cheating on me. I hadn't accepted her apology and never would. I also hadn't counted on her being at school this year. I remembered the day Austin told me Nina's father had taken a job in Florida and that the whole family was moving. I'd thrown a party to celebrate the great news.

Nina said something to Elvira, while Montana listened intently. *Talk about trouble.* That was Nina's middle name. The girl thought she owned the school. I'd been blind to all the bullying she'd done to other girls who'd dared to look at me. In my defense, no one had said a word to me about her antics, and I hadn't witnessed any while I dated her. Sure, she'd snarled at girls if they flirted with me, but I'd done the same to guys who'd flirted with her.

"Dude." Austin's voice snapped me back to the present. "I thought she moved."

I couldn't form words. My jaw hung open. My tongue was dry, and my mind was racing with how the fuck my senior year had just taken a nosedive. She would want to get back together, and that was *not* happening.

"You can't let her coax you into dating her again," Austin said. "I know you had mad love feelings for her. But remember, she gutted you."

Oh, I hadn't forgotten. My mom had counseled me on how first love sucked the life out of a person but that time did heal the wounded heart.

The hole in my heart from Nina cheating on me now had a large fucking steel wall erected around it.

Nina glided down the beach toward me as if she thought she was an angel. "Hey, baby." Her whiny voice hadn't grated on me when we dated, but at the moment, her high-pitched tone was cutting through my skin like a razor blade.

She went to put her arms around me, and I jumped back, holding up my hands. "I am not your baby." And so the fun began.

Austin crossed his arms over his chest. "Get lost, Nina."

She stuck her hands on her hips. "Kind of hard to do. My dad's job offer fell through. So I'm back. Sorry I missed the festivities at school today. My parents had to reenroll me into school before I could attend. But I'll be there tomorrow."

"Where's your Clemson boyfriend?" I asked.

"We broke up. So, Train, I was thinking that maybe we could start over."

Austin snorted. I literally choked.

She inched closer to me. "I miss you. We had such a great time together. I want that again."

I scanned the beach. Everyone was watching us. I shuffled back into the surf. "Nina, you're smoking some heavy dope if you think we're getting back together."

She squinted her gray eyes. "But we had plans for our future."

This time I got in her face. "Until you fucked them up. Stay out of my life. I don't date cheaters. So go find someone else you can cheat on."

Feigning a pout, she touched her heart. "That hurt. But you'll take me back." She stomped away, and by away, I mean she plunked her ass down on the blanket with Montana and Elvira.

"Breathe, man," Austin said.

Derek and Lou ran up.

"What the fuck?" Derek asked. "She's not here, is she? Please tell me she isn't going to ruin our football season like she did last year?"

Yeah, Nina had gotten in my head one too many times during football season last year. If we had a fight right before a game, that fucked me up. It shouldn't have. The anger in me should've grounded me to play the game, and I should have been able to take out my frustrations on the field.

"She's not." I was as sure as I was that water filled the ocean.

Derek slumped his massive shoulders. "Good. Now let's throw the football."

He was all about football. Sure, he had a girlfriend, Jan, who was a cheerleader, and they were inseparable, but we were starting our last high school season. So I had to get serious too. Not to mention, it was time to get physical and blow off some steam.

"Today is not your day, dude," Austin said. "I'm here for you."

"So are we," Derek and Lou said at the same time.

I knew I could count on them. But what could I do with Nina? Nothing. I couldn't kick her out of school. I couldn't do much except avoid her like the plague, and if I knew Nina, she would do everything and anything to get my attention.

I found myself locking eyes with Montana. Her big blues sparkled over the rim of her sunglasses. *Yes, that's my ex you're sitting next to. And watch out for her because she's evil,* I almost shouted. Instead, I released a breath. "Let's gather more guys to play."

Once we had a group of interested men, I said, "No tackles. Touch football." The last thing I wanted to do was get hurt or have any of the guys on the team get hurt. Coach would have a hernia.

As soon as we split into two groups of five, Montana ran down to us. Suddenly, football became history as I tracked every curve on her before settling on her chest.

Thankfully, Austin nudged me out of my lustful stupor. "You sure you don't want to lick that? She would take your mind off of Nina."

Montana's curvy body was taking my mind off of everything. I was dying to shape her hips, feel the silkiness of her skin, her wavy hair, and so much more.

She stuck each guy with a sexy look. "Why don't we play the girls against the boys?"

Derek busted out laughing. "Baby doll, you can't throw a football." His drawl was heavy on the last word. "This game is for men."

She lost the sparkle in her eyes as her nostrils flared. Then she held up one finger. "One, I'm not your baby doll and never will be." She displayed two fingers. "In what world do you think a girl can't throw a football?" She held up three fingers. "And three, are you afraid of a girl beating you at your own game?" She sneered.

Derek grinned, tossing Montana the football. She caught it with quick reflexes. "Then show us what you got."

Montana waved over Elvira and, of all people, Nina. If I was going to keep my shit together and Nina was there to stay, then it was game on. Besides, I felt nothing for Nina except maybe anger.

Elvira nodded at Reagan and Derek's girlfriend, Jan, who were sitting together on a blanket next to her. I thought about protesting but was suddenly interested to see how a friendly football game with girls would pan out, sans Nina. Then again, maybe I should speak up against the game. I didn't want Nina near me or touching me. I wouldn't mind Montana, though. But that wasn't a good idea, either. I would get a boner if Montana even came close to me. Hell, I'd gotten one in the water when I laid eyes on her.

Nina, Elvira, Jan, and Reagan surrounded Montana.

"Are you gals up to a friendly football game?" Montana asked.

"We're in," the girls said.

Derek glared at his girl, Jan. "You cheer, not throw a football."

"Aw." Jan pouted. "Is my hunky man afraid of five girls?"

Derek waggled his eyebrows. "You'll pay for this later."

"If you two want to have sex, then find a secluded spot," I said. "Otherwise, I'm getting a beer." I'd planned to reduce my drinking, but with Nina back, all bets were off on that topic.

Montana twirled the football. "So, you guys pick five, and the rest have to sit this one out."

Austin saluted her as he eyed Reagan. I quirked up one side of my mouth when Reagan blushed.

Austin picked the five guys, which consisted of me, him, Derek, Lou, and Bo, who was another teammate and husky like Lou.

The remaining five guys protested until one said, "It's better to watch."

"Touch football," Montana said. "We'll throw first. The end zone will be past that rock on the beach." She pointed to a large stone about ten yards down. "And the other end zone will be past the volleyball net.

Oh, and anyone who fondles boobs gets a kick in the groin." She pinned me with a glare.

All the guys swung their attention to me. I had no recourse or answer. I was guilty. Regardless, this was going to be a long, long day. As brutal as football practice usually was, I had to say that this touch football game would top my list of brutal.

Chapter 5

Montana

I GATHERED THE GIRLS IN A huddle. "Okay, I can throw a ball, but who's good at catching?"

Reagan raised her hand. "I am. My family always plays a friendly game of football on Thanksgiving."

Reagan, the mousy girl in computer class, wasn't so mousy. She was downright gorgeous with her hazel eyes, long dark-blond hair, and smattering of freckles. Not to mention, her voice wasn't so nails-on-chalkboard cringey.

"I'll cover Train," Nina said.

I bit my tongue as jealousy, hot and fast, coursed through me. I didn't do jealous, although part of me wanted to coldcock Nina for what she'd done to Train. Elvira had quickly given me the 411. Nina had cheated on Train. Nina was supposed to be living in Florida, and the school year might suck with Nina's return. I would've asked more questions, but Nina had parked her scrawny butt on our blanket even though she hadn't been invited.

I didn't want to sit and listen to Nina talk about how she and Train were getting back together and how she missed kissing him. Blah. Blah. Blah. I didn't have any claim to the guy, and I didn't want to get serious with anyone anyway, but Nina's thin voice was definitely grating on my nerves. That was enough to spur me into action. So football it was.

"You're back, huh?" Reagan asked Nina in a pithy tone.

I was beginning to like Reagan. She had some moxie that told me the two of us would get along great.

Nina flattened her lips. "Yeah, I am. Do you have a problem with that?"

"Stay away from Train." Reagan's voice had dropped a couple of degrees. "He doesn't need your cheating ways. And go near Austin, and I'll tear you a new one." The snarl on Reagan's face was priceless.

Elvira, who was sandwiched in between Reagan and Nina, swung one arm out in front of Reagan and the other out to block Nina. "No fights. Let's just have fun."

Aw, I wanted to see Reagan take down Nina. That would have been more fun than football.

"By the way, we haven't met yet," the brunette with the ponytail said to me. "I'm Jan. Reagan and I are cheerleaders. So what do you know about football?"

"I learned a couple tidbits from one of my mom's boyfriends." Joey had played for the Naval Academy. "All right. Elvira, you snap the ball to me. I'll throw to Reagan. Then the rest of us block the guys." *And Nina, keep your filthy paws off of Train.*

"Why don't we distract them by flashing our butts?" Nina asked. "That way, Reagan has a clear line to score."

I would bet that the boys would sink into the sand. I peeked around Nina. Train had a pained expression on his sweat-sheened face. I couldn't say for sure why he looked pissed, but I would guess that Elvira was right. Nina's return had thrown him for a loop. I was curious if Train still harbored feelings for the pretty auburn-haired girl. Then I tossed my curiosity aside. Their relationship was none of my business.

"Girl," Jan said, "while I would like nothing more than to tease Derek, he would freak if I showed any of the other guys my butt."

I wouldn't doubt that, considering he'd all but berated her for wanting to throw a football. Regardless, I had to agree with her that any game should be played fairly, not by distracting a group of guys, plus the large crowd on the beach, with our private parts.

"Come on," Austin shouted. "Today. The beer is getting warm."

"We're playing football, not stripping," I said to the group.

Everyone nodded except Nina. She rolled her eyes, and I wanted to pluck out each of those murky gray eyeballs.

Instead, I clapped. "Let's show them how to play this game."

We got into position, facing off with the five boys. All of them were sweaty and built, all ready to play except Train. He was still sporting a vibe that said he did not want to be there. I couldn't blame him. If Nikko, the boy who had broken my heart, was part of the gang I hung out with, I would be snarling, sneering, and protesting.

With the ball in hand, Elvira got in front of me then bent over at the waist and readied the ball. The other girls fanned out, each matching up with one guy. Nina and Train. *Argh!* Reagan and Austin. Jan and Derek. That left Elvira and me with Bo and Lou. Both boys had big guts, no necks, and scary looks on their faces. Surely, they wouldn't tackle us since we were playing touch football.

"Hike!" I shouted.

Elvira flipped the ball to me. I shuffled back a few steps while Bo was trying to get around Elvira. Lou, on the other hand, was coming at me like a rocket. Reagan had her hands up in the distance with Austin on her tail. I launched the ball at Reagan a split second before Lou's very large hands were on my waist. I stumbled backward, praying Lou wouldn't fall on top of me. I got my wish only because his arm went around me as he pulled me to him.

I let out a breath as our bodies mashed together. "Thank you for not falling on top of me."

He grinned, showing his dimples. "That was some throw. Wow."

Whistles peppered the ocean air. I shrugged out of Lou's hold to examine the field. Reagan had the ball and was running with Austin on her tail.

The crowd cheered and clapped as Reagan held her arms in the air, jumping up and down.

"Touchdown," Jan yelled. Then she stuck out her tongue at Derek.

He grabbed her by the hips and hauled her into the water.

"Hey," she protested. "We're playing football."

"No, you're not," Derek said. "You and I are going for a swim."

Jan giggled as he carried her into the water.

Then, just like that, Nina followed suit, trying to pull Train into the water. He yanked his hand out of hers faster than lightning and stomped back to his blanket.

"Yikes," I said as I watched Train.

Lou followed my line of sight. "Yikes is right. Now that his ex is back, it's going to be a long year and even longer football season." Then he jogged along the shore toward Elvira.

I didn't move. The tension between Train and Nina was as thick as the humid air, and I wasn't even close to Nina or Train. He dipped into his cooler, pulled out a beer, flipped the top, and guzzled the contents. Then he crushed the can. Elvira and Lou were right. The school year would be long and sucky.

Elvira ran up to me. "That was awesome. Your mom's boyfriend must've been good."

"He was the quarterback for the Naval Academy."

As if Train heard me over the hum of the waves lapping at the shore, he whipped his head in my direction, glaring as though he had daggers shooting out of his sea-green eyes. Well, damn. Maybe I upset the sexy Southern boy along with Nina. After all, I had suggested that the girls play. That only served to drive Nina directly to him.

"Let's go swimming," Elvira said.

"You go ahead." I dug my feet into the hot sand, oohing and aahing as I scurried over to Train. Once on the blanket, my burning feet thanked me.

I'd planned on apologizing to him until my stomach did one of those wild somersaults that got even wilder when he sized me up in a slow and languid fashion. Oh hell, if I didn't run now, it would be Nikko all over again. Not that Nikko looked like Train. Actually, there were no similarities between them except what they did to my stomach. Where Train was six feet, Nikko was five ten at most. Train's messy brown hair didn't compare to the blond curls that Nikko had. Neither did the color of the eyes. I didn't have a particular physical trait that I was drawn to when it came to boys. Well, maybe eyes. Nikko's were stark blue, but so full of want and need and pain. With the exception of the color, Train had that same want, need, and pain in his eyes—more so now than when I'd met him in computer class.

I mentally shook off Nikko and Train as the sound of the waves rolling along the shore drew me back to the bubble of hell that I was trapped in as I stood with Train so close to me.

His nostrils flared. "Did you hear me?"

"Come again."

"Normally, I wouldn't repeat myself, but for you, it's important." His tone was deep and serious.

Again, my stomach was riding some massive wave. I wanted to say something, but my tongue seemed to be glued to the roof of my mouth, while my eyes traveled over his delicious chest all the way down to the line of hair that disappeared into his swim trunks. At that moment, all I could think about was one of my mom's detailed descriptions in her book titled *My Heart to Take.*

Train waved his hand again. "Forget it. You're not worth it." Then he grabbed his surfboard, or more like yanked the long board into his hands, and jogged into the water.

That went well.

Nina emerged from the water like some water goddess. She pushed out her small breasts when Train brushed past her. He didn't get far. She wrapped her fingers around his arm. If he was talking, I couldn't hear a thing. I moved over to my blanket, grabbed my sunglasses, and sat down.

Elvira said something to Nina and Train before she returned to our blanket, squeezing water out of her chin-length hair.

Train shook his head at Nina.

With my chin, I motioned at the couple. "Care to share."

"Train's pissed," Elvira said. "Rightfully so. Nina's going to be trouble this year. I can feel it."

"He seems mad at me, though," I said.

She grabbed a towel. "Maybe because you disrupted their manly game, and he wanted to stay away from Nina."

I understood more than anyone how going to school with your ex could be tense and irritating. I'd had to watch Nikko date other girls. Suddenly, nausea settled in my stomach. I didn't want to cause relationship trouble. Not that I could since Train and Nina weren't dating, but all kinds of other thoughts surfaced, like Nina trying hard to get Train back and causing trouble for anyone who wanted to date him. I was all about trouble, but not that kind. My trouble was tagging, not fighting with kids.

"I tried to apologize," I said.

"Give Train a couple of days to get over the shock. Actually, it will take a few days for all of us to get over the shock."

"Do you think he'll take Nina back?" *Please say no.*

"No way."

I let out a silent breath as a Kenny Chesney song pumped out of the speakers close by.

Elvira sat on the blanket then dipped into her bag and removed a comb. "That pass was awesome. I'm in awe that you can throw a perfect spiral like you should be playing football."

I leaned into her shoulder. "Thank you." Not many people gave me compliments. I mostly got sneers or ribbing for things I said or did. The only compliment that kids had given me was for my artwork when I was part of a graffiti crew in New York. It was only my first day with these folks, and I'd already gotten two.

I was enjoying my compliment high, when Nina breezed toward us. She picked up her bag off the sand. "I need to go."

"So you show up to cause trouble, and now you're leaving," Elvira said with some grit in her tone.

"It seems you're not happy to see me either," Nina said. "I thought we were friends."

"In your dreams." Elvira pulled the comb through her hair. "Stay out of our group. And as Reagan said, leave Train alone. He doesn't want you here, and neither do we."

Nina pursed her lips. "That's for him to decide. And he will come around." She hiked her bag on her shoulder and left.

I clapped.

Elvira rested back on her elbows. "She hurt Train. And no one hurts my friends."

I liked Elvira and Reagan. I could get used to having them as friends. But I had to do everything possible to stay away from Train. I had my own heart to protect.

Chapter 6

Montana

I WALKED INTO COMPUTER CLASS EARLY the next day, feeling sunburned after a day on the beach with my new friends. Once Nina had left, that thick pressure hanging over us lifted. The girls had played a game of volleyball, while the boys had either played football or surfed. I hadn't ventured into the water too far, only to dip my toes in and cool off. Between my phobia of not seeing beneath me and not being able to swim all that well, I'd stayed as close to shore as I could. Elvira and Reagan had wanted to bathe in the sun, anyway. So I hadn't felt the pressure to hang out in the water with them.

Aside from Mr. Salvatore at his desk, I was the only student in the room so far. It had been difficult to sleep last night with no air conditioning and a sunburn to boot. Mom had said that the landlord was sending someone over within a couple of days to fix the air conditioner and the toilet. I'd gone from my bed upstairs to a lounge chair on the back deck, but that hadn't lasted long since the mosquitos had been out in full force. The good news—the rancid smell from the broken toilet was gone, thanks in part to the air fresheners my mom had set up around the house.

"Montana." Mr. Salvatore lifted his pen. "A word, please."

I moseyed up to his wooden desk, which was strewn with papers.

He smoothed two fingers over his mustache. "How are you doing after yesterday?"

Considering no one had gotten hurt, I was good. My mom had checked the school's website last night. The post had explained that the experiment Drew had been working on involved sodium and water and that Drew had accidently used the wrong amount of sodium, which had caused the mini boom I'd heard. Luckily, he'd been wearing his safety gear.

"Aside from the sweaty walk to school, I'm cool."

"On another note, I checked your records. Your grades are borderline. From what I've seen, one failed class, and you won't graduate. So I want to reiterate—no trouble from you."

I chewed on my bottom lip, wondering why he even cared about my grades. However, his warning did remind me that my mom wanted me to get a tutor, at least for science and math classes. She'd offered to help me with English if necessary. It wasn't that I'd failed any of my classes at my last school. I'd barely passed my core subjects, which was why my GPA sucked. Hence, no room for errors.

"Yes, sir," I said then found my seat, the same one I'd been in yesterday. I contemplated finding one as far away from Train as I could. But that would mean I would have to take one of the front-row seats that had been empty yesterday. *No, thank you.* I would rather have Train breathing down my neck than Mr. Salvatore. Although if Train were in a mood like he was yesterday, then he wouldn't be bothering me. So I was probably free of any distractions. I giggled. Train was a distraction whether he was speaking, cranky, or none of the above.

Kids slowly filtered in. Behind them, Reagan sashayed in, holding her phone to one ear while she played with the end of her braid. "I'm serious." She slid into her seat as she continued speaking into her phone. "My mom saw Casey Stewart in the grocery store yesterday."

In all the schools I'd attended, I hadn't heard anyone get excited over my mom or even mention her pen name. Of course, Reagan could have been referring to someone else. Listening, I stared at the beam of sunshine spilling in through the window.

"Her latest novel isn't out yet," Reagan said. "I can't wait, either."

I swallowed hard. She was talking about my mom. So much for keeping her identity on the down-low. Then again, Mom and I always knew something like this could or would happen. At least Reagan was excited, although Mom didn't worry about the kids as much as she did about the parents. She'd had a run-in with a group of parents when I was in the tenth grade. They'd felt she was writing the devil's work, which was one of the reasons we'd moved that year—that and I kind of tortured one of the parents' daughters. I'd put a garden snake in the girl's locker with a signed note. Not the smartest move, and it had been my third strike with the principal at that school.

I sat back, blowing out a breath. Calling this town home for more than a year might be rather difficult, especially if anyone started bad-mouthing my mom.

When Reagan hung up, I tapped her on the shoulder.

"Hey, that was fun yesterday," she said. "Well, except for Nina showing up. But afterward, it got better."

"Yeah. I had fun playing volleyball with you gals. So I didn't mean to eavesdrop, but I love to read. Who is Casey Stewart?" I wanted to learn how much she knew of Casey Stewart. My mom had diehard fans who knew her real name, and if we were keeping my mom's profession a secret, I needed to know what I was up against.

Her hazel eyes glistened. "Oooh." She glanced around at the handful of students who sat three rows over. "She's an amazing author. She writes all kinds of steamy and erotic romance stories. My mom is a huge fan of hers."

"Have you read any of her books?"

She wrinkled her nose. "Of course. My mom doesn't mind. She's not one of those moms who thinks sex is evil or shouldn't be talked about. Here in the South, some parents don't like their kids to even talk about sex."

Not talking about sex wasn't relegated to the South, but was common in cities and towns all over the country. "Does your mom know for sure that she saw this Casey author?"

"She went up to her to ask but then backed out. My mom can be a little shy sometimes, especially when she fangirls someone."

The first bell rang.

I made a mental note to talk to Mom after school to let her know that some people knew Casey Stewart was in town.

Students ran in, shoving their phones in their pockets or purses. Voices buzzed through the room as kids talked to their desk mates. Clasping my hands together in my lap, I stared at the door with my pulse in overdrive. Elvira rushed through the door much like she had yesterday when she'd needed to pee. At least the bump on my head had gone down overnight, but it was still sore to the touch.

Elvira waved as she quickly breezed over to me. "I had a great time yesterday."

"I did too. Thank you for bending my arm to join you." Although I could've done without the Nina scene or Train's brooding.

She tucked a strand of her short brown hair behind her ear. "Let's hang out after school."

I nodded as she dashed off to her seat.

The class filled up minus Train, and my pulse slowed until he swaggered through the door at the sound of the final bell. *Well, darn.* He zeroed in on me as he ran his fingers through his damp hair, which was curled at his nape. My pulse sped up, ratcheting up even more as I gawked, wanting nothing more than to run my hands along Train's strong jaw, which looked to be as smooth as a baby's bottom.

His long, thick legs carried him across the room, his jeans riding low on his hips. He wore a gray T-shirt that read Puck This.

My pulse was speeding at a hundred miles per hour as he got closer. If there was air conditioning on in the room, I couldn't feel it. My body broke out in perspiration, and I tried to remember if I'd put on deodorant that morning. But the closer he got, my hygiene and anything else went out the window, especially when he practically snarled at me.

Now my pulse was racing a different tune. I bit my tongue, afraid I might blurt something out and get sent to the principal's office. Then I scolded myself. The principal's office didn't scare me. After all, I was an expert when it came to dealing with principals. I was Montana Smith—spunky, courageous, and brazen. That last word was how my mom would describe me. She'd always said that in the little time she knew my father he'd been brazen.

Train plopped down into his chair, which was, at most, an arm's length from mine. It didn't matter if he was two arms' length from me. His ocean scent knocked me back in my chair, idling my ire for a moment. I would bet he went surfing that morning before school. Or maybe that scrumptious odor was all him with no colognes or salt water.

Mr. Salvatore passed out papers. "Today, we'll discuss HTML coding that will help with your senior computer project."

Papers shuffled around as whispers followed.

I knew how to use a computer. I knew how to get around on my phone, but I'd only heard of HTML from Mom when she was discussing her website with her web designer. She'd explained that HTML was computer language that bolded letters or changed font colors.

I raised my hand.

Mr. Salvatore picked up a sheaf of papers. "What is it, Ms. Smith?"

"I thought we were learning about Photoshop." I'd read that was one of the topics in computer class. I'd been interested to learn the program since an artist could do some neat things with Photoshop.

"You will. But for your project, you'll also need to understand HTML."

I flipped through the two-page document he handed out as he continued to talk. On the top of the first page was the definition of HTML—Hypertext Markup Language.

Mr. Salvatore rested on the edge of his desk as he scanned the room. "You'll pair up with a partner to build an app. The requirements are no games, nothing related to sports, and the app has to be something unique that could benefit an organization or company. For example, think business; think school. What app might benefit a business owner or maybe a college student? Some of your parents run big companies. Start to pick their brains. Go through the App Store and see what's out there. And no copying code from other apps on the web. You'll be given a program that will help you build the app from scratch. But the brains behind it and how you build it come from you and your partner. I want to see a preliminary outline in two weeks. Any questions?"

All I got from his speech was the word "partner." I had to pair up with someone, which meant my partner could be the panty-wetting boy next to me. A droplet of sweat trickled down my lower back.

Elvira raised her hand. "Do we get to pick our partners?"

"I've taken the liberty of pairing you up," he said.

The class protested. "We want to pick our own partners," one boy said. "I don't want my grade affected by someone who isn't going to do the work."

Mr. Salvatore pushed down his hands as though he were bouncing a basketball. "Quiet. I choose the teams. Call it a primer for the adult world you'll be facing soon. You won't always get to work with friends."

Another boy on the far side of the room said, "This is bullshit."

"Mr. Radcliffe, would you like to pass this class?"

The red-haired boy clammed up.

Please don't put me with Radcliffe. I would be in hell trying to get that boy to work with me. *And please don't put me with Train.* Otherwise, I wouldn't learn anything. Instead, my panties would be damp the entire time. Or with my luck, Nina would clobber me for working with Train. Or after the way he'd snarled at me, we would be dueling it out. The latter would be quite fun. But then I wouldn't pass the class.

Mr. Salvatore picked up a notebook. "The partners are as follows." As he began reading off names, nausea swirled inside me. Kids began to whisper their excitement or dread.

"Ms. Smith and Mr. Everly, you two are a pair."

Train choked. The blood drained from my face, I think more because of his disgust when Mr. Salvatore had read my name. I jerked my head at Train. He narrowed his eyes at me, and they seemed to turn a wretched pukey green. *Yippee.* We were going to be a great pair at nothing other than failing. I sneered at him. He grimaced. I was ready to throw down because I wasn't about to fail.

"Okay, I want you to get with your partner and start brainstorming," the teacher said.

Everyone moved around until they were with their partners. I popped out of my chair and stormed up to Mr. Salvatore.

He opened his laptop. "What is it, Ms. Smith?"

"Um. I don't think Train is the right partner for me," I whispered. Thankfully, the noise level was rather loud with everyone talking.

He crossed his arms over his red golf shirt. "And why is that?"

"You said yourself that my grades are borderline, so I assume I would need an A to bring up my grades."

"So you think by working with Train, you'll fail?"

Oh, hell yeah. "He's got football and practice." I couldn't exactly say whether Train was smart or not. That wasn't even the reason for my protest. But I certainly wasn't about to tell Mr. Salvatore that I didn't trust myself around Train. Nor could I argue that Train didn't like me or want to work with me since Mr. Salvatore had said he was teaching us life skills. He also probably wouldn't accept the argument that Train had ex-girlfriend issues I didn't want to deal with.

"Regardless of football, Ms. Smith, Train has to do the work like everyone else."

"But why did you put me with him?"

He studied me. "I'm giving you an opportunity to get a good grade in this class."

"Wait, you think I can get a good grade with Train?"

"Ms. Smith, if you have any questions about Train's capabilities, ask him yourself. Now return to your seat and start brainstorming with your partner."

With all the willpower I could muster, I headed back to my seat, only to find Train with a smart-ass grin.

"Didn't get your way?" His Southern drawl about made me weak in the knees.

I flared my nostrils. "What's your problem?"

"Right now, it's you complaining. I don't want to work with you, either." He pinned me with his gaze as if I were the scum of the earth. "Tell you what. You think of an app, and when you're ready, I'll do my part. That way, we spend little time together." He slouched in his seat.

I ground my teeth together. "I was going to apologize for yesterday, but forget it. I'm glad I suggested football. Or maybe your little ego is also bruised over a girl throwing a football." Derek's had been.

Train let out a low growl.

"Ah, I hit a nerve. Mmm." Maybe all his anger yesterday hadn't only stemmed from Nina's presence. Maybe he was upset over me throwing a football. I nibbled on my bottom lip as I considered him. "You know what? I might pay a visit to your coach and see if I can try out for the team. Girls do play football." Okay, I was stretching things a bit. Girls did play football, but I didn't. Plus, Train was irritating me with his snarl and the disgust written all over his face.

He bared his teeth. *Bingo.* I hit a really deep nerve. He wanted to be an ass. *Well, let the games begin.*

Chapter 7

Train

COACH HOLMES YELLED AT US from the sidelines as the offensive
line huddled together while our defense waited for us to break.
"Get your heads out of your asses and move."

I wished mine were up my ass. Then I wouldn't be replaying how
fucking pretty Montana had looked when she'd gotten all mad and
stormed up to Salvatore to find another partner. I'd thought she was hot
when she walked into class yesterday, setting the classroom on fire as if
she owned the room, even more so after I watched in utter fascination
how she'd thrown the football during our quick game on the beach
yesterday. She hadn't hurt my ego. If anything, her with a football
affected my libido.

Sure, I was trying not to get involved with girls, but I was ornery
because Nina was back. I'd thought my senior year would be smooth
sailing. *Fuck. Not in the least.* On one hand, I had Nina to deal with.
No, you don't. You don't owe her anything. On the other hand, I had a
gorgeous blonde who was fire and ice, a combination that excited me.
But the combination also gave me reason to pause.

Montana could shatter my heart into a million more pieces than Nina
had. The key word was *could.* If things did get serious with Montana
and we broke up for some reason, my gut told me she would flay me in
some way. I was still raw from Nina's betrayal. Regardless, one kiss from
Montana—and I mean a tongue-action, spit-swapping kiss—would fry
me to a crisp. When I thought of her, I thought of a black widow. One
bite, and I was hers.

Derek nudged me. "Are you here?"

I stepped out of the huddle for a second, took a breath, then focused back on the team. "Okay, replay." We would practice the same play until we got it right. If we could get past our defense, which was as tough as the school we were playing on Friday night, then we had a chance to win.

When we broke from the huddle, Derek blocked me. "Whatever you do, don't look at Coach."

"Moron, why did you say that? Of course I'm going to look now."

I glanced over at Coach Holmes, who was decked out in shorts, a Palmetto High T-shirt, a ball cap to match, and a whistle around his neck. My gaze went from him to the girl he was talking to. After a second, I realized Coach was deep in conversation with none other than Montana.

No fucking way. When she'd said she would talk to Coach about trying out for the team, I honestly hadn't thought she was serious. The entire team turned to see what had grabbed my attention.

"You don't think she wants on the team," Derek said.

She certainly did if it meant fucking with me, and it wouldn't be a good fuck. I wasn't against girls playing sports, but football? A girl would disrupt the dynamic of the team. Plus, someone like Montana would get hurt. I'd had to hold my breath when Lou almost fell on top of her yesterday at the beach.

Austin, who was sitting out a play to massage his hamstring, was listening intently to Coach and Montana.

When he darted his gaze to me, I waved him over. "Please tell me she's not asking to try out." My voice sounded as if a pissed-off chick were gripping my balls.

"She gets on the team, I'm out," Derek said.

I slapped him on the back of his helmet. "Montana was right. You are a chauvinist."

Derek pushed me. "So the fuck what? Football is a man's sport. Women don't belong on the field with us. Think about it. Do you want to ram a female? We'll hurt her. Our opponents would have a field day. So if not wanting to hurt a chick makes me a chauvinist, then I'll wear that title proudly."

Lou joined us, his chubby cheeks red and sweaty. "I agree. I'm all for women having equal rights, but I'm not breaking their bones. I almost creamed Montana yesterday, and if I had, I could've really hurt her."

I was kind of jealous that Lou had gotten to touch Montana, as in having his body pressed to hers. "She's not getting on the team."

"Don't be so sure," Austin said. "Coach is listening to her. He wants to see what she can do."

I didn't know what the rules were for girls on the football team, but the teams we'd played didn't have any girls on them. I removed my helmet. "Let's break for water."

Coach would be mad we weren't practicing our plays, but I didn't care. Hydrating was key; at least that was my excuse.

I jogged up to Coach as Montana was leaving. She swayed her sweet hips over to Elvira, who was waiting in the end zone.

"What's going on, Coach?"

The team fought for cups and Gatorade from the cooler we had sitting on a chair.

He lifted off his cap, ran a hand through his sweat-soaked black hair, then returned the cap to his head. "The new girl in school wants to try out for the team," he said in a pained voice.

"You're not going to let her, are you?" I held my breath. I agreed with Lou about women's rights and all, but I also agreed with the guys about not wanting to see some brute from another team pummel a girl into oblivion, Montana no less. That wasn't happening while I was captain and quarterback of this team.

She could stomp her feet, pout, shout, and do anything else to get her way, but she was not stepping foot on this field as a Titan. No way. No how. Granted, I'd acted like a dick to her in computer class that morning, but she had no idea how much of a dick I could be.

She tossed her wavy hair over her shoulder along with a glare, which she followed by sticking her tongue out at me. I smirked when I should have been running in the opposite direction. The blue-eyed bombshell brought out a wild side of me that I never knew existed.

Coach blew his whistle. "Two laps around the track then hit the showers."

I poured myself a cup of Gatorade. "Well? Are you?"

"I have to at least see what she has to offer," he said.

"No way. Tryouts ended two weeks ago."

"If I don't, she could make a stink with the school board. Flynn won't like that."

I knocked back the cold liquid then threw my cup in the trash can beside the cooler. "Do you hear yourself?" I asked, my voice rising. "She's a girl who could get hurt."

One side of his mouth quirked up. "Are you afraid she'll show you up?"

Yes. "No. Of course not." So she could throw a football like a pro, but that was only one throw in a relaxed environment. I shouldn't be worried. She wasn't about to take my position, although she would definitely distract me from the game.

"Hit the track," Coach said.

Instead of joining the team, I jogged in the opposite direction toward Austin, who was talking with Montana and Elvira. When I approached, the threesome broke up. Montana and Elvira beelined up the hill toward the school. I almost ran after them to shake some sense into Montana. Instead, I decided to cool off.

"Coach is giving her a shot," Austin said. "Can you believe it?"

Hell no. "Do you know where she lives?"

"I'll text Elvira," he said.

"Send it to me when you get it. I've got to do my laps. By the way, how's the hamstring?"

"Sore, but I'll be ready for Friday's game."

I hoped so. Austin was our best wide receiver. He was my go-to man on the field along with Derek. I left Austin and finished my laps. Then I hit the showers. The locker room droned with Montana's name bouncing around.

"Calm down," I said to the team. "Coach is only letting her so he doesn't get shit from the school board."

"But you saw her throw," Derek blurted out as he tore off his shoulder pads.

"There's more to making the team than throwing a football. She's got to know the game. She's got to do all the drills that we had to do.

That's the only fair way. Right?" I wasn't sure how much she knew about the game.

Lou scratched his matted blond hair. "Who are you trying to convince—us or yourself, dude?"

"Both," I said.

The entire team broke out in a fit of laughter. I groaned.

"You're afraid of her," Derek said. "You like her too. And don't deny it. I see it in your eyes. You're hungry. I got that vibe yesterday on the beach after Nina left."

I groaned again, mainly at the Nina reference. At that moment, I decided to stop snarling every time Nina's name was brought up. I couldn't walk around biting off heads, especially those of my team. They needed me to be the captain they believed in. Not only that, but Derek was right. I hadn't stopped ogling Montana when she jumped to hit the volleyball or when she dove, trying to keep the ball alive. She certainly was taking my mind off of other people.

I stripped down. "So Montana is hot. Doesn't mean I want anything to do with her," I protested.

Derek folded large arms over an even larger chest as he eyed me with small brown eyes. "Take her to bed. Get her out of your system, or else you're going to be shit on the field. She might help you get over Nina too."

I *was* over Nina. I just didn't like her assuming that she and I would be a couple again. "Isn't happening, man. In fact, absolutely no girls for me this year." I walked my bare ass into the showers.

"I'll believe it when I see it," Derek said at my back.

The entire locker room broke out with barbs and laughter. *Whatever.* I was sticking to my plan of no girls. No distractions. I was going to concentrate on football.

Austin poked his head in as soon as I stepped under the shower. "Derek has a point. Get Montana out of your system."

I squirted soap in my hair. "When the sky falls, I will."

"I tried, guys," Austin said, his voice fading.

Guys booed while I finished showering. Then I toweled off and wrapped the terry cloth fabric around my waist on the way to my locker. Montana's name dropped from someone's lips.

I stood up on one of the wooden benches. "First, chill about Montana. Coach knows what he's doing." At least my fingers were crossed on that. "Two, I'm not going to use her to get my rocks off because you think that will help us win a game or to get over someone else. We'll win on Friday night based on our skills, provided you morons have *your* head in the game. Remember, Charleston High is one tough motherfucker of a team. So we need defense in tiptop shape. We also need the offensive line to do their job, and I will do mine." Then I hopped down.

One by one, they nodded. Several slapped me on the back before they left. Finally, when the locker room was empty with the exception of Austin and me, I dropped down on the bench.

Austin leaned against a locker opposite me. "I'll be one hundred percent. Don't worry about me. I texted you Montana's address. What's your plan?"

"I'm going to talk. Then afterward, I'm getting drunk." Or maybe I should get laid. Then maybe I wouldn't be sexually frustrated around Montana.

"Your mind is going a mile a minute," Austin said.

He knew me too well. "It's only the second day of school, and I feel like I've been in hell both days. If this is what senior year is going to be like, then I will need tons of girls and booze."

"There's my friend." He grinned. "Celibacy never helped me."

Chuckling, I got off my ass and dressed. "Since when has the girl magnet been celibate?"

"You got a point. Do you want me to come with you to Montana's?"

"No. I won't be long." My plan was to dissuade her from football. I couldn't have the guys on edge, and I had to keep order on the team and in my head.

Austin and I chatted about football all the way to my truck. After I was on the road for the one-mile ride to Montana's house, I turned up the Grant Lee Buffalo song on the radio, although I wasn't listening. I was debating what to say to her, but all I could think about was throwing her against the wall and kissing the fuck out of her.

I pulled up to the two-story plantation home with the wraparound porch. It looked like every other house in the neighborhood. The engine idled. *Get out of your vehicle and be the polite Southern boy you're known to be.* I'd had that illustrious distinction for most of my life until I'd put that Clemson quarterback in the emergency room. Then polite had gone out to sea.

I got out of my Hummer, absorbed the humidity, and strode up the driveway to the path that ran parallel to the house. After I climbed the four steps onto the porch, I raised my hand to ring the doorbell then paused. Montana's singsong voice floated through the screen door.

"Someone saw you in the grocery store yesterday," Montana said. "They know you're here."

"We'll deal with it," a voice that sounded almost like Montana's said.

I glanced at the Lexus in the driveway, trying to decipher what the heck was going on. When I turned back, Montana was staring directly at me through the screen door.

Chapter 8

Montana

I GLARED AT THE YUMMY QUARTERBACK. His hair was damp, his cheeks were red, and his impish smirk was sinful. "Are you a stalker?" I asked with my hands on my hips.

"Who is that, honey? The air conditioner man?" My mom's footsteps slapped on the tiled foyer as she came up behind me.

"Do you know how to fix air conditioners?" I asked Train. My body was tingly from his tantalizing male scent floating in through the screen door.

"Oh, hi," Mom said. "You're not the AC man."

"I'm one of Montana's classmates." Train's raspy Southern accent only enhanced the tingly sensation in my belly.

My mom pushed open the door as Train skirted to the side. "Come in." Then she glared at me. "Where are your manners?"

Train traipsed in. "Yeah, Montana. Manners." Then he batted his long lashes at my mom. "Hi, ma'am. I'm Train Everly."

She craned her neck up at him. "I'm Georgia." She planted on a warm smile. "Would you like something to drink?"

"No, ma'am. But it's deathly hot in here. Do you have someone coming to fix your air conditioner?"

"The landlord said it would be a couple of days," Mom said. "I think Montana and I might have to go to a hotel until we get it fixed."

That would be wonderful. Then I could get a good night's sleep.

"I could call my father. He owns a contracting business with a team of workers that have all kinds of skills. I'm sure he could get someone over here."

Mom's blue eyes beamed. "I couldn't ask you to do that."

"Why not?" I chimed in. "If it gets someone out before the they find our bodies shriveled up in here." Comfort was more important than ignoring Train at the moment.

Mom dragged her fingers over her forehead. "Honey, don't be so dramatic. And Train, if you don't mind calling your father that would be great. I'll let you two talk. I'll be in the kitchen." Mom breezed away.

Thank goodness her brain had cleared to accept help.

Train and I entered into a stare-down. Another minute of taking in all that was Train Everly was too much for my system. He made the heat in the house hotter with his presence.

"If you're here to talk me out of football, then leave. My mind is made up." I didn't care to play. My goal was purely to mess with him. Sure, I could think up other ways to screw with his head, but Derek's chauvinistic comment had stuck with me, and I got the impression Train agreed.

He pursed his lips together—lips that I couldn't take my eyes off of.

He snapped his fingers. "You want to kiss me. Don't you?"

I almost dropped my jaw then clamped it shut. "Not in this lifetime."

He inched closer with that smile that about made my knees buckle. "Do you always lie?"

I inched backward until my butt hit the bannister. My breathing ramped up as I threw my hands behind me to latch onto a spindle.

He raked his gaze over my face then lingered on my lips. "And what else is your mind made up about?"

"That it will be a cold day in hell before you kiss me," I said weakly.

He leaned down so his steamy breath was tickling my ear. "The way I see it, you'll be throwing yourself at me." He nibbled on my ear. "You have no willpower."

I lost my breath, my vision, and all sound of my mom, who had been making noises clinking glasses together. I planted my hands on Train's hard chest. "You're an asshat." Then I tried to push him away. *Tried* being the operative word.

"You're not playing football." His mouth hadn't left my ear.

56

The lust coursing through me gelled as I balled my hands into fists. "Get your ego out of your pants and think for once that women have equal rights."

That got him to step away with a scowl. "So if you can't show Coach what you got, you're going to the school board?"

I hadn't thought about that, but he had a good idea. I lifted a shoulder.

"Do you really want to make a spectacle of yourself?"

"If I got it, why not flaunt it? Besides, it might bring down all those egos on the team."

A muscle jumped along his jaw. "I'll make you a deal. You lay off the football, and I won't spread the word on who your mom really is."

I squinted at him as though we were standing in the bright sunshine. Reagan might've put the puzzle pieces together and blabbed to him, Elvira, and others. I'd always found it amazing how rumors spread so quickly through high school. The problem was my mom's identity wasn't a rumor.

My mom cleared her throat. I swung my gaze to her, hoping she could read my mind. *A little warning before you enter a room.*

"Did you happen to speak with your father?" Mom asked.

"I'm sorry, ma'am. I'll call him now. Excuse me." Train went out onto the porch.

"What is going on between you two? Are you dating?" Mom asked in a singsong voice.

I gently pushed Mom into the family room. "Shh. No. He's an ass."

"A handsome ass, Montana. And he's so polite."

All fake. "He's mad because I asked the football coach if I could try out."

My mom's red lips opened, her jaw almost slamming on the white carpet. "Since when do you play sports? Wait. You need to get your grades up. And what about a job and art classes?"

"I am taking an art class as one of my electives."

"Montana Smith, you are not playing football. You'll get killed when those boys tackle you."

I was hoping that Train would tackle me, but at that moment, I wanted to show him that girls could do what boys could do. "You sound like the football team."

She gave me one of her mom expressions with tight features and lines fanning out around her eyes. "They're right. You'll get hurt."

Footsteps clobbered into the house. "Excuse me," Train said. "My dad is making a few phone calls. I've got to run, but I'll call Montana when I hear from him."

"Does he have your number, honey?" Mom asked me.

I swiped Train's phone. If it weren't for the dire need of cold air, I wouldn't be punching in my number on his cell. When I was finished, I shoved his phone into his chest.

A barely there grin emerged. "It was nice meeting you, ma'am. Montana, we'll talk soon." Then he waltzed out with a swagger that I wanted to punch holes in.

I huffed. "I'm going to my room."

"It's okay to like a boy. Not everyone will break your heart like Nikko," Mom said, raising her voice as I climbed the stairs.

I could return with a barb about one of her boyfriends, how she'd gotten hurt a time or two, and that she should consider a steady man in her life. But I wasn't one to give advice. I'd only been hurt by Nikko. Still, a broken heart hurt, and I understood why my mom saved her love affairs or giving her heart away for the pages of her books.

I dodged one of the unpacked boxes as I threw myself onto my unmade bed. The cool breeze from the ceiling fan did nothing to relieve the anger that was burning my insides. Train had the gall to threaten me. I wanted to know how much he knew about my mom.

Then the blood rushed to my feet. Maybe Train did know, which was the reason he'd been sexually forward downstairs. And if he thought I was easy because my mom wrote erotica, then others at school would think the same thing. It wouldn't be the parents I would be worrying about or my mom's reputation. It would be my reputation on the line. With an entire school year ahead of me, I wasn't certain how I would handle the backlash of boys ogling or asking me out just to get laid. Sure, I was all for a date here or there or a one-night stand, but I didn't want to be dubbed a whore. I was beginning to understand why my mom wanted to protect me and my social life. I should find out what

Train knew about my mom. Then Mom and I could prepare for any onslaught of rumors.

I got up, retrieved my phone from the clothes-infested window seat, then texted Elvira for Train's address. I imagined she was the one who had given Train my info, so she shouldn't mind returning the favor.

Within a minute, his address was on my phone.

Thank you, I sent back.

Good luck, she replied.

I laughed out loud. Luck wasn't what I needed. Willpower was key. I had to refrain from throwing myself at him. *When you get there, get straight to the point.*

I checked myself in the mirror. My skin glowed with a sheen of sweat. My mascara was smudged underneath my blue eyes. And my hair was frizzy, as though I'd stuck my finger in an electrical socket.

Great. I'd officially looked like hell in front of Train. I quickly freshened up, brushed out my hair, twisted it into a bun, splashed on some blush—mainly to absorb the sweat—then went in search of Mom.

She was in her office, which was situated off the kitchen. I poked in my head. "Mom, do you mind if I borrow the car? I forgot to ask Train about our computer project. We're partners, and we should be working on it."

A warm breeze seeped in through the sliding glass door that overlooked the well-manicured backyard. Like my bedroom, her office had boxes littering the large space.

She lifted her gaze from her laptop. "Can't you call him?"

"I gave him my number, but I didn't get his."

"Fine. Don't be too late." She resumed typing on her computer.

I snagged the keys off the kitchen counter on my way out the door. I punched Train's address into the GPS on my phone then got on the road. The GPS said it was a two-minute drive. Before long, I was in Train's driveway. My heart beat in my ears as I cut the engine. I shouldn't have been so nervous. I talked to guys all the time.

I climbed out of my mom's air-conditioned Lexus. Dusk was setting in, but the sunless sky didn't change the temperature one degree.

I rolled back my shoulders and headed for the two-story brick home, complete with columns and a stone porch. I pushed the doorbell and let my gaze wander to the porch swing. Ooh, one of those would be nice on our porch. *Note to self: ask Mom to get a porch swing or rockers.*

The door opened, and a blast of cold air hit me along with a slew of welcomed shivers. I almost threw myself at the brown-haired lady in the wheelchair.

She smiled, showing perfect white teeth. "May I help you?" Her voice was dainty and very Southern.

"I'm here to see Train. I'm Montana."

"Sure. Come on in." She rolled back her wheelchair.

I entered the large, elegant foyer decorated with flowered wallpaper, an oblong glass table that had a vase of eucalyptus on top, and a fabric wicker bench adjacent to the door.

"Hi, I'm Train's mom, Lucy. I've met all Train's friends. Are you new in town?" Her red-painted nails stood out over the white capris she was wearing.

"My mom and I moved down from New York over a week ago. We're renting a house on the other side of Palmetto Plantation." I was curious as to why she was in a wheelchair, but it would be rude of me to ask.

She turned her chair and wheeled herself to the massive family room that looked out over the golf course. "Train!" she called out.

Heavy footsteps trudged from above, growing closer before Train appeared in a doorway off the family room. "I told you I would call when my dad got back to me." His tone was snooty.

"Train, you don't talk to girls like they're beneath you." His mother's tone went from sugary to salty.

Ah, someone was on my side.

His hard features softened. "Yes, ma'am.

"What's going on?" Lucy asked, her dark eyes appraising Train.

"Montana's air conditioning isn't working. I thought Dad might be able to help."

"Call him again," she said, holding onto the salt in her tone.

Train gnawed on his lip as he stomped away like a boy who had gotten scolded.

"Follow me," Lucy said. "We were about to eat dinner. Would you like to join us?" She wheeled herself down an open hall and through the same doorway Train had come in from.

I crossed the threshold into the gourmet kitchen, which also had a view of the golf course. "I didn't mean to interrupt your dinner. I can come back."

My mom had rented a beautiful house, but Train's was gorgeous and looked expensive. I wasn't that surprised, considering he drove a Hummer and the plantation homes were upscale.

She pushed a button on the arm of her chair, and it rose to the height of the marble counters. "It's no trouble." She pulled out a plate from a cabinet adjacent to the stove. "I love New York. Did you live in Manhattan?"

I inched in further until I was standing behind the island. "Yes, ma'am."

"When I think of New York City, I think of Wall Street. Is your dad a big-time executive?" she asked.

"My mom is. Dad died in Iraq."

"What does your mom do that would bring her from the big city to a small Southern town?"

"My mom works from home. Marketing." Not exactly a lie. Books required sales; therefore, my mom had to market herself, even with a big-time publisher.

Train trudged in. His shoulders were stiff. "She's not staying, Mom."

"Young man, I told you to watch your manners," she said tersely.

He sighed heavily as he locked eyes with his mom. I didn't see too much resemblance between them except the lips. Hers were as full as Train's.

Train crossed the kitchen and kissed her on the cheek. "I left Dad a message. I need to talk to Montana about our computer project. I'll be back in a few. Okay?"

Liar. Although we'd both told our moms the same excuse as to why we needed to talk. So I was a liar too.

Lucy's rosy face brightened as though she was the proudest mom. "Don't be too long. I'll keep your dinner warm."

Train opened the sliding glass door. "We're going for a walk along the golf path." He prodded me with his eyes. "After you, Montana."

Argh! The boy was... I couldn't think of a word except asshat. "It was nice to meet you, Lucy."

"You're welcome anytime," she returned.

Anytime meant never if Train had any say.

Once outside, the scent of freshly cut grass floated on a light breeze. Train stomped down from the deck to a flower-lined stone walkway then to the black tar path along the golf course. An old man was hitting a ball from the sand onto the green.

"I told you I would call you." Anger laced his words.

I clenched my fists at my sides. "So it's okay for you to show up at my house unannounced, but I can't show up at yours without an invitation?"

He ran a hand through his hair, his sea-green eyes seeming to darken. "We didn't have anything else to talk about."

"Computer project comes to mind." Of course, that wasn't the reason I was there, but with his defiance, now wasn't a good time to ask him about my mom. He would sense my fear and use it to his advantage. I had to wait until he at least got rid of his grumpiness.

"We're never going to be more than two students working on a project," he said.

I had the urge to scream at the top of my lungs. Instead, I pushed him. He stumbled into a cluster of bushes.

"Get off your high horse. I wouldn't date you if..." I couldn't think of a word.

That asshat grin started to show. "If what, Montana? Cat got your tongue all of a sudden?"

More like a tall sexy quarterback sucked me in with one look that said, "I want you, but I hate you too."

"Why do you get on my nerves?" I asked.

"Because you want me, and you're afraid to admit it."

True. I rolled my eyes. "You do nothing to wake up my jumanji."

"What the fuck is that?"

I pointed to my crotch. "Some girls call their lady parts hoo-has or whatever. I call mine jumanji."

He roared with laughter as he brushed off the leaves that had clung to his shirt. "That's one for the books. I also can't believe you told me that. You sure aren't shy."

I said what was on my mind and didn't care what people thought. But suddenly I did care what he thought, and for that, my cheeks flushed. Mom had always said never let them see you sweat. Now it was my turn to laugh. Sweating was an everyday thing here in the South.

He turned. "Are you laughing at yourself?"

I shrugged. "I guess I am."

He laughed harder. When he did, I did. Then the tension between us snapped. We strolled along the golf path, the freshly cut grass lingering in the air as the snakelike hiss of the sprinklers sang their tune.

"Why do you call your puss jumanji?" He tightened his lips, trying not to laugh.

"A friend and I had been talking about names that girls call their lady parts, and I came up with juji. Then she fired back with jumanji. So the name stuck. Why did your parents name you Train?" He had an odd name, and I could think of all sorts of innuendos about it that would make it fun to rib him.

The crack of a golf club hitting a ball echoed.

We weren't in harm's way of getting clobbered from a golf ball since we were beneath a cluster of trees, but we both checked behind us. The ball soared through the air and landed in the middle of the fairway.

Train shoved his hands in the pockets of his jeans. "My paternal grandfather's middle name was Train. His father was a conductor, and his wife thought the name would be unique. When I was born, my dad wanted to keep the name in the family."

We passed beautifully landscaped backyards and two men putting on one of the holes. No sooner had we cleared a curve in the path than a familiar voice shouted Train's name.

We both whipped our heads to the yard on our right. Nina jogged up, sporting a bikini and wet hair. The humid air suddenly got as thick as a brick.

A muscle ticked in Train's jaw. It was clear he was fighting some inner demons. Elvira had said on the beach that Train would never take Nina back, but I wasn't so sure.

She glared at me then set her confused attention on Train. "Are you dating Montana?"

"It's none of your business," he volleyed back.

One side of her nose twitched. She reminded me of a rabid dog about to attack her prey—that prey being me.

"He's right," I said. "It's none of your business." I couldn't just stand there and let her think I was scum. Sure, I could've told her the truth. But I didn't think she would believe me, and I didn't like her.

"Train isn't over me," she said with a tone as sure as the grass was green.

I tilted my head. "You cheated on him. On what planet do you think he'll take you back?" Okay, he could take her back, although that would make him a fool in my book. I believed once a cheater, always a cheater.

Nina's orange lips split into a smile. "I know he will."

Train rubbed the nape of his neck. "Montana's right. I will never take you back."

She knitted her perfectly shaped eyebrows at him. "Not even to take me to the debutante ball?"

Either the girl wasn't the sharpest knife in the drawer, or she really believed she could get Train back.

"You're a piece of work," Train said to Nina.

A little girl called to Nina.

Train tipped his head at the girl with bright-red hair. "Your sister wants you."

Nina regarded me. "Train will never stay with you. You're just a distraction." Then she twirled on her bare foot and marched back to the pool.

I ground my teeth together as my body stiffened. Then I shrugged off her comment. I wasn't dating Train. So whatever she'd said shouldn't bother me.

"Let's get back. I have to help my mom." His tone matched his grimace.

Quietness hung over us all the way back to his house. Train kept his head down. Meanwhile, my stomach clenched. Nina could be trouble even if I weren't dating Train. After all, she was a jealous ex.

When we reached my car, his shoulders finally relaxed. "Why didn't you tell her we weren't dating?"

"Would it have mattered what I told Nina?"

He clutched the back of his arm. "No." His tone was even. "Thank you for having my back."

"No problem."

A beat of silence stretched between us until Train's next-door neighbor started his car and the muffler backfired. I flinched a little.

A strand of hair fell over Train's forehead. "So why did you come over? Did you think about my offer?"

And we were back to that. "Before we were rudely interrupted, I was about to ask you what you knew about my mom."

"Are you going to push this football thing?" His tone was husky, his expression deadpan.

The camaraderie we'd had in the few moments where we laughed and shared personal details about ourselves vanished. The anger and frustration I'd harbored on the way to his house was front and center.

"Seriously?"

"I'm waiting," he said.

Wow, this dude was moody, although I could be too.

"Screw you." I opened my car door, but he cocooned me with his body.

He planted one hand on the roof of my car, while he tucked a stray hair behind my ear. The butterflies and nerves rushed back stronger than before. The boy had a softer side. The boy had manners, although only when his mom was present. The boy had a way of making my heart race, my belly ache, and my palms sweat. He was probably right about one thing—I would be throwing myself at him, especially if he kept showing subtle hints of niceness.

"I'll call you when my dad has a refrigeration guy pinned down." Then he pushed off the car and hurried toward the house as though I were some kind of demon that was there to take his soul.

I stomped my foot. "Train, wait."

The house door slammed shut, and I jumped. I couldn't make heads or tails about what was transpiring between us or what had happened in the last hour or so. All I knew was my stomach hurt, and not from lack of food. The guy drove me mad. If he thought I would cave on football or jumping his bones, he was in for a rude awakening. I was about to bring out the big guns.

Chapter 9

Train

DARK CLOUDS SKATED ACROSS THE sky, but every now and then, the sun would make an appearance, albeit briefly. Football practice happened rain or shine, especially the day before a game. Two solid days had passed since Montana came to my house. I'd been taken by surprise that a girl I barely knew would have my back like she had when we'd run into Nina. Maybe I could trust Montana. Maybe she wasn't the type of girl to stomp on my heart. I also liked Montana a little bit more for not asking why my mom was in a wheelchair. That told me she didn't pry into other people's business.

In the four short days since I'd met her, she was making it difficult for me not to break my own promise of no girls this year. Not to mention, she'd traded T-shirts and jeans for low-cut semi-see-through blouses, colored bras, and short shorts. Granted, most girls wore short shorts to school. The principal didn't have a strict dress code unless a girl's butt was hanging out. Regardless, Montana wasn't most girls, not with her long, long legs. Not only that, she'd been wearing her hair up, displaying a smooth neck that drew my attention to her cleavage—big, round, and inviting. If her physical appearance hadn't caused me to walk around with a semi-boner, her stubborn and feisty attitude pulled me to her yet pushed me away.

"So what did you want to talk to me about?" Austin asked as we walked out to the field. "Is Coach sticking to his guns about Montana trying out for football?"

"Didn't bother to ask Coach." I also hadn't broached the subject again with Montana. I was trying like a motherfucker to stay away from all girls, although I was having a hard time since Montana sat next to me in computer class and I thought about her constantly.

"So you didn't get Montana to drop football?" Austin asked.

"Dude, I want her to drop her pants. Okay, I said it."

He slapped me on the back. "Feels good to get that off your chest, doesn't it?"

Not as good as I would feel getting laid, and by no one but Montana. I knew if I had sex with some chick, I would be envisioning Montana, and that wouldn't be cool. "I overheard something at Montana's house that I probably shouldn't have. It's been bugging me."

Austin shifted his helmet from one arm to the other. "Please tell me she has an older sister."

I nudged him with my elbow. "You like Reagan."

"That I do, but I can look."

"Anyway, Montana said to her mom, and I quote, 'Someone saw you in the grocery store yesterday. They know you're here.' Odd. Right?"

"Her mom is hiding from someone?"

"That's what I'm thinking, and I threatened Montana to drop football, or I would blab about her mom. Yet I really don't know anything about her mom."

He chuckled. "Dude, you're messed up. But that's what I love about you."

"Yeah, we were made for each other." I rolled my eyes. "I've done some research on her mom and Montana but can't find anything on the Internet." Not that I'd expected to, especially if her mom was in the FBI or CIA, although I doubted she was employed by either organization. The way Montana had sounded led me to believe her mom was running from someone or something, maybe an ex-lover or the federal government or the law in some state.

The team, Austin, and I gathered on the field and started in on our stretches and pre-warm-up routine.

Austin bent his upper torso over his legs so that his hands were touching his cleats. "Tell Montana you were eavesdropping and ask her about her mom."

I joined Austin doing the same stretch, and the entire team followed suit. "Seriously? I'm trying to get her to not try out. The chick is stubborn."

"Here's an idea," he said. "Ask her out. Get on her good side. Then she'll not only come clean about her mom, but she'll give up on football. You've always been good about weaving a spell that chicks fall for."

I grunted as we continued stretching. Maybe he was right. I should ask her out for many reasons other than football. Or maybe I should let the cards fall where they might, although I wasn't ready to ask her out. If she said no, I would only become more of a dick, and if she said yes, then I would be breaking my no-girls rule and could set myself up for heartache. The latter scared me more than her on the team.

Coach Holmes jogged out from the sideline then blew his whistle. "Listen up. After a discussion with the administration, Montana Smith will be trying out."

"No way," Derek said on my left.

Austin laughed.

I scowled.

The rest of team complained.

Coach blew his whistle. "Enough. With Adler gone and Cruise hurt, we could use a good kicker. That is if she can kick."

A drone of grunts, growls, and mutters peppered the air.

Coach walked in between and around us. "A girl on this team might do you boys some good. Maybe she'll show you a thing or two. Anyway, she'll be down on the field after we finish practice. Right now, get your asses up. We're facing one of our toughest rivals tomorrow night."

We hopped to attention. While everyone separated into defensive and offensive lines, I ran up to Coach. "We don't need Montana. Austin can kick." Austin was a great kicker, but he was better as a wide receiver.

He pierced me with dark eyes. "What are you afraid of?"

"Honestly, she'll distract me. The girl drives me fucking crazy. And since I'm being completely honest, my dick stays hard when she's around."

He chuckled. "You're a teenager. Your dick should be hard all the time."

I didn't know about that. "Also, have you thought about her safety?" Then again, as a kicker, she wouldn't be in harm's way.

"Practice. Let me worry about her safety."

Reluctantly, I joined the offensive line. I wanted to argue more, but with Coach, arguing only got a person fifty more laps around the track. Not that I was a wimp since I ran outside of football. I just didn't want to croak before the game tomorrow night.

"Well, what did Coach say about Montana?" Derek asked.

"Forget Montana. You heard Coach. We have a tough rival tomorrow."

We ran through play after play after play. We had just gotten into formation for our last play when I spotted Montana walking toward Coach. All the guys saw her too, some muttering their disapproval.

Ignore her. Play the game. A wild fucking laugh broke out in my head. Montana had made it impossible to ignore her on any given day. I was about to obey my conscience, when off to my left, I spotted my old man. I didn't know what was worse—Montana showing up, making me want to tackle her and do things to her that I'd been imagining since I met her, or my old man showing up to watch me then tell me everything I was doing wrong on the field.

Then it dawned on me. I hadn't heard from my dad about a refrigeration guy to fix Montana's air conditioning.

"Are we playing?" Lou asked.

I placed my hands behind Lou's legs. "Set!" I yelled as I scanned the offensive line. "Red twenty-five!" I turned my head to my right. "Red twenty-five!" I turned my head to the left. "Hut! Hut!"

Lou snapped the ball. I shuffled back as I honed in on where Austin was going to be. In football, the quarterback threw the ball where the receiver would be, not where he was. My dad had drilled that into me at an early age.

But my focus wasn't anywhere on the field. My dad and Montana were shaking hands. Several swear words went off in my head. Then before I could release the ball, I was tackled by two of the players from the defensive line.

Some of the guys started yelling, but the loudest person was Coach. "Fuck, Everly. That fucking head of yours is up your fucking ass again."

"Yeah, man." Lou held out a hand. "It's not your head, but your eyes were on someone's ass."

I got up without his help, ignoring my old man. I could hear him now. "You're not going to get into USC if you play like shit. That was a moronic play. Blah, blah, blah." I'd heard all his rants, and they never went in one ear and out the other. Nope. They only angered the fuck out of me.

I flared my nostrils as I flipped the ball back to Lou. "Again!" I barked, not looking at anyone beyond the guys.

We huddled as I blew out a breath.

"Don't worry about your old man," Austin said.

Derek chuckled. "He's not worried about his old man. He's got his dick pointed at Montana."

"Can it," I said. "All of you. Let's run the play again." *Fuckers.* They were right on both counts.

We practiced the play again, and this time, I built tunnel vision around the field. Granted, the tunnel was thin since I could see out of the corner of my eye. Montana was talking with Coach, while my father seemed to be listening. Once Austin caught the ball, he ran only to be tackled about five yards from the end zone.

"All right," Coach called. "Take five laps tonight around the track. Then get some rest for tomorrow. Everly, front and center."

Everyone removed their helmets, grabbed some Gatorade, then headed onto the track. Before I met Coach, I got a drink, checking on Montana, who had fallen in line with Austin, jogging around the track in her tight yoga pants and a workout bra that kept her tits firmly in place.

Whatever you do tomorrow night, do not look for her in the stands.

I knocked back the Gatorade as my old man came up to me.

Tall and lean with a light-brown goatee, my dad, Lawrence Everly, was a formidable man. "What kind of junk are you playing?" He narrowed his green eyes, enhancing the lines on his face. There was no question that he and I were related. "USC won't take you if you play like that."

Then don't allow a fucking girl on the team. The words blared in my head, and I wanted to scream them at Coach.

I snarled. "Are you here to coach me? Because if you are, don't bother. I have a coach."

"I'm here to speak with Coach Holmes and you. I managed to get the USC scout out to the game tomorrow night."

"You could've called me." My tone was full of acid but quickly dissipated when it clicked that the USC scout would be at the game. "A scout, huh?"

"I thought you would be happy," he said.

Over the fucking moon. "I am. Thank you." I really had to get my head in the game. "Why haven't you returned my call about the refrigeration guy for Montana Smith, the girl you were shaking hands with?"

He raised his eyebrow. "Son, she called me. I took care of that yesterday. I also sent someone out to her house this morning and then stopped by to make sure the AC was working."

"Montana called you?" I wasn't sure I'd heard him. Then again, I shouldn't have been surprised. Montana wasn't the type of girl to wait for anyone.

"Why is that a surprise?" he asked. "My company is listed on the Internet."

Everly Architecture and Design was listed on the Internet and in big bold letters on the door of the building my dad owned in downtown Charleston.

"Never mind. Coach needs me." He needed to squeeze my balls until I was keeling over. Or maybe Montana would do just that when she sashayed onto the field to show us what she had.

Dad walked with me. "We have dinner tonight at six at Dominic's in Charleston. Our first-game-of-the-season tradition. Remember?"

Not really, thanks in part to my screwed-up life, compliments of girls. But we did have a tradition—the night before my first football game of the season, we would have dinner and chat about plays, the other teams, and anything related to football. But since my dad and mom had divorced, our tradition had been him talking and me tuning him out. Maybe tonight, I would listen since the scout would be at tomorrow night's game. After all, my father knew the game well and had been the quarterback for USC in college. So he was an expert.

"I know. Mom gave me the message."

Again, why he hadn't texted me or called me had me scratching my head. I suspected he knew I would decline, but I wouldn't and couldn't say no to my mom. She had insisted that I at least try with my dad. After all, he was the one paying for college and everything else in my life.

"I might be a few minutes late. I have to stop by the bookstore and pick up a book for English." I needed CliffsNotes.

Coach dropped his clipboard on a chair as he and my old man exchanged a handshake. "All right, Train. I want you to throw the ball to Montana."

My dad's eyes widened. "What's going on?"

"Coach is letting a girl try out," I said in a not-so-nice tone.

"Tryouts are over," Dad said. "And she could get hurt."

My thoughts exactly.

"We need a kicker. I'm giving her a shot." Coach waved at Montana then turned to me. "Get the ball and get out there."

The team settled around the field, while Montana ran toward me with a boner of a smile on her face.

I was screwed.

Chapter 10

Montana

I SLOWED TO A WALK AS I kept Train in sight. He looked as scrumptious as ever in his football uniform minus the helmet, although I preferred him in swim trunks. He palmed the ball, glowering at me. Coach had asked me earlier that day if I was still interested in trying out. I'd debated for the last two days on whether to go through with the tryout or not. I could throw a football, but that was where my talent ended. Honestly, when I'd spoken to Coach, he didn't give any indication he would give me a shot, although the scuttlebutt from Austin said otherwise.

But since I'd made such a big stink, puffing my chest out as though I were queen of the field, I couldn't back out now even if I made myself come off as a twit, jackass, and all the other words that would describe my inability to play football.

But my Nana Smith had always said, "Do as you say you're going to do. Otherwise, no one will trust you."

I might not have cared how I looked on the field, but trust was important to me. Deep down, I wanted Train to trust me.

Out of the corner of my eye, I spotted Elvira walking down to stand next to Austin. I'd texted her to come support me, but I wasn't sure if she would. We were in the infancy stages of our friendship, and we hadn't discussed in detail what her thoughts were on me trying out.

I settled in front of Train with my pulse sprinting.

"You seem nervous," he said, sounding relieved.

Understatement of the year. "Not at all."

"None of the guys want you on the team. I know you're only doing this to piss me off." His tone was snide.

"Do you want me on the team?"

He studied me for the longest moment. "You don't belong on the team."

"Why? Because you think girls should be barefoot and pregnant?"

He squinted his beautiful peepers at me. "Coach wants us to throw. So go long."

I'd watched enough football to know that I had to run and keep my eye on the quarterback at the same time. The problem was I had a wandering eye. I checked on the team, who were all holding their breath. When I flipped my gaze back to Train, the ball was soaring in the air, a perfect spiral, heading right for me. I held up my arms, my stomach knotting and nausea ready to spurt out, as I darted right then left, hoping and praying I could catch the ball. *I can do this,* I chanted until the ball landed square in my chest, punching the wind out of me as I fell on my ass.

Titters and snorts ensued from the football team. I was grateful the whole school wasn't there.

"Don't let them bother you!" Elvira shouted. Maybe she was on my side.

I brushed myself off in an attempt to soothe my ego as I picked up the ball then threw a perfect spiral back to Train.

Someone whistled.

"Austin!" Coach yelled. "Get out there and set her up for a kick on the twenty-yard line."

Oh, this ought to be fun. Not. I didn't know the first thing about kicking.

Train tossed the ball to Austin as he ran out to me.

"I have no idea what I'm doing," I said to Train's best friend. "I can throw a football, but that's about it. I only wanted to mess with Train. God, now I look like an idiot."

"No, you don't," he said. "Trust me when I say there are guys out there who would get excited to see you throw the ball the way you do. Hell, I'm one of them. And Train is another. But don't do this unless your heart is in it. The team has put their heart and soul into every season. To be frank, we don't need a person—guy or gal—on the team who doesn't want to be here."

"I'm not a quitter. I had to at least follow this through."

"You're not done yet. Let's see that kick." Austin set up the ball. "Please don't kick my arm."

I busted out laughing. "Then you've been warned."

I focused on the ball and thought about all those NFL kickers I'd watched kick a football. I shuffled back about five feet then ran forward. Just before I reached the ball, I pointed my right foot down toward the ground then kicked. When my foot connected with the football, pain shot up my leg. I bit back any screams or swear words while I watched the ball dribble down the field from my pathetic kick.

"Montana!" Coach shouted.

"You did okay," Austin said.

The muted laughs trickling onto the field from the team stung just a tiny bit. "I was horrible." Even though I was embarrassed, I held my head high. I was proud that I hadn't backed out. I dared not look at Train, though. Otherwise, I might have curled up on the field and begged the earth to suck me in.

Austin leaned in to me as we trekked over to Coach. "Don't worry. Train isn't laughing, but he is sizing you up."

I rolled my eyes. "That doesn't help."

Austin headed toward Train. "See you later."

I would bet they would have a good laugh in the locker room. *Whatever.*

"All right, everyone. Showers. Get some rest tonight," Coach said to the team.

Elvira walked up. I couldn't wait to hear what she had to say.

With his car keys in his hand, Mr. Everly said, "Young lady, valiant effort in trying. Great throw." His tone was polite and soft. "Coach, see you tomorrow night." Then he was gone.

I was dying to know what Train thought. *Maybe not.*

Coach played with the whistle around his neck. "How do you think you did?"

"Horrible. Coach, I want to apologize. I only tried out because someone made me mad." There was no point in lying. "I really didn't think you would let me, anyway."

He scrubbed a hand along his unshaven jaw. "I had every intention of scolding you for wasting my time, but honesty and an apology keep me from doing just that. Now, I will say that if you had practiced more in your younger years, you could've had potential, especially with your arm. Where did you learn how to throw a football?" he asked.

Stress oozed off of my shoulders. "Joey Dennison."

"*The* Joey Dennison?" Coach's voice rose in pitch. "The guy who played quarterback for the Naval Academy then was a first-round draft pick for the Saints?"

"You know him?" I asked.

"Who doesn't? He blew his knee during a summer tour with the military overseas. Came home, and the doctors said he needed a lot of therapy. So the Saints let him go."

I wiped the sweat from my forehead. "He seemed fine when he was dating my mom. Again, I'm sorry if I stirred up trouble."

"I was hoping you could kick a football."

Elvira hung close, listening. I didn't mind. I wasn't hiding anything, anyway.

"Yeah, that didn't go well. Just to be clear, I'm not on the team?"

He began gathering his clipboard and a gym bag. "I'm afraid not."

I scanned the field. Train was gone, as was the entire team.

I sighed. I didn't have the energy at that moment to banter with Train. "Was everyone laughing at that kick?" I asked Elvira.

Her sparkly eye shadow glinted in the sun. "I think the guys were relieved you couldn't kick."

"I was too. Are we still on for a trip into Charleston later?"

She bobbed her silky head of hair.

After I quickly showered and changed, Elvira and I drove into the city. The sun dipped behind the buildings in downtown Charleston as we strolled along the Battery, a historic defensive landmark that stretched along the Cooper River. The purpose of our trip was that she wanted to take me on a tour and I wanted to fill out job applications, which I'd done at two local art galleries.

"Do you think you and your mom will stay in town after you graduate?" Elvira asked.

Two weeks ago when Mom and I had gotten there, I would've said no way. Quiet towns, small towns, and claustrophobic places weren't my shtick, but Mom and I were finding that the sun, the ocean air, and the plantation-style living were rather nice. The area wasn't as small as I'd originally assumed. The city had a lot to offer, including a college right in the heart of Charleston, and I was digging the friendship that was blossoming between Elvira and me and even Reagan.

I lifted a shoulder. "We'll see. My mom's marketing job will dictate what happens next. But I do plan on graduating." Unless I didn't make the grades or got expelled for some reason. I made a mental note to see the guidance counselor next week. My mom had been on me to see if the school could recommend a good tutor. I needed help with Algebra II, and I might need help in computer class if Train and I didn't come to some form of platonic friendship, if that was even possible. The pull he had on me was powerful, and maybe he was right that I would cave and jump his bones.

Elvira and I settled on a bench that overlooked the rippling water. "Are you going to college?" I asked.

"Absolutely. I want to be a doctor. I've applied to Duke University and other schools. But Duke is my top choice. I have the grades, and my dad went to Duke. But I'll be home during the summers."

"A doctor. Wow, girl. That's awesome. I want to be an artist."

"Hence why you like graffiti," she said.

Oh my God. I hadn't thought about tagging since the first day of school. Then again, my mom hadn't given me a reason to, and no one had hurt me enough for me to lash out. But graffiti wasn't about lashing out. I could succumb to peer pressure if my friends were into it. "Art isn't just about graffiti, but the cool paints and the large murals make graffiti fun. So I noticed on the beach that first day that you and Lou looked chummy. Do you like him?"

The water rippled in the distance as a small boat floated by.

"He's cute," she said. "And he is the sweetest boy I know."

I didn't know him well, but he had saved me from being crushed by his massive body. "Do you think Train still likes Nina?" I couldn't read

Train well. One minute, he was growling at me, then he was nice, then he was coming on to me. Case in point: I firmly believed he'd cocooned me up against my bannister because he knew about my mom. Over the last two days, I'd wanted to ask him again what he knew, but I decided that the more I pushed him to answer, the more he would use my fear of him knowing about my mom to his advantage.

"You like him, don't you?"

"He gets on my nerves."

She bumped my shoulder with hers. "That means you like him."

A couple with a large-lens camera strolled by, the middle-aged lady pointing to something out over the water.

"Physically, he's got the looks down. He oozes sexiness. But emotionally, I don't know. His ex is back. That scares me. I'm protecting my own heart, anyway. The last breakup I had ruined me. Since then, I've been a little shy of anything steady."

She patted my leg. "So sorry, girl. You two might be right for each other after all. You can heal together."

I giggled. "Are you a psychiatrist?"

"Not yet," she said. "Anyway, Train is a little rough around the edges right now. He assumed he wouldn't be seeing Nina this year. Yet she's back at school. And she's a troublemaker. Last year, she had the nerve to show up at a party with the guy she was cheating on Train with. Train went haywire, beating the guy into the ER. Then Train was thrown into the back of a police cruiser."

"Yikes." I might've done the same if I'd found out Nikko had been cheating on me. I couldn't say for sure if he had. Nevertheless, the reason we had broken up was because he'd wanted to date other girls.

"Exactly. And if she's touting that her and Train are getting back together, then she's got something up her sleeve."

"Hence why I'm staying away. Not only because Nina is trouble, but what if he took Nina back?"

"He wouldn't. I've known Train a long time, and once you break his trust, you're history."

Maybe he was rough around the edges with me because he too was afraid of what could happen between us. But I wasn't a cheater. *He doesn't know that.*

"Give Train some time," she said. "We should go. It's getting late."

I fiddled around in my bag for my keys as I got up.

Elvira rose gracefully, smoothing her hands down her tan shorts before hiking her bag over her shoulder. "Since we're talking about Train, I want to be honest with you."

My stomach twisted at the curtness in her tone.

Her pretty features hardened. "I like you a lot. And Train is one of my dear friends. Don't toy with his head. If you want Train to notice you in a good way, then don't pull crap like Nina would. That display on the football field wasn't a way to get a guy to like you."

Whoa! I wasn't sure how to respond, although I didn't disagree with her. But my ego and my anger had gotten the best of me. Nevertheless, hearing her words kind of stung. "I get how you protect your friends. I'm not here to cause trouble. And I kind of suck at making friends."

"I get that. You're cautious."

She had me pegged. I half-smiled, but I was throwing up inside. Normally, others didn't see the true me, except my mom, and it felt weird.

The car ride home was somber as we listened to music. I'd been quiet since Elvira gave me her two cents. As much as I was screwing with Train's head, he was also playing with mine.

His words rang in my head. *Stop football, and I won't tell people about your mom.* Not that he had any leverage over that threat anymore.

"I upset you, didn't I?" Elvira asked.

Gripping the steering wheel as though I were trying to crush it, I wheeled into our development. "Why do you think that?"

"Because your knuckles are bright white." Elvira started to laugh, like uncontrollable laughter. She patted her wet eyes. "Relax, Montana. I'm not out to get you. I'm only being a true friend."

Maybe that was my problem. I never really had a true friend. The moment anyone got close, I pushed them away.

After several turns, I pulled up in front of Elvira's house. "True friends don't mock."

"I'm sorry for laughing." Her pink lips curled downward. "But I'm not sorry for speaking the truth. I'll see you in school." Then she got out of the car, leaving me dumbfounded.

I navigated the streets until I was parked in my driveway, staring at my white knuckles. At every school I'd attended, I had been able to blend in, even with my spunky attitude. But at Palmetto High, not so much. *You can't blend in if you make a fool out of yourself on the football field. Whatever.* I couldn't fault Elvira for speaking her mind. I did the same. We were alike. She had moxie, like me. She'd been the one to ram the door into my head—by accident, of course. She'd been the one to tell me outright that she had to pee. Kids didn't tell strangers that much personal information, like I had done with Train when I told him about my jumanji.

As I got out of the car, I lost all thought when I came face-to-face with Lucy Everly and my mom. I should've questioned what Train's mom was doing at my house. His dad had every reason to visit us to examine our air conditioner, but Lucy? Instead, I said, "You're walking." I quickly covered my mouth then lowered my hand. "I'm sorry. That was rude."

She beamed from ear to ear. "That's okay. I get that reaction a lot."

My mom appeared confused.

"I didn't tell you, Georgia. I sometimes use a wheelchair. My rheumatoid arthritis can get the best of me." Lucy set her sights on me. "I'm also surprised you didn't ask why I was in a wheelchair when you were at the house the other day."

"It's none of my business," I said as I spied a proud smile on Mom.

"All the more reason you and Train would be a good fit for the debutante ball."

I reared back. "Come again?" Nina had said something about the debutante ball and going with Train.

She glided up and took one of my hands. "Your mom will explain everything."

My mom had better do more than explain. I hope she told Lucy I didn't do balls or whatever she'd said.

"It was nice chatting, Georgia. We'll talk soon." Then she walked to her Mercedes as though she were modeling her cute leather sandals and crisp outfit, which included a sleeveless white blouse and a knee-length skirt.

My mom waved at her. Once Lucy was gone, my mom sat on the

top step then patted the spot beside her. "This may sound weird." She twisted her hair up on her head then secured it with a band she had on her wrist. "I've met Train. I've met Mr. Everly, who came by with his AC man this morning, and now Lucy. I think the universe is trying to tell us something about the Everly family."

I cozied up next to her. "Are you trying to tell me you've given my hand in marriage to Train?" I asked jokingly.

Our neighbor, an older gentleman across the street, was washing his truck.

"Well—"

I chomped on a nail. "Mom, what did you do?"

"Lucy sits on the debutante committee. One of the moms had to back out, and she asked me to help. She thought since I was new to the area, that maybe I would like to get to know some parents. She also wants Train to go to the ball, but she knows he's not interested, although she believes that you might be able to persuade him."

I laughed as hard as Elvira had been laughing at me. "The boy hates me."

"According to Lucy, he's quite taken with you. I do have to agree. I saw how he was looking at you when he was here."

Tears streamed down my face from giggling. "Why does she want him to go to a dance?"

She shrugged. "Train's parents are divorced, and according to her, he's been in a bad place, even more so since he broke up with his girlfriend. So she thinks a fresh and pretty face will brighten his spirits."

If Nina has her way, then Train would have a date to the ball. "I don't understand how I will be able to convince Train Everly to go to a shindig."

"Honey, don't shortchange yourself. You are sweet, well mannered when you want to be, and you certainly are gorgeous. I'm only relaying our conversation. I'm not going to force you to go or do anything you don't want to do. I did offer to help out with decorating, though. If we're going to live here, then let's build that foundation we talked about."

Train wouldn't be taking me to the dance.

"On another topic, I tried out for football today."

"*What?*" Mom's voice sounded like nails on a chalkboard.

"I shouldn't have done that. I looked awful out there. Actually, my throw was great, thanks to your ex, Joey Dennison."

Mom sighed. "He was a good player. But that's not the point. Tell me more about the tryout."

"Coach was interested in me if I could kick, and I can't. I only tried out because Train made me mad and because one of the guys on the team made a chauvinistic comment on the beach the other day about how girls don't belong on the football field."

She draped her arm around me. "Please tell me you apologized to the coach for wasting his time."

"Yes, ma'am. But I might be ridiculed in school tomorrow."

She pulled me to her. "I love you."

Whether people looked at me funny or whispered about me at school the next day, I would worry about that tomorrow. For the moment, I was with my mom, and it was one of the best moments I'd had in a long time. "Ditto."

Chapter 11

Montana

THE HUMIDITY THE NEXT MORNING on the way to school hung in the air like a thick winter blanket. I thought back to New York and how the weather in September would be cool or even cold. Part of me wished for cold. I debated if I should beg my mom to let me miss school for one day. Then I could stay snuggled up under my blankets in our very cold house. Mom had lowered the thermostat before she went to bed, which helped me sleep for the first time since we'd moved in. It also helped that my sunburned shoulders were no longer bothering me.

I smelled my armpits as I was approaching school.

"Did you not use deodorant this morning?" Reagan asked, her glossy lips shining in the morning sun as she came up beside me.

Thankfully, my scented cucumber antiperspirant was working, at least for now. "How do you stand the heat?"

With both hands, she motioned to her blue shirt. "Cotton, and I've lived here all my life. What's up with your blouse buttoned up to your neck?" She arched her eyebrow. "Are you hiding a hickey?"

I touched my neck. "Oh God. No. I'm not dating anyone." Although I wouldn't mind Train's lips on my neck. "The slutty look doesn't suit me." I had dressed in some revealing blouses lately, hoping to garner Train's attention, but our little exchange on the football field yesterday had been the extent of our interaction since I'd been to his house. But something had to give soon since we had our computer project to work on.

"I beg to differ. Your wardrobe has been tasteful compared to other girls in this school, although not today."

"You don't like my ankle-length skirt and blouse?" I asked in a playful tone.

She scrunched her nose. "If you're going for the 'I'm a virgin' look, then it works."

I was about to make a retort, when a group of girls we passed on the front lawn of the school pointed at us, snickering. Maybe they had something to say about my outfit. Or maybe word had gotten around about my pathetic display on the football field yesterday.

"I heard through the grapevine about your football tryout," Reagan said.

"Yeah. I think everyone else has too." I caught several other kids gawking our way and wasn't watching in front of me. I bumped into a boy with a carrottopped head of hair. "I'm sorry."

He stared at me like a deer in headlights.

Reagan tapped him on the shoulder. "Drew, are you okay?"

"Oh, you're the boy who had the experiment gone bad," I said.

His freckled face became as red as his hair. "It was an accident. So you're prettier than my cousin gives you credit for."

I raised an eyebrow. "Who is your cousin?"

"Nina," Drew and Reagan said at the same time.

I wasn't sure what to make of that comment. "Thank you, I guess."

He tucked his head to his chest and darted off.

"That was weird," I said to Reagan.

"Drew is a nerd, if you haven't noticed."

I would have said shy. "I guess Nina doesn't think I'm pretty."

"Not if you like Train. You're her number-one enemy if she knows you like him."

"She cheated on him," I said more to myself than her.

"That's Nina. She probably thinks she can get Train back."

There was no "probably" about it. She firmly believed that Train would take her back. I hoped he wouldn't. Elvira swore Train would never go back to Nina. Even Train had said something similar to Nina during our conversation with her behind her house. But people gave others second chances. Right now, I couldn't worry about Train or Nina. I had a computer project and other schoolwork to think about.

Reagan and I started for the entrance.

"On a different topic, what books of Casey Stewart's have you read?" I wasn't about to share the truth. I was still leery on the subject of my mom. But I was curious.

The halls were teaming with kids talking, banging their lockers shut, and hurrying by as though they were late for a fire even though we had about fifteen minutes before class started. Reagan and I banked left toward computer class. The halls quieted as all eyes diverted to Reagan and me. Whispers hummed as we passed.

"I guess the whole school heard of your tryout," Reagan said.

"Or they're ogling my virgin outfit."

When we approached computer class, a boy of average height with long sideburns pushed off a locker he'd been leaning against. "Montana," he said, undressing me with his eyes.

I glared at him. "Who wants to know?" *Be nice.*

"I'm Ferris. I was told you needed a tutor."

My eyebrows went up as I lost my snarky attitude. "Ferris?"

"Don't you dare laugh at my name. I've been in hell since I entered grade school."

I pressed my lips tightly together so I wouldn't break out in hysterics. "Except the sideburns, you remind me of Matthew Broderick in *Ferris Bueller's Day Off.*"

"No, I don't. Look, Ms. Shepard told me how to find you. She also explained you need a tutor. Do you?"

My mom had mentioned last night that she had spoken to the guidance counselor but told me to check in with Ms. Shepard. "I do. Can we meet after school on Monday?"

"I'll meet you in the library, and don't be late." He bounced off.

"He's up for valedictorian," Reagan said.

I guessed I was in the right hands, then.

When we ambled into class, Reagan poked me in the arm. "That's the last Casey Stewart book I've read." She pointed to the back of the classroom.

It took me a second to realize she was not only pointing at my mom's book, whose face was plastered on the back cover, but at the person who was reading *My Heart to Take*. I shook my head as I squeezed my butt cheeks so I wouldn't poop my pants.

"I'm shocked that Train Everly is reading that book," Reagan said as we both froze, staring at the sexy quarterback, who had his head buried in the pages.

Ditto. Ditto. Ditto. I honestly didn't know what to make of Train reading my mom's book other than wondering how he knew. So he *was* coming onto me because of my mom's erotica books.

"What's wrong?" Reagan's strawberry-scented shampoo drew me out of my funk.

If the cat was out of the bag, then I shouldn't lie. I might lose both Elvira and Reagan as friends. But I wasn't certain if I was ready for the school to know. Then again, Train might have blabbed the news already. "For one, Casey Stewart is my mom," I barely whispered near her ear.

"Shut up." Her pretty hazel eyes grew as big as damn basketballs. "Oh, I got to call my mom."

I grasped her arm. "I get your excitement, and thank you for it. My mom is awesome. But I barely tell people, only because some can be—"

"Assholes," she said. "Don't worry. I got your back."

A warm feeling covered me. It was good to know I had someone on my side. Now to deal with Train.

As Reagan began texting, I sat down and swiveled to face the boy who twisted my insides in a good, bad, and irritating way. "Is it a good book?"

Lazily, he flipped the page as he smirked. "The best. I see why you're rather forward."

My stomach knotted. "You're judging me based on a book?" My suspicion as to why he had come on to me slowly became a reality.

He folded a corner of a page then swung his head my way. His lids were heavy, and his eyes were full of... something. "Not any book. Your mom's book."

If anyone in class was listening, I couldn't tell. I didn't want to break eye contact with Train. "Operative word in there—my mom's. Not mine. How did you find out?"

"Austin tells me that you tried out for football to fuck with my head. How did that go for you?"

I knew he suspected the reason I had tried out, but suspecting and hearing the truth were two totally different animals. "I'm breaking barriers. How about you? Oh, wait. I got it. You're reading my mom's book to learn how to have sex. I guess I won't be jumping your bones after all. I like a guy who's experienced." My mom could be quite graphic in her sex scenes.

A handful of students who were in their seats got whiplash trying to watch the exchange between Train and me. I wasn't sure if I wanted to tell all of them to mind their own business, hide in a dark hole, or brag that my mom was a *New York Times* best-selling author.

Reagan, however, giggled. "She's right. You could learn a few things. It's her mom's best work to date."

I loved Reagan.

Train shot daggers at her. She rebutted with more giggles.

"Hannah Montana, or whoever you are, stop making a spectacle of yourself." His raspy drawl hardened. "It's not pretty."

I was conflicted. His harsh tone set off butterflies in my stomach, but at the same time, a pain stabbed my heart. I told myself he wasn't trying to hurt me, but Elvira had said something similar last night. Nevertheless, I thought of unicorns and rainbows to stave off the urge to burst into tears. I wasn't a crybaby. I could take anything thrown my way, or so I thought. *His words hurt because you like him.*

The bell chimed, breaking up our spat. Elvira breezed in and waved as she slid into her seat. More students spilled into the classroom, followed by Mr. Salvatore. I pulled out a notebook and opened it to a blank page.

Mr. Salvatore held up his hands. "Quiet down. I want to remind you that a preliminary report on your student project is due next Friday."

I huffed. Train and I hadn't even discussed what type of app we would create.

"Today, I want you to get with your partner and work on your projects. While you're doing that, I'm going to list what I want to see in your report."

Fan-fucking-tastic. I had to collaborate with a boy who wanted nothing to do with me.

Chairs shuffled around, creating a buzz amid the voices. I didn't have to go far, although I was thinking of an excuse to go to the nurse's office. But then we wouldn't get anything done, and I could fail the class.

I slid my chair closer to him. That knot in my stomach was tighter than before. "We don't have to like each other to work together," I said. "You want a good grade. Right?" He had to want to pass the class. His dad had mentioned to my mom that his son was headed to USC on a football scholarship. "Let's brainstorm. You write down some ideas, and I will too." That way, I didn't have to hear his sexy drawl.

He flipped his notebook open to a blank page and began writing.

I noodled on the question. What kind of app could we create that would help a college student or business owner? I thought of my mom and what her author business could use as an app. She had a website, which was a landing point for any of her fans that wanted info on her and her books.

Train waved his hand in front of my face. "Hey."

I blinked.

The asshat smirked. "You want to throw yourself at me? That's why you're staring at me?"

I couldn't help but roll my eyes. "Get off your high horse. Besides, it will be a cold day in hell unless you learn how to treat a lady."

"Ladies don't play football," he said.

"Train." My voice hardened to ice. "It's clear we've got something going on between us. What? I'm not sure. And right now, I don't care. We have a project to do, and I would like to pass this class. Don't you have a scholarship to worry about?"

He narrowed his yummy sea-green eyes. "Fine."

I slumped my shoulders. For rest of the class, we jotted down the notes that Mr. Salvatore had written on the whiteboard, and brainstormed ideas. Train came up with an app for oceanographers. I suggested an author app for my mom that would complement her website. He scrunched his nose at that. Then he suggested an app that could benefit his dad's contracting business—in particular, an app to help consumers troubleshoot a problem with their air conditioning.

"Aw, how sweet," I said. "You're thinking about me."

He brushed me off by checking his phone.

With a couple of minutes left until the end of class, I dipped into my bag for one of my acrylic markers, flipped to a clean page in my notebook, and started drawing. The act helped me to think.

Train stabbed a finger at my notebook. "What is that?"

I didn't know if I wanted to tell him. But his tone was nice and not condescending. "It's my signature. I use it on my artwork." He didn't need to know that all taggers had a signature on their graffiti, and my signature was the word "Spunk," minus the u. I'd merged the letters S, P, N, and K into a cool design. Just looking at my design gave me the urge to find a large blank mural. It had been months since I'd tagged anything, and as frustrated as I was, I needed an outlet. The notebook wouldn't be enough.

"S-P-N-K," he said.

"Yeah, Spunk."

He chuckled. I liked when he was nice like he had been for a brief moment when were walking along the golf course the other day.

When class ended, Train ran out as though he had to put out a fire. Elvira came over before I could get out of my seat.

"Can I tell her?" Reagan asked.

I shrugged.

"Montana's mom is a big-time writer. She goes by the pen name of Casey Stewart. And Train found her mother's book and was reading it in class. He's screwing with Montana."

I almost blurted out, "*See? Train is trying to get in my head too.*" But that would be catty. Still, I wanted to kiss Reagan for backing me up.

"Ah," Elvira said. "Now I know why your mom looked familiar when I met her. I think my mom has one of her hardback books that has her picture on the back. How come you didn't tell me then? Or why didn't your mom say anything to me?"

"You know how people around here can get kind of wonky about sex in books," Reagan said.

"I'm sorry I didn't tell you," I said. "My mom and I have been on

89

the bad side of rumors and glares and fights with parents about what she does. Sometimes it's better to keep her profession out of my social life. That's why I told you she was in marketing. And she kind of is with her books, in a way."

"That's okay. What your mom does is none of my business," Elvira said. "About last night, I wanted to apologize again. Are you mad at me?"

"Nah. You were only being honest, and you're right." I got out of my seat and hugged Elvira then Reagan. "Thank you. I haven't had any girlfriends who stuck up for me."

"Okay," Elvira said. "What's with the church-going outfit? It looks horrible."

"I was trying to turn over a new leaf." I didn't think Train even noticed me, though.

"Don't. And we need to go shopping."

Mom had bought me a couple of pairs of shorts that I'd been wearing, but shopping did sound fun. And if the South was going to be my new home, then cute sandals were in order too. Suddenly, I remembered Lucy Everly's brown leather sandals along with the debutante ball.

"Tell me about the debutante ball." The way things were going with Train, I doubted he would even ask me to the ball. I was curious about the shindig, though.

Reagan and Elvira exchanged a giddy look. Then Elvira launched into a dissertation on the event as we headed to our next class. By the time we arrived at English, I'd learned that the ball was a rite of passage for the ninth grade girls who were celebrating their adulthood. The ball took the place of homecoming but was always scheduled for the Saturday after the last football game of the season, which was seven weeks away. And each year, Mrs. Everly hosted the ball.

"Simply put, the ball is a tradition," Elvira said. "But in the last three years, Mrs. Everly hasn't focused so much on a coming-out party but rather a charity event."

"This year, I believe the charity she's sponsoring is Feed The Hungry," Reagan added. "All that aside, the event is fun. We get to dress up, dance, and have a good time."

"Train's mom wants me to go with him," I said matter-of-factly. "But Nina thinks she's going with Train."

"Train won't be taking Nina," Elvira said, sure and strong.

"Tell that to Nina," I said.

Nina and the ball became a distant memory when Derek stalked up to me with a smirk on his face. So far, I'd endured the looks and whispers of kids but not the team yet.

"Say it," I said.

He covered his large hand over his mouth and chuckled. "I'm proud you stuck to your guns. We all know why you tried out. I'm proud to report that you are officially stuck in Train's head. I'm also glad you're not on the team. I would hate to see you get hurt by a big guy like me." His sweet tone was a far cry from the way he'd acted when I first met him on the beach.

"So if we're being honest, Derek"—I peered up at him—"you spurred me on too with the chauvinistic comment you made."

"Now you know the reason I made it. Anyway, Coach wanted me to tell you to meet him in his office after school."

I knitted my eyebrows. "For what?"

He shrugged massive shoulders. "Got me."

I racked my brain, trying to drum up a reason. I was drawing a blank.

Chapter 12

Train

I THREW OPEN THE DOORS TO the locker room. The school day had sucked the big one. I couldn't wait to get my ass in my uniform and pound some heads at the football game later that night. Right now, I needed to find a bathroom stall and jerk off to release all the pent-up fucking energy I had, especially after reading a sex scene in that book, *My Heart to Take*. My mom read romance books, and I didn't want to imagine if those were the kinds of books she read. I didn't need to have my head buried in a book, either. I should have been trying to score some tits and ass.

I checked the locker room. All was quiet. So I locked myself in a stall and unzipped my jeans, when Austin and Derek's voices trickled in.

"Yo, Everly," Austin called out. "Are you in here?"

"I'm beating off. Go away." My voice bounced off the walls.

"I just read that scene in the book you told me about," Derek said. "I think I need to do the same."

I grunted as I sighed. Then I zipped up my jeans and walked out. "Can't a guy get some relief before a big game?"

Derek wagged the book in front of me. "This shit is good. Montana's mom can write."

"Go away and get that fucking book out of my face." I stormed over to my locker and started undressing. We had four hours before the game, so a run around the track would do me some good.

"Dude, you're not supposed to beat off before a game," Austin said at my back. "We want you ready to explode for the game."

I spun around to find Derek scratching his short brown hair as he read that book. Austin was leaning against a locker with his white-blond eyebrows lifted, almost waiting for me to unleash my anger on him.

I drove my hand through my hair. It wasn't his fault that I was sexually frustrated and angry. Nina's return had done a number on me, but the wordplay between Montana and me was hitting my groin and psyche.

"Man, Ms. Stewart knows how to write from a guy's perspective," Derek said. "Listen to this."

I snatched the book from him and threw it in my locker, the sound exploding in the room. "Enough. We need to get ready for the game. The rest of the team will be here soon, and I don't want everyone walking on the field with a hard-on."

Derek grabbed his dick. "It's too late for that."

I changed into my running gear as Austin settled on the bench next to me. "Give in. Ask her out. Take her to The Music Farm tomorrow night. Skylar Grey is headlining."

Not happening. "No girls this year. I'm going for a run." If I couldn't jerk off, then pounding my feet into the track would release some energy.

Derek untied his shoes. "Take Austin's advice."

I readied my headphones. "For the love of our football team, no. She gets under my skin."

They both chuckled.

Derek waggled his thick, dark eyebrows. "You mean that you want her to be under your skin."

I wanted a lot of things, but nothing more than to tear into her so she could cool the fire burning inside me. I clenched my jaw as I left them behind.

"Not everyone is like Nina," Austin shouted.

Nina's return had fucked with my head. Her cheating on me topped the list of reasons why I was cautious with girls, and for that, I despised my ex. I wanted Montana as badly as I wanted my USC scholarship. I couldn't shake her long legs, nice tits, and the image of her in a bikini. I even enjoyed our sarcastic taunts and, more than anything, her spunk, as she'd dubbed her signature for her artwork. She had the balls to show up to try out even though trying out was a way to fuck with me. I'd smiled at her when she tried to kick the football. I hadn't been mocking her but was proud of her for following through on her threat.

I wouldn't make it past the weekend if I didn't get laid or beat off. And since I'd given up on girls, beating off won. Otherwise, Coach would be right. I would have a hard-on twenty-four, seven.

Once on the track, I stuck my earbuds in and turned up the volume on my phone. "Broken-Hearted Savior" by Big Head Todd and the Monsters blared in my ears as I jogged slowly to warm up, trying to erase Montana from my mind. After one lap around, I'd finally rid my brain of the sexy girl. I sifted through plays for tonight's game as the music blared. But as I rounded the track, Montana popped into my brain again. Not only was her body on my mind, but her words had been on repeat all day. *"You're reading my mom's book to learn how to have sex."* I wouldn't say I was learning, rather I was adding details to my repertoire and moves I would like to try on Montana.

The cheerleaders practiced their routine on the field beneath the afternoon sun. The track was quiet save for the cheerleaders, but they were staunch in their work to make sure their routine was perfect, which meant they wouldn't bother me. Reagan waved as I jogged by. I didn't acknowledge her. She was as bad as Montana, goading me that morning in computer class.

Football plays. But as I made another lap around the track, Nina glided toward me. *Holy fuck.* She wasn't a cheerleader. However, she did have friends on the squad. I ran past her as I picked up my pace, but she ran up beside me and wrapped soft fingers around my forearm.

Keep running. Walk away. If I did, I might drag her alongside, and that wouldn't be good or gentlemanlike, no matter how much I despised her.

Nina wouldn't let go. I spun around, taking one earbud out. "What? I'm in the middle of a workout."

She twirled a strand of auburn hair between the fingers of her free hand. "I heard you're taking Montana to the debutante ball." Her tone was harsh.

I lifted my T-shirt and wiped the sweat off my face. "I am not going to the ball with you. We are not getting back together. When are you going to get that through your head?"

She dug her nails into my arm. "I want you back, Train. I can't tell you how I screwed up. Please, give me another chance."

Begging didn't look good on her.

She might have thought she was inflicting me with pain, but it was just the opposite. Her nails in my skin were keeping me from losing my fucking shit. I eyed the cheerleaders, who were now watching intently. At least I had witnesses if I needed them. I'd known Nina a long time. She wouldn't cry abuse, but she had changed last year into a person that I didn't even know anymore. So all bets were off, and I wasn't taking any chances. "Let go of me," I said as nicely as I could.

She drilled her evil gray gaze into me. "You never wanted me to let go of you when we were screwing."

"What do you want?" I knew what she wanted, and I only asked because I was a gnat's ass away from pushing her.

"I want you to take me to the ball. We can start there. We had future plans together. Remember? College and maybe marriage."

Nausea shot up to settle in my throat. "We were kids with a pipe dream. Oh, and you cheated on me."

Her features grew dark, or maybe it was a cloud skating in front of the sun. "I'm not giving up. And I'm not letting a new girl steal what's mine." Her bitchiness grew with every word.

I threw my head back, inhaled, then slowly righted my head. "I don't belong to anyone."

She huffed and finally let go of me. "We'll see about that." Then she stomped away.

Sucking in a much-needed breath, I checked my arm. I had red imprints. I wiped the sweat off my face then wanted to scream. Instead, I growled out, "Women."

I started a slow jog, pounding one foot then the other into the hot pavement. My head slowly cleared as I honed in on the game—a very important game against a tough team. And I had a scout attending tonight's game as well. So I decided to run one last lap then hit the showers. When I came around the track alongside the bleachers, I spotted Drew, Nina's cousin. His carrottop seemed blinding in the afternoon sun. I slowed to a walk. "Hey, Drew. How are you after that lab accident?" I liked the tenth grader. He'd always been nice to me when Nina and I were dating.

"Good," he said, picking at his fingers.

"What're you doing out here?" Drew was a nerd who was into science and building things. If anyone were looking for the kid after school, he could be found either in the science lab or the library ninety-nine percent of the time. Maybe he was finally getting over his shyness to ask a girl out. "Are you interested in one of the cheerleaders?"

He shrugged. "Maybe."

I grinned. "Good luck, man. I got to run." I blew past the cheerleaders and didn't stop running until I was outside the locker room. I was a little calmer, although a long shower would do the trick. But when I entered the quiet room, I skidded to a stop.

Half of the football team was crowded around Derek and Montana while Derek read a passage from Montana's mom's book. Man, I opened a can of worms with that book.

I cleared my throat as I pushed two players out of the way.

"My heart beat faster anytime she was in a room," Derek read aloud.

The guys were riveted, while Montana wore a happy expression or maybe a proud one since her mom was the author.

I snatched the book from Derek. "Stay out of my locker. Now all of you get dressed." I stuck a glare on each player then Montana. "You, out." I didn't want to ask what she was doing in the locker room in the first place.

Her stunning face radiated with a menacing glow. "Still pissy, I see." She'd changed out of her nun-style outfit and into short shorts.

"Are you looking to practice some moves that your mom outlined in her book?" That appealed to me, especially if she wrapped her long legs around me.

"Nah. I know those by heart. I'm here to make your life miserable. In fact, that's my mission between now and graduation."

I grasped her arm. "Come with me." It was time to settle whatever was happening between us. I knew what my body wanted, but my brain was shouting at me to stay away from her. *She's trouble. She'll break your heart.*

She giggled. "Kidnapping won't look good on your college applications."

I growled as I opened the door to the weight room, which was tucked in the back of the locker room.

She swayed that sweet ass of hers inside.

I bit my bottom lip. "You're not protesting or running." I followed her into the jock-, sweat-, and feet-scented room.

Austin popped up from the weight bench, lifting an eyebrow.

"Hey, man. Can you give us a minute?" I asked my best friend.

He grabbed a towel. "The room is all yours." Then he hurried out.

Montana crossed her arms over her tight tank top. "So what do you want to talk about?"

I stalked up to her. "Who said anything about talking?"

She giggled as she inched back until her body was up against the punching bag. Her chest rose and fell as she batted her long lashes at me.

I snaked my hand around her head, grabbed a fist full of her thick hair, and tugged gently so I had full access to her delicate face. Her sweeping mascaraed lashes fluttered as her blue eyes sucked me in. She gulped loudly, her tongue darting out to lick her lips, and within a flash of a second, my gaze dropped to her mouth. I lowered my head until my lips were barely touching hers. Her breathing increased, as did mine. I anchored my free hand on her hip to keep myself steady, but my fingers had a mind of their own, shaping the curve of her waist. I wanted to explore every part of her.

Dial it back, dude. You're forgetting you don't want to get involved.

My hand slowly traveled around her waist to the small of her back, where I dipped my fingers underneath her top. As soon as I touched bare skin, I lost control. I jerked her to me until she was flush against my sweaty body. She moaned, a sound that made my groin react instantly. I dragged my lips along her jaw, down her neck, and settled on that sensitive spot behind her ear—the spot her mom had described in that sex scene in her book.

As though one of the guys dumped a cold bucket of Gatorade over my head, I released her and backed away.

She stumbled slightly before she angled her head. Her cheeks were beet red as she lasered her angry but disappointed gaze on me. "What's wrong? Afraid? Not sure what to do?"

I spun around so my back was to her and adjusted my boner. I conjured up images of football and ramming our opponents, but that did nothing for relief.

She came around, glanced down at my crotch, then back up to me before she rolled her eyes. "Please. I've seen a hard-on before. What spooked you?"

Oh, the fact that I was trying out one or two moves from your mother's book made me feel weird.

"I shouldn't have done that," I said. "You're not my type." I headed for the door, itching to turn around and take her on the weight bench. But that would have been a colossal mistake for both her and me.

She muttered expletives under her breath. "I told you you're not my type, either."

She had said that on the first day of school.

"Then we're in agreement." I stalked out and found Austin and Derek and a couple of other guys with different expressions that I didn't have time to figure out. Then I noticed Drew among the players.

"Man, that was hot," Derek said. "You learned those moves from the scene in that book."

I clenched my jaw. "You ever hear of privacy?" I'd forgotten that the door to the weight room had a window. "And what are you doing in here?" I asked Drew. Again, he was a nerd into science shit, and the locker room was definitely not a science lab.

On second thought, I didn't want to know. I darted into a bathroom stall until Montana left. Even then, she didn't really leave. Her coconut scent lingered in the air, and I swore it made the guys act weird. My mission after the football game was to burn that book, burn any memory of sex, girls, and especially Montana. Which would be impossible after that hot scene in the weight room. With her flush against me, my hands on her, her thick bottom lip between my teeth, all I'd wanted to do was suck the sweetness out of her.

"Bye, Montana," Derek said loudly.

"Train," Drew said.

Fuck. This kid had hardly spoken to me in school, and in the last thirty minutes, he was in my face.

I threw open the stall door. "Make it quick. I've got to suit up." *Or jack off first.*

He looked away, nervous. As Austin had said, Drew did shop at a different mall. "I need some advice. I want to ask one of the cheerleaders to the debutante ball. But I'm not sure if she'll say yes. So maybe you can give me some pointers."

I almost busted out laughing—not at him, but because he thought I could help him. I was the worst person to ask for advice. "Drew, roll your shoulders back, keep your head up, and make eye contact. Then ask her." I didn't want to know who the chick was. It was none of my business, and I didn't want to get involved, considering Drew was related to Nina. "I've got a game."

He nodded his head a few times. "Thanks." Then he rushed out.

I scratched my head. He'd never asked me for advice before. But I traded thoughts about Drew for other important things like a big football game. After I suited up, I left the guys and headed for Coach's office, which was two doors down from the boisterous locker room. The closer I got, the louder Montana's voice got. I lingered in the hall, listening.

"Did you change your mind about me being on the team?" Montana asked and then snorted.

I held my breath as I scanned the empty and dimly lit hall.

"No. Actually, I wanted to ask a personal favor. If you say no, I completely understand. You said your mother knows Joey Dennison. Is she still in contact with him?"

That name sounded vaguely familiar.

"I don't think so," Montana replied. "Why?"

"I had an idea that would fire up the team. Maybe Joey would be open to joining us for a practice to show the guys some plays."

"I could talk to my mom."

"It's not a big deal. I just thought I would ask." Coach sounded like a little boy who wanted desperately to meet his idol.

I heard rustling.

I inched closer until I was standing in the doorway. "What's going on?"

"I'll get back to you, Coach." She shoved me out of the way, or more like I let her, then she vanished.

Coach snagged his ball cap from his desk. "Lover's quarrel? I don't want to know. Let's talk about the game."

I sat down on the warm seat, and despite Montana's lingering scent, football dominated the conversation and my thoughts. Coach and I dove into the details of plays for that night's game and talked about the USC scout. Before long, we were on the field, playing among a packed house of parents, students, cheerleaders, the band, and a few from the media. I played the game, thought about the game, and refused to look in the stands for the scout, my old man, or even Montana.

After a grueling win by the skin of our pants, we marched to the locker room, slapping high fives and talking shit about the game. Our opponents had a fucking tight defense. I'd even gotten sacked twice. I was certain my old man would have something to say about that. Regardless, a win was a win. Besides, Coach would work us hard during the next practice to make sure we closed the gap on our offense.

Austin and I trailed behind the team, discussing our plans for the weekend, then we both stopped short. The team parted, opening up a chasm, as though Austin and I were some prominent leaders.

"What's going on?" I asked.

Derek's big physique blocked the door. "You're not going to like this, man."

Please tell me Montana is not behind that door. I was riding my high from our win, and I might do something drastic like ask her out.

Derek slid to one side, revealing a huge heart. Inside the heart were the words "Train sucks."

Austin touched the letters. "It's dry. Someone had to do this right after we left for the second half."

The door had been clean when we came in for halftime.

"Maybe Montana did this because of the weight room scene," Derek said.

Highly possible, considering her feistiness. She'd shoved me out of the way when she left Coach's office. Then a loud *ding, ding, ding* went off in my head. She was an artist, a "tagger" as she called herself. But I didn't see her cool signature of "Spunk" that she'd drawn in computer class earlier that day. Maybe she didn't want me to know what she'd done. Either way, she'd given me another reason to rattle her nerves.

Chapter 13

Montana

I VENTURED INTO THE KITCHEN, EXPECTING an empty room since it was Monday morning. Mom sat at the island with her laptop opened and her fingers tapping the keys. The *click, click, click,* sounded like a soft drumbeat.

I gathered a bowl, spoon, the box of Cheerios, and the milk then sat across from her. "Did some crazy idea pop into your head in the middle of the night?"

One whole week had passed since I started at my new school, and in that time, I had enough drama in my life for my mom to use in ten books.

She barely regarded me as she flicked a strand of her messy hair out of her face. "Since we've been here, the story I'd been struggling with is pouring out."

I filled my bowl with cereal. "You've been at it all weekend."

She even canceled the Saturday night dinner we were supposed to have as part of us spending time together. I'd been looking forward to us wandering around the city, window-shopping, and eating at a cool restaurant. But at the last minute, she'd dumped me. I'd felt as though we were back in New York, where all of her weekends consisted of writing or dating. Normally, I would have huffed and puffed then tagged. But not this time.

She took a sip of her coffee, and then she bent over, lifted her computer bag, and set it on the counter. Disappointment washed over her face as she removed a paint can... my paint can. It was the one I'd had in my schoolbag, the one I used for tagging. I was waiting for her to show me the other can, but she only set the one down.

My heart stopped beating for a long second.

"Are you tagging again?" she asked.

I swallowed the fear ball that was lodged in my throat. "Where did you get that?" My schoolbag was in my room, or so I thought. "Did you go into my room?"

"That's not an answer." Her voice matched the anger swimming in her eyes.

"It's not what you think." I'd had every intention of tagging something on Friday night. Train had had me so flipping frustrated. And during halftime, I'd wanted to tag his locker, but I didn't know which one it was. I'd almost settled for the locker room door, but then I thought about what could happen to me. And Train wasn't worth me getting expelled. I'd also heard voices. So I'd torn out of the school like white lightning. "I carry them in my bag. That's it."

Mom stared at me over her coffee mug. "So you didn't tag anything?"

"I promise. I didn't. Besides, I've been here all weekend. Remember? You dumped me." So I'd locked myself in my room. Otherwise, I probably would've colored the city with my artwork, which was one of the reasons I hadn't accepted Elvira's offer to go out with her to the Music Farm. I'd also declined since Train would be there. I wasn't ready to deal with him—not that I was afraid of him. I was more afraid that I would either kick him in the balls or throw myself at him in a desperate need to lock lips with him.

I shoved a spoonful of cereal in my mouth. After I swallowed, I hopped off the stool and deposited my half-eaten bowl of cereal into the sink. I wasn't hungry anymore.

My mom caught my arm. "Montana, you better not be lying to me."

"I'm not. You should write, Mom."

The lines around her face softened. "Hey, I'm sorry about canceling on you this weekend. I'm trying to meet my deadline. But something tells me you're bothered by something else as well. It's that boy, Train. You like him but don't want to admit it."

Busted on that count. "I need to get to school."

She set down her cup and swiveled on the barstool. "Honey, talk to me. I might be absorbed in the story I'm writing, but I'm not dead. I get that you're upset with me, but you could've gone out with your new friends this weekend."

I hated that she knew me so well, although I wasn't sure she believed me when I said I hadn't tagged. "Okay, here's the deal. I like Train. But he's an asshat. He gets under my skin and stays there."

She rubbed my arms. "Which is the reason you want to tag? But didn't, right?"

I huffed. "I didn't tag, Mom."

She mashed her lips. "What does he do that makes you mad?"

"He says things like I'm not his type, yet he gets in my face like he's going to kiss me then storms off. I'm also afraid that if he does kiss me, that I'll fall for him like I did Nikko." Train had barely nibbled on my lips in the weight room. I was talking tongue action.

She frowned. "You shouldn't be afraid of feeling for someone. Yes, the breakup with Nikko hurt. All first loves do. It's your senior year, honey. Train is a good-looking boy. Have a little fun. Maybe go to the ball with him."

"It takes two, Mom."

She placed her hands in her lap. "Give it time. He'll come around."

I shrugged. "So how do I have fun without letting my heart get in the way? How did you date so many men without feeling for them?" Then it dawned on me that I had to ask her about Joey Dennison.

She gave me a weak smile as she swept my hair from my shoulder. "I did have feelings for a couple of them, but their values weren't my values. Honey, we've been through a lot in the last month. You've got a new school, we haven't completely unpacked, and I have my book deadline looming. So things around here will be a little tense for both of us. So please bear with me. Okay?"

I understood that her books were what kept food on the table for us. However, it still hurt that she'd blown me off. It also didn't help that all the drama at school had me in a funky mood. "I'll try."

She wrapped my arms around me. "I love you."

I hugged her back. "Same here, Mom."

She grabbed her coffee cup and went over to the counter to fill it.

"Speaking of old boyfriends," I said, "Coach Holmes seems to be in awe that we know Joey Dennison. He wanted to ask if you still had contact with him. He mentioned that he would love to see if Joey would be interested in giving the football team some pointers."

She poured milk in her coffee. "He emails me every now and then. I could ask. I wouldn't mind seeing him."

"Thank you. Also I have my tutoring session this afternoon. Oh, and I'm supposed to hear back from one or two of the art galleries."

She set down her cup then kissed me on the forehead. "Speaking of the job, I decided you should concentrate on school and your grades. I'd rather you not work. But that's entirely up to you."

"I'll think about it." I liked one of the places that hosted sip-and-draw nights, where a group of folks came together to paint one scene and sip wine. I thought that was a cool way to attract people to the gallery.

"By the way, I probably won't be here when you get home. I have a meeting with Train's mom about the debutante ball."

I should at least warn her that a few students knew who she was, which meant parents would know she was an erotica author. "Mom, word spread on Friday that you're Casey Stewart. So be prepared." I wasn't sure how many kids knew, but the football team had been salivating over her work.

She sat back down in front of her laptop. "How? Did you say anything?"

I chewed on the inside of my cheek. "Not a word. Train was reading your book in computer class on Friday morning. I didn't ask him where he got it, though."

"His mom might read. But my books are in stores. So any backlash for you?"

"I think the school would rather talk about my football tryout." Then again, maybe word hadn't spread yet about my mom. "I've got to run." I darted up to my room and snagged my bag then left.

When I finally arrived at school, I was perspiring but not dripping with sweat. Maybe the steamy weather was growing on me. Cars were parked in the lot, and students gathered in groups, while others headed in the air-conditioned building. I didn't see any sign of Reagan or Elvira or even Train.

I trailed behind a group of girls who were talking about the debutante ball. At least today, kids had moved on to other juicy gossip rather than whispering about my pathetic public display of kicking a football.

The halls were light with traffic for a Monday morning as I made my way to computer class. When I rounded a corner, I came face-to-face with Nina.

Her auburn hair was pulled up in a high ponytail, and her makeup was painted on to perfection. "So your mom writes smut for a living. Is that why you're a slut and attacked Train in the weight room on Friday?"

So much for not getting any backlash about my mom's profession. "Someone is quite jealous." I skirted around her scrawny frame. I wasn't about to get into it with her.

She caught up to me, digging her long red nails into my arm. "You won't get Train. I've been asking around about you. You're nothing. I own this school. And I'll do what I can to make sure your life is hell."

I got in her face. "Bring on hell, then." I stuck my nose in the air and left her standing in the hall with her mouth open.

Snickers and snorts zipped up and down the hall from nosy bystanders.

She could burn me at the stake, spread rumors, or do whatever she pleased. I wasn't about to let her or anyone else get to me. Besides, I'd seen girls like Nina in the other schools I'd attended. Most of them were all talk.

Mr. Salvatore nodded at me when I entered. "Good morning, Ms. Smith. Have you and Train come up with your app for your project?"

"We're working on it." *Liar.* Our preliminary report was due this Friday, and the mood Nina had dumped me in might have been what I needed to light a fire under Train's ass.

More students piled into class. None of them were Train or even Elvira. As I headed to my desk, I sent a quick text to Elvira. *Where are you?* Then I pulled out my notebook and pen. A minute later, her response popped up on my phone: *Running late.*

Reagan bounced in, her hair loose and flowing, and wow. For the last week, she had worn her hair in either ponytails or braids and dressed conservatively in cute capris and cotton shirts. Today, she wore a short skirt, exposing tanned legs, wedge sandals, and a shirt that dropped to her butt and hugged her curves. She beamed from ear to ear as though she'd gotten laid over the weekend.

"You look amazing," I said.

She blushed. "Thank you. I decided to let my hair down, literally and figuratively."

"Does your awesomeness have anything to do with a guy? Maybe Austin?" She'd been quite territorial, telling Nina to stay away from Austin.

She hung her arms over the back of her chair. "Austin and I hooked up at the Music Farm on Saturday," she whispered. "He asked me to the ball. By the way, we missed you. Elvira said she texted you, but you were busy."

Busy brooding and being frustrated over Mom, school, and Train. "After Friday, I needed some time to recharge. The first week of school was crazy." I wasn't lying.

"Are you going to the debutante ball? Maybe with Train?"

"Ha. You're funny." If my mom was going, then I should go too, and I was curious to see what a Southern ball was all about. "Tell me more about Austin. Why haven't you guys hooked up before now?"

She shrugged a small shoulder. "I'd always been afraid to approach him. He's such a man whore. But on Saturday, something between us clicked." She sighed with a dreamy look. "His eyes are like melted chocolate, and he has a smile that makes my stomach flutter."

I knew that feeling all too well, only the guy I was swooning over had the greenest eyes I'd ever seen and brown, shaggy hair that curled at his nape. And the way he'd handled my body in that weight room had soaked my panties. I still couldn't figure out why he'd pulled away, though.

Reagan studied me. "You know Train likes you."

I busted out laughing as I sat back in my chair. "What planet are you on? Have you seen how he talks to me or treats me?"

"That means he likes you, but he's afraid. Nina screwed him up. Give him a chance. He'll come around."

I doubted that, but I couldn't help but flash back to Friday and his erection poking through his gym shorts. *Yum.*

No sooner had I sighed than Train swaggered in as though he didn't have a care in the world, zeroing in on me and only me.

"See how he's looking at you?" Reagan whispered.

I was concentrating on his denim-encased legs. Scratch that. I was riveted to his groin. I couldn't get the image of his hard-on out of my head until I read his T-shirt. In bold black letters, the word "punk" popped out against the white fabric. What had me angling my head and pinching my eyebrows was that it appeared he had taken a red Sharpie and wrote the letter S in front of the word punk. *Odd.* He'd seen me draw my tagging signature in my notebook during class on Friday. But I didn't understand why he would wear a shirt with Spunk written on it.

"I told you he wants you," Reagan whispered. "I've known Train a long time, and his eyes are screaming for you."

All I saw was a guy who was ready to start trouble.

Train dropped his notebook onto the desk. The sound reminded me of someone slapping bare skin.

"Where's that novel you were reading?" Reagan asked in a mocking tone. "Did you learn anything?"

I loved her.

Train grimaced. "I learned plenty. Didn't I, Montana?"

Reagan turned her head toward me so fast, I would be surprised if she didn't get a kink in her neck. "Do tell."

"There's nothing to tell. Train tried a move or two from one of the scenes in my mom's book then petered out." I licked my lips. "Didn't you?"

He raked his gaze over me. "I see you ditched the good-girl outfit. Please tell me you burned that ugly blouse."

"In your honor." I leaned over my desk. "What's with the wording on your shirt?"

He pulled out his phone then proceeded to text something on it.

My phone vibrated in my lap. I opened the text from Train. *I know what you did. So if you keep teasing me, I'll make sure Principal Flynn knows that it was you who vandalized school property.*

I shot a glare his way then typed a reply. *How am I teasing you? And what do you mean I vandalized the school?* I was dumbfounded to say the least.

First, my mom accused me of tagging. Now Train was under the impression I'd done something to school property.

You're showing me your cleavage. And come on. You tagged the locker room door with "Train sucks."

Horror careened through me. *I DID NO SUCH THING*, I typed out in all caps. I'd wanted to tag but hadn't.

The final bell rang, and a handful of students ran in.

Mr. Salvatore droned on as he wrote on the whiteboard. "This week will be more lectures. Also a reminder that your reports on your senior project are due this Friday." He set down his marker then began talking about coding and HTML.

I took notes, but I also zoned out. It was weird that the locker room door had been tagged when I'd almost done it myself but backed out. *What are you worried about? You didn't do it. So what if Train thinks you did. But what if my mom gets wind and thinks I did tag when I promised her I didn't?* I wasn't taking the blame for something I didn't do. Not only that, Train was threatening me by going to Principal Flynn if I kept teasing him, and I could become the number-one suspect since Principal Flynn had my records from my last school.

My phone buzzed in my lap.

It was a text from Train. *So how's your jumanji after Friday?*

I tapped out a reply. *We need to talk. Meet me at my house after school.* It was time to clear the air with him. I also had to find out more about the door. I couldn't start asking around. Otherwise, I might look guilty. I didn't need to have more people pointing the finger at me.

You want me. Don't you?

I wanted to type out, *Duh.* Instead, I texted, *I'll show you how much when you meet me at my house after school.* I didn't want to give him any reason to not show.

Out of the corner of my eye, I saw his mouth drop open.

Bingo.

He growled beside me. *I'll be there.*

Double bingo.

I tabled the mystery of who tagged the locker room door. Instead, I focused on taking more notes and learning how certain keystrokes returned a color, capital letter, or larger font. The class flew by as I got into the cool language of coding. I was also patting myself on the back that I understood the coding language. Maybe the class wouldn't be difficult. *Oh yes, it will when you have to work with Train.* That was another reason to chat with him in private and not in front of friends, the team, or anyone else. Just him and me. Then I would have his undivided attention.

I peeked over at him. Pain and happiness waged war on his handsome face. Maybe he was sporting a boner, but I couldn't tell. When class finally ended, he didn't give me the time of day. But I would definitely have his full attention at my house after school.

Chapter 14

Train

I CLIMBED THE PORCH STEPS TO Montana's house. I'd been thinking about her all damn day. I'd been thinking about our weight room scene and how fucking great she'd felt against me when I'd all but attacked her body. And I couldn't stop thinking about how she'd moaned ever so lightly, which had my dick permanently hard. Lastly, my mind drifted to our little tit for tat in computer class that morning.

I swore I'd read her text a million times throughout the day. *I'll show you how much when you meet me at my house after school.* Out of all that, I was scratching my head at how shocked she'd appeared when I told her about the locker room door. She was the only person I knew who tagged. She'd even asked me about tagging on the first day of school. The funny part was I believed her when she said she hadn't done it. One thing about Montana was she wore her feelings on her sleeve.

With a racing pulse, I was standing on her porch like a moron who wanted to be tortured. I hadn't hesitated when she invited me over, although I had wrestled with the idea of not showing up. But I wanted to hear what she had to say and see what she had in store for me. I couldn't avoid her forever. After all, my grade in computer class depended on her.

I rang the doorbell.

She answered, sucking on a lollipop.

Kill me now. Get your mind out of the gutter. I laughed as I entered. She was going to make it impossible for me to think straight. Was this her idea of showing me how much she wanted me? No. This was payback for coming on to her in the weight room. *Holy fuck!* As I looked at her mouth, all I kept imagining was what her lips would feel like around my dick.

She plucked the pop out of her mouth, the sound sending a stream of fire down to my groin. "What's so funny?" Her tone was polite, a stark contrast to what I was used to from her.

"What do you want that you couldn't tell me in a text or in school?" I asked through gritted teeth.

She shut the door. "Come with me." She wiggled her round ass into the family room. Then she motioned with her lollipop to the leather couch that was facing the TV over the fireplace. "Sit down there."

I hesitated for a second, eyeing her up and down. Her painted toes sank into the white carpet. Her short shorts were frayed on the ends, and her tank top stretched across her awesome tits. "I'm not sure about this, but I'll bite."

She muttered something as she stuck the lollipop back in her mouth.

I dropped down on the couch, hovering on the edge of the cushion, my gaze on her unwavering.

She sucked on the lollipop as she sat on the large square coffee table within an arm's length from me. "What I'm about to do is something that needs to be done. I need your assurance that you won't flip out."

My breath caught in my throat as my heart rammed against my chest. I couldn't say she was scaring me. I was more afraid of myself, and what I would do if she touched me. I nodded.

"I need to hear, 'Yes, Montana, I won't flip out.'"

I quickly scanned the family room then kitchen behind us.

"My mom isn't home if that's who you're looking for," she said.

I leaned forward. "I won't flip out."

She placed her lollipop on a silver plate beside her on the coffee table. Then she pushed me back against the couch and straddled me.

"What the fuck? Are you taking advantage of me?"

She pressed her fingers into my chest as she gnawed on her bottom lip. "We've been dancing around each other for over a week. I'm tired of it. I need to get good grades this year. I have to pass computer class. I can't have you screwing up my chances to graduate. So I'm taking matters into my own hands."

"I see that. But you can't handle me." Or maybe I couldn't handle her.

She dragged a fingernail up my chest, along my neck, then stopped on my lips. "You're so wrong. But that's not up for discussion. We need to clear the air between us. I need you, and you need me. Or else we fail computer class."

Goose bumps coated my arms as she ran her thumb over my lips. I wasn't going to last a second before we were both naked. "Is this about you tagging my name on school property?"

"That's the other reason I asked you over here. I want you to tell me what happened."

My dick was beginning to betray me. "Again, you could've asked me this at school."

"Sure. But then you would've only shunned me or made a snide comment. Then we would be arguing. This way, no one's around. It's just you and me. Do I have your undivided attention?"

I loved fucking with her mind. I loved the banter we had between us. I'd never dated a feisty girl like Montana. At the moment, I couldn't focus on anything other than keeping a boner from happening, and I was failing miserably.

I touched the sides of her thighs, soft and silky. "I'm not exactly in a position to do much." Well, I could have, given my strength, but I would have been a moron not to listen to what she had to say or see how she was about to torture me. "The floor is yours." Or rather, I was all hers. Maybe after she was done with me, I would realize we weren't good for each other or, even scarier, that we were good for each other.

My fingers coasted up and down her thighs. Her eyes became heavy as she rubbed against my groin.

I lost my breath, my mind, and almost my vision. I shaped her hips before my hands were underneath her tank. "Um, is this your way of talking?"

"Maybe." Her voice was breathy.

"I like it," I said.

She stopped moving on me. "Tell me about the locker room door."

"Someone tagged a heart and 'Train sucks' inside the heart. I assumed it was you. You asked me about tagging the first day of school, and then

I saw you drawing in your notebook. But why are you worried if you didn't do it?" Something wasn't right.

She picked at her tank top. "Because one of my paint cans is missing. I think I left it on the floor outside the door."

"When the team returned after the game, there wasn't a paint can anywhere around there. Besides, it's not like Principal Flynn will send the can to a forensics lab." I chuckled.

"Maybe not. But he has my school records from my last school with how I defaced school property." She dropped her gaze to my stomach, which was showing because my T-shirt had ridden up. "He might assume it was me, and I can't prove I didn't do it."

"Why do you tag?"

Her gorgeous blue eyes flashed with excitement. "It's my way of dealing with things. Plus, I get a huge adrenaline rush when I tag. Some people get high on drugs. I get high on graffiti. And you irritate me. There, I said it."

The feeling on my part was mutual. I was getting high being around her. She was slowly becoming my addiction.

She slouched in my lap. "But I swear I didn't do it. I almost did. I stood in front of the door with my paint can and realized I couldn't go through with it. I got thrown out of my last school because I painted an entire wall in the gym. I also promised my mom I wouldn't tag. Then I heard voices in the hall. So I ran. Do you have any enemies?"

I dropped my hands from her. "Everybody loves me," I teased.

Her tongue slid out to lick her bottom lip. "I don't." She wiggled on me.

"Wait." I smirked. "You must. You jumped my bones as soon as I walked in."

"If that's the case, then you love me since you were all over me in the weight room."

I locked eyes with her. "I told you. You're not my type."

One side of her mouth went up. "So if I gave you a blow job right now, you would stop me? Or if I stripped down right now, you wouldn't react or have your way with me? Or if I bent my naked body over the table, you wouldn't do anything? You would simply walk away? Or—"

I grabbed onto her waist as I hopped up then threw her on the couch before I got on top of her.

She giggled.

"What do you want me to say? That I want to suck on your tits until you're squirming and screaming? Or maybe you want me to drag my tongue up and down your naked body before I capture your clit in my mouth and tease you to an orgasm."

Her cheeks turned bright red as her breathing grew shallow. The only thing red on me was my dick, or at least I would bet it was since my erection was straining to get out of my jeans.

A car door slammed.

We both looked at each other with horror.

"My mom's home."

We both vaulted off the couch. She smoothed out her hair, grabbed a laptop off the chair near the fireplace, then plopped back down on the couch. "Sit with me."

I did as she said. I didn't have to worry too much about my hard-on since the thought of getting caught had deflated any sexual tension in the room.

The door opened. "Montana!" her mom called.

"In here!" Montana said. Her hair was mussed as though I'd had my way with her, but I didn't have time to tell her to fix it.

Her mom came in, grinning at us as if she thought we were the cutest couple. "Hi, Train. Are you two working on your computer project?"

No. Your daughter is torturing me into jacking off as soon as I leave here. "Yes, ma'am."

"Good. I had an idea for your app as I was driving home."

Montana closed the laptop screen. "Great."

"What if you two were to build an author app for me? I could post updates and other information similar to my website, but with the app, they wouldn't have to type in my web address. They could just tap on the app."

I glanced at Montana. "That might be a good idea."

Montana slapped my thigh. "You didn't like that idea when I suggested it in class on Friday."

I hadn't been listening.

Ms. Smith tilted her head. "Honey, are you okay? You look a little out of sorts."

"Fine," she said quickly.

I pushed to my feet. "I should go."

Montana got up too. "I'll walk you out."

Ms. Smith said good-bye as I was almost running out of the house. When Montana and I were on the porch, I said, "Our preliminary report on the app is due Friday. So let's get together and outline the specifics."

She stuck her hands on her hips. "Now you want to work with me?"

"We both need to pass." And if working with her meant she would straddle me, then I would be a fool not to do my part.

She sighed. "So did Coach say anything about the door?"

"Montana, don't worry about that. If you didn't do it, relax. And Coach bitched for a few minutes." He couldn't blame any of the team. We'd been playing the game.

"Any idea who might have?" she asked.

"Maybe if you straddle me again, we can brainstorm ideas on who done it."

"That was a one-time deal," she said so seriously.

Maybe I should consider asking her out, then.

Chapter 15

Montana

I SAT IN ART CLASS, MY last class of the day, working on a drawing. The teacher had given us an assignment to pick one historic piece in Charleston, draw out a rough sketch, then submit it at the end of class. I'd decided to sketch out the Battery along the Cooper River since Elvira and I had been there.

"Montana," Ms. Ingram said as she loomed over me.

I lifted my pencil and looked up at the young woman, who I guessed to be in her thirties.

"That's a great sketch. Your angles are perfect. And who's the boy leaning against the railing?"

To add a little something to my drawing, I'd also sketched in the boy who made my stomach flutter, made me a pile of mush, and made me want to punch and kiss him at the same time, especially after last night when I'd been straddling him on my couch.

"His eyes are amazing," Ms. Ingram said.

I smiled at the sea-green eyes I'd colored in amid the muted colors of the rest of the picture.

"Is he a boyfriend?" she asked.

Train was far from a boyfriend, although we'd broken the ice a little bit more after I spilled my guts to him about how I'd almost tagged the door and why I tagged in general.

I never blush, but my cheeks heated. "A friend," I said. "It's not quite done yet."

"See me after class." Then she moved on to the next student behind me.

I couldn't tell from her tone if I was in trouble or not. I hadn't done anything. And I was trying to take Train's advice and not worry since I wasn't guilty, but the culprit probably had my paint can, although the can couldn't be tied to me.

The bell signified the end of class.

After I gathered my things, I ambled up to Ms. Ingram's desk and handed her my drawing as other students did the same. Once the class emptied out, she sat back in her chair.

"Am I in trouble?" I asked.

She arched her thin eyebrows. "Did you do something to be in trouble?"

I shook my head.

"Good. Every assignment you've turned in has been impeccable, and I wanted to chat with you about college. Are your sights set on an art school?"

"I would like to find a good art program, but my grades aren't great."

"That doesn't mean you can't apply. Sure, colleges are tough on their admission requirements, but if you're interested in attending, then you should fill out the applications. And I would do that now."

I seriously hadn't thought about college since Mom had asked. College had been one of our many topics during our road trip from New York to South Carolina.

"Do you think I could get in?" I asked.

Her face brightened. "There's a possibility that if you brought up your grades, you could get a small scholarship."

I opened my mouth. "I wouldn't even know where to begin." My stomach tumbled at the mere notion that I could go to college and study art. I mean, I knew colleges had art programs, but I'd never considered that I could get into one with my expulsion record and grades. *Oh no. Expulsion records.* My last principal had counseled me that my expulsions would hurt my chances of getting into any college program.

"Are you okay?" Ms. Ingram asked.

I shifted on my feet. "I'm good." I didn't need to rehash my past. I had to study hard and ensure that my school record while attending

Palmetto High was near perfect. "Thank you. I got to run. I'm meeting with my tutor."

She smiled from ear to ear. "Good to know you have a tutor."

I was deep in thought on my way out, when she called my name. "Oh, one more thing I meant to ask. Do you know anything about someone painting the boys' locker room door?"

"No, ma'am."

"Very well. I'll let Principal Flynn know. He wanted me to check in with all my students."

He was smart to ask the art students. Maybe the guilty party was in my class. Maybe Train had an enemy he didn't know about. As I left class, I also left the whole door-tagging thing behind. I needed to switch my brain from the creative side to the analytical side to learn algebra.

The library was teeming with students at tables, studying or playing on their phones. Ferris was whispering to none other than the girl who had threatened me to stay away from Train. Upon first glance, I thought he was tutoring Nina. But the table was devoid of books and notepads. He looked as if he was trying to pick her up. Or maybe she was moving on to other guys since she was tracing a finger over his lip.

I settled my stance at their table. "Maybe you two should get a room."

Ferris reared back as though he was guilty of something. I didn't know the black-spiked-haired boy that well. I'd only had one tutoring session with him earlier that week.

Nina kissed him on the lips. "Remember what we talked about."

Ferris flicked his chin at her. Once she gathered her purse, she brushed past me on her way out.

I slid into a chair next to him, when a boy with a ball cap ponied up to the table.

"Are you Montana Smith?" he asked.

"Greer, get out of here," Ferris said in his deep voice.

Greer checked on two other boys who were sitting at a table not far from us. Both boys looked to be holding in a smirk. "Rumor around school is your mom writes sex books."

Ferris popped to his feet, about to chase off Greer, but I held out my hand. "I would like to hear more. Where did you get that info?"

"Everyone is talking about it." His tone changed from cocky to polite. "Is it true that your mom is Casey Stewart?"

The boy had to be either in the ninth or tenth grade. "Did your friends dare you to ask me?"

He shrugged. "Yes. But my mom is a fan. She would like your mom to autograph her books."

It seemed that my mom had a few fans among the moms. "I'll let my mom know." I wasn't about to promise him anything.

"Get out of here," Ferris said.

He scurried away, and his friends laughed.

I pulled out my algebra book. "So, you and Nina, huh?" I asked Ferris.

"Not really. Let's get to work." He opened the book and began sifting through the pages.

Odd. They had sure looked chummy, especially when Nina pecked him on the lips. What was even more odd was her desperate attempt to get Train back, yet she was smooching on Ferris. Maybe she wanted to make Train jealous to get him back. I didn't have time to worry about it because algebra was calling my name.

For the next hour, Ferris explained algebraic equations, then I worked through problems. I was solving my last problem and ran out of room. So I flipped the page.

Ferris's eyes grew wide. "Whoa! That's a cool pic. What does it say?"

"Spunk without the u." I flipped to a blank page then finished my math problem.

"So do you have a date for the ball?" Ferris asked.

I scrunched up my nose. "Are you asking me?"

Ferris was a good-looking guy but not as handsome as Train. "Maybe."

"What about Nina?"

"Her and I are friends. She wants me to help her with a subject she's having problems in."

My intuition was telling me to stay away from anyone who was close to Nina. I was so focused on trying to read Ferris's blank expression that I didn't hear or see Train until he sat down.

"Tutoring session over? Train asked in a hard tone.

Ferris sprang to his feet. "Yep. Montana, think about what I said. See you Friday. Same time." His long legs ate up the distance from the table to the door before he vanished.

"He likes you," Train said.

My tongue hadn't untied yet from Ferris asking me to the ball.

Train snapped his fingers. "Montana, what's wrong? Did he threaten you?"

The worry in his tone jolted me back. "No. He asked me to the ball."

"What did you tell him? Are you going with him?" Train sounded as though he didn't want me to go with Ferris. Train confused the hell out of me.

I had a sarcastic retort on the tip of my tongue, but I decided not to goad him. Maybe then he would open up more.

"I didn't get a chance to answer him," I said.

"I think you should stay away from him. His mission is to screw every girl in school before he graduates."

"Is that your way of saying you don't want me to go with him because you like me and want to ask me yourself?"

He leaned over the table, his hair falling over his forehead. "Seriously. Watch out for him." He got a pen and a notebook out of his bag. "Let's work on our report."

Maybe there was some truth to his warning since Ferris had been cuddling up to Nina. I flipped open my notebook to the place where I'd jotted down the list of items that Mr. Salvatore wanted to see in our report. I'd also made a list of the topics that Mom had suggested for her author app, from new releases to author events and other things associated with her books.

For the first time since Train and I met, we dropped all the drama and sarcasm and concentrated on our project. I scooted closer to him while he broke out his laptop and began typing up the report. Since this was just a preliminary report, we didn't have to make it too perfect. The report was Mr. Salvatore's way of making sure we were on track.

I pointed at the screen. "Back up. You typed teaser wrong."

He swatted at my hand. "Don't touch my screen. Fingers leave an imprint that's hard to get off sometimes."

Oooh kay.

As he typed, he said, "By the way, I'm having a beach party on Saturday night. Do you want to come?"

I did a double take. "Are you asking me out?" Maybe he'd had an epiphany during the last hour.

"Pfft. No. It's a party. If you come, bring an overnight bag and make sure you bring your blue bikini." He licked his lips, and his eyes seemed to darken.

"I'll think about it." I knew my answer, but he didn't need to know I was silently pumping my fist in the air because I would be spending the night on a beach with Train among the partygoers, although I did have to clear the overnight part with my mom.

Chapter 16

Train

I GRABBED A BEER OUT OF the cooler off the back deck of my parents' beach house, which overlooked the Atlantic. I'd gotten permission from my old man to use the place. He was in the process of renovating the sprawling structure, but the only room that was torn up at the moment was the upstairs master bedroom, which was off-limits. The rest of the house was intact but with minimal furniture, which for a high school party was perfect.

Music pumped out of the large speakers that Austin and I had set up on the deck. The neighbors on both sides of us were far enough away that they wouldn't hear super loud music, not with the waves crashing along the shore.

I took a swig of beer as I watched a group of girls below me on the sand sway their hips to Coldplay. I searched the rest of the crowd for one girl in particular, but I came up empty. I'd invited Montana, and she'd confirmed with me in computer class on Friday after we handed in our report that she had gotten approval from her mom.

Overall, I'd had a great week. Nina hadn't been in my face, and I'd spent most of the time practicing football. We'd even won our game last night. The only thorn I had stuck in my side was Ferris. He'd asked Montana to the ball. I didn't know whether she'd said yes or not, and I hadn't asked. Part of me didn't want to know. The other part of me wanted to shove Ferris's spiked head into a toilet.

Austin ponied up to me with a beer in his hand. "Man, Montana's here."

I quickly scanned the beach, the patio, and the living room behind me. "Where?"

"Down, boy," he said. "I thought you swore off girls."

"Shut up."

He held up his hands and gave me one of his smirks that said *I knew you couldn't go without a girl.* "Tonight might be a perfect night for you to make your move, then."

"Maybe to talk." Hell, there wouldn't be any talking between Montana and me.

"Fuck talking," Austin ground out. "Look at her."

At that moment, she glided up to Elvira and Reagan as though the sand beneath her bare feet were ice. Her hair was up and off her shoulders. The blue bikini top revealed the swell of her breasts, and the frayed short shorts hung low on her hips. My balls were officially blue. I grinned because she'd worn the blue bikini. When I'd mentioned that she should wear it, I was expecting her to return a sarcastic comment like *In your dreams. I'm not wearing that.*

I downed half my beer to clear the dryness in my throat. "You might be right. Talking is overrated."

Elvira handed Montana a beer.

"Put your tongue back in your mouth," Austin said at my ear.

I couldn't. I was finding that Montana had the perfect makeup of beauty, confidence, and attitude. My mom had always said a girl should have beauty inside and out, they should carry themselves as though they could fight off an army of men, and they should have an attitude that could adapt to anything on a dime. Montana certainly measured up to my mom's advice, unlike Nina.

As if my mind had conjured up Nina, she appeared with her cousin Drew. I growled.

"Easy, dude," Austin said. "You knew she would be here."

"I didn't invite her."

Austin swigged his beer. "Seriously? It's a high school party. Tell one, and the whole fucking school shows up."

I stifled a growl and the urge to jump off the deck and escort Nina right the fuck off the premises. But those thoughts floated out with an ocean wave when Montana ran a hand down her chest as though she was wiping something off. The innocent act jolted every muscle in me until, out of the darkness, Ferris sauntered over to the ladies. He proceeded to drape an arm around Montana, who smiled at him.

What the fuck? Maybe she had said yes to his offer. Maybe they were officially dating. I fisted my hands at my sides. *So much for a great fucking week.* I was deciding what my next move would be, when Montana giggled at Ferris.

"You might be too late," Austin said. "Ferris seems to have garnered your girl's attention."

It was time to get my ass in gear and snag the girl who'd rocked my world since she'd shown up to class on the first day of school. The same girl had my stomach in knots, had me jerking off in my shower every morning, and had me practically running to school each day to see what tango we would dance to. My problem, though—I wasn't sure I could trust another girl again.

Austin gripped my shoulder. "As your best friend, I'm telling you to go down there and hang out with Montana. Take the bull by the horns and live a little."

Montana shrugged out of Ferris's arm, peered up at me, and gave me one of her ball-tightening smiles. At the same time, Nina joined their group.

Derek came up on the other side of me. "What's cooking?"

"Numbnuts here is still a pansy-ass and afraid to ask Montana out," Austin said.

"For fuck's sake, do it already. That scene between you two in the weight room still burns brightly in my head." Derek chugged a few gulps of beer.

I grinned at Derek. "You're sick if that scene gets your rocks off," I said.

Derek ran a hand through his thick hair. "Aren't we all? Coach says our raging hormones are good for football."

Whatever works.

Austin cleared his throat.

Ferris again draped his arm over Montana.

I growled.

Derek and Austin busted out laughing.

"Time's ticking," Austin said in between snorts.

"Fuck off." I stormed off the deck, down the stairs, then over to Montana. But before I reached her, Nina blocked my way.

"Hi, Train. Great party." Man, her voice grated on my nerves.

"I didn't invite you."

She planted her hands on my chest. "It's a high school party."

I inched back. "And your point?"

She moved closer. "I thought we could talk."

I couldn't touch her, didn't want to touch her. I flicked my gaze up to Austin and Derek on the top deck, trying to send them a telepathic message to get the fuck down here and help out a friend. Instead, of all people, Montana waltzed up.

"Hey, what's going on?" Montana's honeyed voice coated my nerves.

Nina wrapped an arm around my waist. "You're not part of our conversation. Go back to your boyfriend."

I was in hell with the fire burning me at the damn stake. I moved away from Nina so fucking quickly that I stumbled forward. I caught myself before I fell, though.

"My boyfriend?" Montana asked. "You mean Ferris? The guy *you* were kissing in the library the other day?"

I gave Montana an "I told you so" look, but I didn't think she caught it.

"You're the one all over him," Nina countered.

I snagged Montana's hand. "Let's go."

Nina's face darkened to a deep red beneath the spotlights spraying out from the house.

Montana huffed, and I was almost in a jog, trying to catch my breath. Never in my life had I despised anyone as badly as I did Nina. Man, I'd thought I would marry the witch someday. Thank the romance gods for her cheating ways. The more I was around Nina, the more my heart hardened to steel.

"Um, Train? I do need my fingers to draw," Montana said.

I came to an abrupt halt a good distance from the party. As dark as it was, no one could see us, which was perfect because if I had to deal with Nina anymore tonight, I would throw myself in the violent ocean.

I tugged Montana to me, my body heating hotter than the warm sand beneath my bare feet.

"Train," she said my name softly. "If you're about to pull a weight room move, then you better finish what you start."

"Are you dating Ferris?" I asked.

Her small hands settled on my lower back, warm and energizing. "God no. And I'm not going to the ball with him, either."

I held her to me. "Then why did you let him put his arm around you?"

She dragged her nails lightly over my back. "Maybe to make you jealous. It worked, didn't it?"

I couldn't think with her hands on me, or the way her nails felt along my skin, tingly and nice. "So you were late. Everything okay?"

"I was having dinner with my mom, and then I got a call from one of the art galleries I applied to for a job. I'll be starting next week."

We held an unblinking stare in the faint light from a neighbor's house behind us. "I was curious if you wanted to go out sometime?"

Her blue eyes, framed by thick lashes, widened. "For real?"

I was dying to kiss her, but I wanted to wait until she said yes. "Maybe we can go surfing. Do you know how to surf?"

She glanced past me to the water then back up at me. "I can barely swim, let alone surf."

"I didn't mean tonight." The surf was rough. "Tomorrow, though." I wanted to spend some time alone with her away from the group and party. I wanted a chance to get to know the real Montana. She'd shown me a glimpse of her sweet side and a ton of her feisty side. But I wanted to see more. "I'll teach you."

"Train, what changed your mind about me?"

"I can't give all my secrets away tonight. Say yes, and I'll tell you in the morning."

Her lips parted slightly as she studied me.

I could've told her that her spunkiness, the sweetness she'd displayed with my mom, her bold attitude, her curves, her legs, and her tits were all the reasons I was attracted to her, but I was having fun, especially catching her off guard.

"Well, then. I'll tell you my answer in the morning."

I went to say something, when Elvira ran up. "Reagan and Nina are fighting."

I bolted back to the house. When I got to the group surrounding the fight, I pushed them aside. Reagan was yelling. "You're such a slut. I told you to keep your paws off of Austin."

My best friend shook his head at me. I wasn't sure what he was trying to tell me.

"Nina, leave," I said in a tight voice. "You weren't invited, anyway. So get out."

Nina stuck out her chest and opened her mouth.

I held up my hand. "Don't make threats you can't cash."

She stomped past me then snarled at Montana before she disappeared. I flicked my head at Derek, who I realized was standing next to me. "Make sure she's gone."

He saluted me.

I blew out a huge sigh. *Time for a beer.* Austin and Reagan disappeared down the beach. The rest of the partygoers resumed talking. I didn't see Ferris, and frankly, I didn't care to see him. Elvira and Montana went down to the fire pit while I got a beer.

Derek returned two minutes later. "She's gone. Her and Drew drove off. That girl is evil with a capital E."

I agreed as I drank my beer. "Did you see where Ferris went?"

"I think he left," Derek said.

Derek's girl, Jan, couldn't come tonight, so we both commandeered two lounge chairs on the patio. We drank and talked football.

By ten that night, the party was in full swing. The music continued to pump out of the speakers, a group sat around the fire pit, others danced on the patio below deck, and couples disappeared down the beach. I was the key master, which meant I had all car keys. No one could leave without checking in with me. Then again, our parties on the beach were all-nighters, and kids who came to our parties showed up prepared with sleeping bags.

Derek ended up down by the fire pit with Austin and Reagan. I mingled, always keeping my eye on Montana. I didn't want to crowd her space, but every time I saw her talking to a guy, including Lou from the football team, I wanted to kidnap her and take her to my room so we could pick up where we'd left off at her house. But I decided to take a break from obsessing over the blond goddess. Tomorrow would come soon enough. So I headed down the beach to find a place to take a piss. A long line of girls had been waiting earlier for the downstairs bathroom. I could've used the bathroom in my bedroom, but I was lazy and didn't want to give anyone any ideas that they could follow me.

I was about to whip out my dick, when a girl screamed. A loud commotion ensued. *Fuck.* I bolted toward the firelight and the spotlights beaming out from my house. A group of kids ran down to the water's edge.

When I got there, I pushed everyone out of the way. "What's going on?"

Austin was dodging waves as he headed into the water.

A girl pointed out. "Someone is in the water, screaming for help."

I spotted Derek. "Man, in the trunk on the patio, get me a flashlight and my rescue can." A surfboard wouldn't work, not for rescuing anyone, anyway.

Derek jumped into action while I waded in a ways, watching Austin the best I could in the low light from the moon.

"Hey, man," I called to Austin. "I'll have my rescue gear in a second."

Derek returned quickly, splashing water as he came up to me.

"Keep the light on Austin." I dove into the water with my rescue can in front of me then kicked like a motherfucker out to Austin. Between my lifeguard training, surfing, and growing up on the water, I knew how to handle the waves. So did Austin. However, even with his expert lifeguard skills, he would need all the help he could get with the violent waves.

As I swam out, I heard choking and coughing on top of the word "help." When Derek beamed the light on Austin, I sucked in a sharp breath. Just beyond him, Montana was trying to swim toward him. The operative word was *trying*. She had had a beer in her hand for most of the night, and she'd said earlier that she could barely swim. If that was the case, then how did she end up in the water?

After a battle with the surf, I finally reached Montana, who was holding on to Austin's neck for dear life. He didn't stand a chance if she choked the life out of him. A wave came at me, smacking me to one side and pushing me away from Montana and Austin. I gulped in a large amount of water and began choking. Once the wave passed and my lungs were clear, I attempted to get closer to Austin and Montana.

Austin reached out with one hand. "Hurry, Train. Another wave isn't far behind."

I swam closer with my rescue can perpendicular to the shore, which was hard when the waves pushed me in that direction.

"Montana, I want you to grab on to this rescue can. Then I'm going to pull you in." We were at a lull before the next wave. "Do it now." I raised my voice. "I got you, baby." I didn't see any cuts or bleeding, but it was hard to see.

Austin held her as best he could while she grabbed the rescue can.

"Austin and I will help you in." Then I pulled her. "I want you to stay calm."

She nodded.

Austin swam alongside Montana, while I swam and pulled her to shore. When we were close to shore, Derek, Elvira, Reagan, and others raced in to help us. I let out a breath as I pushed to my feet. As soon as I was out and upright, I stalked toward Montana, ready to yell, but stopped in my tracks.

Tears flowed down her face as she shivered endlessly.

Without a word, I lifted her in my arms and marched right into the house and up to the bathroom in my bedroom. As soon as I set Montana down on the sink, Reagan, Elvira, Austin, and Derek came in.

"Austin, can you start the shower?" I asked.

Reagan snatched a towel off the rack and brought it to me.

Montana's teeth chattered as I wrapped the towel around her. Then I checked her body to make sure I didn't need to call 9-1-1. But I saw no cuts on her feet, legs, or anywhere else.

"What were you thinking? I asked, trying not to bite off her head. I had to remember that she wasn't a local. We knew when to stay away from the rough surf and how fierce the undercurrents were. I glared at the girls. "Did you not see her walk down to the shore?"

Steam filled the medium-sized bathroom, which felt tiny with everyone crowding in.

"I went to use the bathroom," Reagan said.

"And I was talking to someone," Elvira said. "I'm sorry, Montana."

Montana's teeth chattered. "It's... not... anyone's fault... but mine.

"I ought to tear off your head." I glared at Montana's blue lips. "You've been drinking. We don't drink and swim."

Austin wiped himself down. "Yeah, girl. It's just as bad as drinking and driving."

"I wasn't trying to swim. I went down to the edge of the water, but when I stepped on something, I fell. The next thing I knew, the ocean was dragging me out."

"I got to run," Derek said. "Jan should be getting home from her family outing. Montana, I'm glad you're okay."

"You've been drinking," I said to Derek. "So no keys."

"That's cool. I'll stop by tomorrow," Derek said as he left.

"The shower should be ready," Reagan said.

The girls could handle the rest. I needed to quiet my shredded nerves. Man, if something had happened to Montana, I didn't know what I would've done.

Both fear and relief flashed in Elvira's big brown eyes. "Why don't you dry off? Reagan and I got it from here."

Austin and I headed for the door.

"Train, don't leave," Montana said softly.

Reagan's hazel eyes went wide, while Elvira's jaw dropped.

"Will you stay? Please." Montana sounded desperate as she shivered.

I was at a loss for words.

The sides of Reagan's lips curled. "I think you should."

"I'm with Reagan," Elvira added.

Austin poked me in the side.

Before I could respond, Austin, Reagan, and Elvira shuffled out, closing the door behind them.

Suddenly, I didn't know what to do until a tear ran down her cheek. This was a new side of Montana. The tough girl did cry.

I went over to her. "Are you certain you want me in here?"

Another tear ran down her cheek. "I'm sorry. Thank you for saving me."

I wiped the tear away with the pad of my thumb. "You scared the fuck out of me."

She threw her arms around my neck and started crying. I lifted her off the sink and walked us into the shower. I had on my swim trunks and T-shirt, but we were both soaking wet, so it didn't matter. I set her down on two feet but held on to her as the hot water cascaded down on us.

She stayed in my arms while I rubbed her back. Her chattering teeth quieted.

"Your heart is racing," she whispered.

"Well, I just saved a beautiful girl from drowning."

"I *am* drowning," she said.

I eased back, placed my hand underneath her chin, and guided her face upward. "Explain."

"You confuse me and terrify me and make me angry. But all I want to do is kiss you."

I grinned like an ass before I mashed my lips to hers. I'd been dying to really kiss her too, not nibble her bottom lip or kiss her neck or her ear. But I'd been desperate to slip my tongue in her mouth and kiss the fuck out of her until our lips were red and raw.

As soon as I got my wish and our tongues collided, I groaned, pressing her up against the stone wall. She moaned as she explored my mouth, and for a second, I let her take control of the kiss, enjoying how she suckled my tongue and my lips until I was bursting at the seams.

I lifted her up. "Wrap your legs around me."

She giggled.

I shut off the shower then got out with her in my arms. As I made my way to my bed, I untied her bikini top at her back. She untied it at her neck. Then she slid down my body before she stripped out of her shorts and bottoms.

I took a step back to admire the girl who was making my heart race faster than a horse at the Kentucky Derby. She smiled shyly as she twirled around like a model on a runway. I chuckled at the freeness and confidence she had about her nakedness in front of a strange guy. Granted, I wasn't a stranger, but in a sense, we really didn't know each other all that well. Yet I felt as if I'd known her forever.

"Would you like me to model too?" I teased.

Clapping, she dropped down on the edge of my bed. "That's a great idea."

I laughed as I took off my shirt, twirling it around my head in an awkward fashion. Then I threw the wet fabric at her. She let out a squeal, and my dick jerked. Then I grabbed the band of my swim trunks and slowly turned, facing the door as I pushed my trunks down, exposing my butt a little at a time.

"More." The giddiness in her voice was doing crazy things to my body.

I whirled around, swaying my hips to the muted music on the deck as I pushed my trunks farther down, exposing my full-on erection.

She gasped as her blue eyes traveled down to my dick, where she became mesmerized. I kicked out of my swim trunks then inched over to her, my pulse pounding in my ears.

"Can I touch him?" she asked.

Who was this girl? I didn't remember having this much fun with any girl, even Nina. The only foreplay I'd had was kissing and groping. *Fuck.* What we were doing was amazing.

"He might spit."

She snorted as her tiny fingers touched my dick, then she immediately withdrew.

"Something wrong, baby?"

She sank her teeth into her now pinkish lips. "I'm afraid if I touch him, I'll want to lick him."

I held back a laugh. "And that would be bad?"

Her wrinkled nose and the fact that feisty Montana was a bit polite were too darn sexy. But her answer was downright blinding. She closed her mouth over my dick, and I literally saw stars. I tensed as I fisted my hands at my sides. In a million years, I would never have expected the night to include Montana and me naked in my bedroom. I wasn't complaining. I was moaning as she was sucking and licking and driving me to the edge. I couldn't let her take me over the edge. A blow job was the bomb. But my old man had taught me that when it came to sex, a man always pleased a woman first. Unfortunately, that would have to wait. As much as I wanted Montana, she'd been drinking.

I eased back, withdrawing my dick, the act making a popping sound as though Montana had that lollipop in her mouth.

She licked her lips. "Something wrong?"

My voice was strangled. "Get on the bed."

She scooted back, her legs falling open.

My dick jerked. "Tease." I climbed on the bed with her. "I don't think we should do this."

She dragged her nails up and down my chest. "Why not? Don't tell me you're going to be a gentleman."

"Montana, I want you so fucking bad right now. But you've been drinking. You almost drowned, and I don't want us to get caught up in the moment only for you to regret this tomorrow."

She pouted. "I'm not drunk. I have my wits about me, and I do want to date you."

I rolled off and lay next to her, propping up my elbow to rest my head in my hand. "This is not how I envisioned our first date. Tell you what, if after our date tomorrow, you still see me as a hot guy you want to bone, then we can replay tonight minus you almost drowning."

"Bone?"

"Jumanji?" I returned as I pinched her nipple.

Squealing, she jumped up, kissed my dick, which hadn't lost its hardness, then trampled into the bathroom.

I sat up, shoving my hands through my hair. I was a jackass for turning her down. But as much as I wanted to be inside her, I had to be sure she knew what she was doing sans alcohol.

Chapter 17

Montana

I OPENED MY PEEPERS ONLY TO slam them shut at the blinding sun pouring into the room. After a second, I bolted upright, surveying my surroundings. The living room was littered with people in sleeping bags. But the person next to me made my pulse kick into gear as though I'd had several cups of coffee.

I poked Train in the side. He groaned as he rolled over. Then he stretched out his arm, and before I could move, my front was pressed to his front, and *oh my*. He was as hard as he'd been last night. *Oh shit. Last night.* I wiggled to escape. *Wait.* I wanted him. He'd asked me out on a date. I swallowed the ball of fur in my throat. I'd sucked on his penis. We had gotten naked. *Oh double shit.* I'd almost drowned last night.

"Mmm. You smell good, even in the morning," he said in a sleepy voice.

I gave up on my escape plans. I wanted him. He wanted me. And I wasn't one to shy away. So I curled my arm underneath my head as I lay on my side. "Care to tell me how you ended up next to me? And what did you do with Reagan?" When I'd fallen asleep, Reagan and I had been talking. Elvira had gone home because her parents wanted her home for Sunday church service.

"She's on the other side of me with Austin," he said through half-lidded eyes.

I lifted up slightly to peek over Train. Austin winked at me, while Reagan slept in his arms. I could see why Reagan swooned over him. He was a looker, and those eyes of his sucked a person in.

Train tapped on my face. "I'm the one you should be drooling over."

I returned to my position. "Jealous?"

He trailed a finger over my lips. "Something you should know about me—I don't like when a girl's eye strays or when a guy touches my girl."

Whoa! "Am I your girl now?" I had been truthful when he asked me about Ferris. During my last tutoring session with Ferris, I'd given him my answer of no. In part because of Train, but also because Ferris didn't give me a warm and fuzzy, not after I'd seen him and Nina together in the library that day.

A wolfish grin lit up Train's handsome face. "I did a striptease for you. So yeah."

Austin snickered. "Way to go, man."

Train grinned.

My cheeks burned at the image of him taking off his clothes. "But we haven't had a date yet."

He leaned in. "You had your mouth around my dick," he whispered. "So I would say we progressed a bit quickly to the dating phase."

I rolled my eyes. "What now? Are you taking me surfing?"

"Nah. I need to make sure you can swim better than you did last night." Concern filled his sea-green eyes.

"I'm sorry I scared you, and thank you again." I rose up a little and peeked at Austin. "You too. Thank you." I didn't get a chance to thank him last night. Train had consumed my thoughts with how visibly shaken he'd been. Then when I'd finally dressed in dry clothes and went in search of Train and Austin, they were nowhere to be found. "By the way, you left me in your room. Then when I came out to the party, you were gone." He'd asked me out. Then we had gotten naked. So I thought we would have at least snuggled up to the fire.

"I went for a walk down the beach. When I returned, you and Reagan were deep in a conversation. So I sat down by the fire with Austin. Then the next thing I see is you snoring on the floor."

"Pfft. I don't snore."

A crease formed in between his eyebrows. "Why did you go down to the water?"

I huffed. "The area around the fire was hot, and I wanted to think. I thought dipping my toes into the water and listening to the ocean would be nice." I shivered as I remembered getting swept in. I'd tried to get up, but the pull was too strong. Then I was under a wave, panicking, gulping down water.

I mashed by body into Train's. "It was scary. I have this phobia of not being able to see what's under me."

He nibbled on my chin. "The only thing that should be under you is me."

I wouldn't argue with that.

He kicked off the blanket and stood, holding out his hand. "Come on."

I skimmed my gaze over his muscled chest, arms, and abs. Yeah, he wasn't wearing a shirt, but sadly, he was wearing swim trunks. The green swim trunks seemed to brighten his sea-green eyes.

"Baby, my hand."

His pet name for me jarred me from my drooling state. "Baby?" I took his hand.

When I was upright, he buried his hands in my hair. "Not a fan of the word?"

"Whatever trips your trigger," I teased. He could call me anything he wanted to as long as my body was flush with his.

He laughed.

"Hey, man," Austin piped up. "Are you making breakfast?"

Train flicked his head at Reagan, who was just moving under the covers. "Go back to your girl. We're taking a walk. Then we'll talk about food." Train ushered me outside.

Breakfast did sound good.

More bodies were cocooned in sleeping bags around the fireless pit. The sun sat slightly above the horizon, while the water was calm—a sharp contrast to the rough surf last night.

Train and I ventured down the desolate beach and walked along the shore, sinking our feet into the wet sand. The only sound for miles was the push and pull of the barely there waves that slid along the sand and, at times, over our feet. We meandered for about five minutes before I broke our silence.

"What are you thinking about?" I asked.

"You. Me. Us."

"Again, you confuse me. You said you would tell me this morning why you changed your mind about me."

He picked up a seashell. "If I'm being honest, you scare the fuck out of me. I've never met a girl like you."

"I'm not sure how to take all that."

His tone was genuine. He did like me. Otherwise, he wouldn't have slept next to me. Even if he just wanted sex, he still had to at least like me. I couldn't have sex with someone I didn't like.

A seagull cawed overhead.

His eyes sparkled in the morning sun. "Nina was my world. I seriously thought I would marry her someday. We were inseparable. We've known each other since grade school, and it wasn't until the ninth grade when we started dating. Then at the end of our junior year, I was in Charleston, visiting my dad. I was walking to my truck, when she came out of a nearby restaurant with a guy. I watched as she kissed him. When I confronted her, she said the guy was a friend of the family. You don't tongue a guy who is a friend of the family. The kicker was I knew the guy. He's the starting quarterback for Clemson, who wasn't a friend of her family."

"Elvira said you put him in the hospital?"

"After Nina and I broke up, she decided to show up to a party with the dude on her arm. I was drunk and lost my shit." He stared out at the water.

I grasped his hand. "I can't tell if you're not over her or still hurt by her or both."

He switched his gaze from the water to me. "Neither. But I was shocked when she showed up on the beach on the first day of school. Over the summer, her father took a job in Florida, but I guess that didn't work out. I thought I didn't have to see her at all during my senior year or ever."

"Hence why you've been cranky," I said.

"I'd sworn off girls this year. But that lasted all of two weeks." He chuckled. "Some blonde who thinks she owns the universe blew into computer class and blindsided me."

His admission explained why he'd been pushing me away.

He snaked an arm around my back. "I do like you. You have this personality that attracts me to you, and you have a way of getting me to do things I would never do."

A butterfly winged in my stomach, but I tamped it down. "You mean like stripping."

"Fuck. I would've never done that with another girl. Not to mention that weight room scene. That's not me, although your mom's book spurred me on."

I slipped my fingers just inside the band of his swimsuit. "Why did you get spooked in the weight room?"

He sucked in a breath. "I was making moves your mom wrote. It was weird."

"So I guess we're dating now," I said.

"Is that your answer?" he asked.

After everything we'd been through, especially last night in his room, God yes. But just to seal the deal, I grabbed his hard-on. "Yes."

He lowered his eyelids then quickly removed my hand. "And Ferris isn't going to be a problem?"

I giggled. "Don't like my hand on your boner?"

His teeth sank into his bottom lip. "I'd rather have your mouth. But back to Ferris."

"Ferris isn't a problem, but he is my tutor."

He made a noise in the back of his throat.

"Train, there's something you should know about me. I was hurt by a guy once. He broke up with me to play the field. So I'm as scared as you. Let's date and have fun. If sex happens, then it happens. But just so you know, I love sex, and I'm not a virgin."

He lost the jealous attitude and smirked. "You say the boldest things."

"So how about a lesson in swimming?" I asked. "If we're going to date, I guess I should learn to like the water, but only if you're with me." I wasn't sure if I could get over my phobia of not seeing what was below me, but I was willing to try with him.

"Come on. Let's eat first. Austin gets cranky when he doesn't eat."

Two hours later, after our food had digested, Train and I were in the ocean in an area where we could see and touch the bottom. We hadn't gone far out at all. He'd been watching me swim and teaching me the

139

different swim strokes. Again, I could swim but not to save my life. Train said that was because I was panicking. But after an hour of the doggie paddle and regular swim strokes, I was tired.

He grasped my waist and lifted me in his arms. My legs went around his waist, while I locked my hands behind his neck with my front pressed to his front. We floated out a little ways until I couldn't see the bottom.

"Okay, time to go in," I said.

"This is where you need to learn."

"It freaks me out that I can't see the bottom."

He pulled out a set of swimmer's goggles. "Put these on. Then take a peek."

He held me while I slipped on the goggles. Then I dipped underwater. All I could see was a sandy bottom and nothing else. I popped up.

His cheeks were getting sunburned. "Nothing to worry about. Right?"

I lifted a shoulder as I lowered the goggles, letting them hang around my neck. "I still need you to hold me."

He raised an eyebrow. "Why?"

"So I can do this." I jumped into his arms and kissed him.

He clutched my hips, then his tongue was in my mouth. He tasted salty but oh so good. I melted into him, letting him take as much as he wanted. He grabbed a handful of my hair with one hand and gently cupped my face with the other as we floated.

My hands slid around his neck, and I dug my fingers in to hold on for whatever ride he was taking me on, and he was teasing my tongue, willing me to engage. I was in heaven, letting him have his way.

"Kiss me, baby," he said, biting on my lip.

I mewled in time with the sound of the seagulls overhead. I sucked on his tongue until he was groaning and pressing his hips into me. As we kissed and groped in the ocean, I knew without a doubt that I would fall for Train Everly.

Chapter 18

Train

FOOTBALL PRACTICE HAD FINISHED UP, and I was jogging around the track, doing more laps than Coach had ordered. Four days had passed since I gave Montana swimming lessons. She wasn't as bad at swimming as she'd made it sound. The fun part was making out while we were floating in the water. I'd wanted to take her back to my room, but I didn't want to rush things. And if I were being honest, I was afraid to do more than kiss and grope because the minute I was inside her was the minute I would be a goner.

I checked my watch. I had about thirty minutes before I met Montana. She was in her tutoring session with Ferris. I wasn't exactly pleased, but I couldn't order her not to work with Ferris. I could tutor her, but we probably wouldn't get any work done, and I had to trust her, though I was having a hard time. Besides, Ferris had the smarts to make valedictorian. I did as well, and I understood why Salvatore had partnered me up with Montana. He wanted me to help her since her grades were nothing to write home about.

The sun burned my back as I jogged the last lap. Then I slowed to a walk, regulating my breathing as I collected my football gear. When I started for the showers, I spotted my old man waving at me on the other side of the goalpost.

He slipped his hand into the pocket of his khakis. "I talked to the USC scout."

My heart punched my ribs. "And?"

"He hasn't said yes yet, but your scholarship looks promising. He wants to see how the next two or three games go."

I wiped the sweat off my forehead with my T-shirt. "Is he hung up on something with me?" Maybe I wasn't as sharp as I should have been. I'd also gotten sacked twice in the first game, although I'd played a great game last week.

Lines fanned out underneath his green eyes. "Nothing like that, son. Scouts just like to be sure, and the football coach wants to see the tapes of your games again. My advice is to play like you did last week."

I had thrown four touchdowns and hadn't gotten sacked. But we had six games left in the season.

"I got to run," I said. "I'm meeting Montana. We're having dinner with Mom."

His tanned forehead creased. "You're dating again?"

"Is that a problem?"

He fiddled with his car keys. "Don't let your head wander from the game because of a girl. You know what happened last year with Nina."

I couldn't argue too much with him. Nina had driven me to drink many times last year. But Montana wasn't Nina. Montana didn't nag like Nina. Montana didn't whine, either.

I clutched my helmet guard. "I got a handle on things."

His tone was even. "I hope so, son. The USC scholarship is important, and I'm not bailing you out again. I've used all my favors with the USC sports director."

My insides twisted into a knot. "You know, Dad, if anyone is going to screw with my head, it's you. You ride my ass constantly about football. 'You didn't throw the ball right. You should've thrown the ball to so and so. You can't make plays like that and expect the scouts to give you high marks.'" My voice was shaky.

He grabbed the back of his neck, one of the signs that I was hitting a nerve or he was getting pissed. But I wasn't hanging around to get into a huge argument. A blowout fight with my dad would put me in a terrible mood, and I had a date with my mom and my girl, although it felt good to finally get that off my chest.

"I got to run. I need a shower before I meet Montana. I'll see you at the game tomorrow." I jogged up to the school and went directly to the showers, stewing over how a conversation with my old man could go from zero to sixty in two seconds flat. I understood that he was busting his ass to help me get that scholarship, but man, he wasn't about to tell me who I could or could not date.

After I washed off the sweat and anger then dressed, I darted through the empty school halls. Montana had told me to meet her in the library. Before I went in, I glanced through the window above the door and stiffened. Ferris was way too close to my girl as he leaned in close to her, pointing to something in her notebook. I swallowed a lump in my throat as red coated my vision. *Dude, don't go ballistic. Your old man just warned you about girls and that football scholarship.*

"Mr. Everly," a deep baritone voice said from behind me. "Are you lurking?"

I spun around to find Principal Flynn heading toward me. "No, sir. Just waiting on Montana."

He settled in front of me, his large gut protruding out while he loosened his tie. "Good. I'd planned on talking to her tomorrow, but since she's here..."

My antenna went up. "Is something wrong?"

"Not sure. Do you know who could've painted your name on the locker room door?"

I thought that incident had blown over. It had happened two weeks ago. The graffiti had been cleaned, and word from Coach was that the administration had no suspects. "No, sir. Do you think Montana did it?"

He regarded me from his six eight height. "Do you know if she did?"

I didn't get a chance to answer, when Montana came out of the library with Ferris. She swung her confused gaze from the principal to me. "What's going on?"

Fear washed over Ferris's face.

"Let's take a walk, Montana," Principal Flynn said.

Her sun-kissed cheeks paled. "Can Train come with us?"

Principal Flynn's loafers clicked along the floor. "If you don't mind him listening to our conversation."

"Go," I said to Montana. "I'll catch up in a minute."

She joined the principal.

I blocked Ferris. "Why do you look like you're guilty of something?"

He pursed his lips. "I don't know what you're talking about."

"I swear, dude. If I catch you trying anything with Montana, I'll shave that spike right off your head." I almost threw him up against the wall, but Montana's voice was fading, and I was curious to hear the conversation with Principal Flynn. I sneered at Ferris before I took off.

Principal Flynn was ushering Montana into the empty chemistry lab. I didn't have chemistry this year. But the rumor was that the lab accident hadn't done too much damage. Mainly, a small fire had ruined a lab bench, although I didn't see any signs of damage.

"Montana, I understand from your school records that you have a talent for artwork, where you defaced a gym at your last school. Is that true?"

Montana clung to her book bag as though it was her lifeline. "Yes, sir."

"And have you done anything like that at this school?" Principal Flynn asked.

Her eyes never wavered from his. "No, sir."

He studied her with his hands in his pants pockets. "You realize that graffiti can warrant legal action?"

"Has someone accused me of doing something like that?" Montana asked.

"Not at all. But it came to my attention that you had been in the locker room earlier the day of the first football game. So I pulled your records."

"I was down in the area talking with Coach Holmes," she said.

"Did you see anyone other than the football team?" Principal Flynn asked.

"No," she said.

"Very well," he said. "You both can go."

She rushed out as though she couldn't breathe.

"Mr. Everly, good luck at the game tomorrow night," Flynn said.

I nodded as I hurried to catch up with Montana. We didn't speak until we were standing next to my Hummer.

"Oh my God," she blurted out. "I knew he would check my records."

I guided her chin up. "You didn't do it. So let it go." I nibbled on her bottom lip. "We got other things to discuss before we get to my house. My mom's going to ask if we're going to the debutante ball together. Do you want to be my date?" I had refused to attend, but that was before Montana.

Her mouth opened slightly before her delicious lips curled upward. "Why, sir," she said in a sweet Southern accent. "I do believe I would love to." She flicked her hair over her shoulder then held out her hand like a lady would do when waiting for a gentleman to kiss the back of it.

I placed my palm under hers, bent over slightly, and kissed her hand. "Thank you, madam. It will be my honor to escort such a lovely woman to the ball." Then I pulled her to me and crushed my mouth to hers.

For the moment, nothing else mattered but kissing her.

Chapter 19

Montana

THREE WEEKS HAD COME AND gone since Train and I had had dinner with his mom and Principal Flynn had questioned me about the graffiti. The subject had all but died. Even Nina hadn't followed through on her idle threats that she would make my life hell or get Train back, which wasn't a surprise to me. Girls like Nina were all talk. And for now, I had other things to worry about, like the upcoming ball that was two Saturdays from today.

My stomach rumbled with giddiness and nerves as Mom and I shopped for dresses. She'd taken a breather from writing and kept her promise that we would spend the day together. The city was bustling with tourists and locals. I couldn't remember the last time Mom and I had hung out on a Saturday afternoon. I did have to work at five for a couple of hours. Train had plans with his dad and the football coach for USC.

Mom had found her a simple black-and-white dress that fell to her ankles with a slit that traveled up to just below the knee on one side. She was checking a rack in the small dress shop, while I ducked into a dressing room with an A-line floor-length princess-style dress. I shucked my clothes and stepped into the garment, then I walked out to show Mom.

"What do you think of this one?" I twirled around, holding the lace fabric that fell over the satin skirt.

She covered her hand over her mouth as her eyes watered. "Face the mirror."

I turned and smiled. "It's beautiful, isn't it?"

"You're beautiful. I love the lacy long sleeves and how the bodice sits well off your shoulder. You can use grandma's pearls."

Aw. I teared up. I missed my grandma. She died when I was in the seventh grade. She used to watch me when Mom traveled to promote her books.

"Do you think Train will like it?" I asked.

She grasped my shoulders from behind as we locked eyes in the mirror. "Of course he will. And I love burgundy on you. It makes your blue eyes pop."

I held my stomach. "Oh God. I'm suddenly nervous." The hottest guy in school was taking me to a big shindig. I'd never been to a dance, let alone a ball.

"Have you two not had sex yet? Is that what makes you nervous?" she asked as though she were my best friend and not my mom. We had an open mother-daughter relationship. She knew I wasn't a virgin, and she'd made sure I was on the pill.

"We haven't." Not that we didn't want to. We'd been busy with school, his football, and my job. Plus, anytime we'd been at his house or mine, our moms had been home. Even though my mom was cool with me having sex, I didn't feel comfortable getting naked with Train in my room. "But that's not it. I've never been to a dance. And things have been going so well between Train and me that I feel like I might lose my glass slipper like Cinderella." I didn't think Train would ever go back to Nina, but weird things did happen in the world.

She spun me to face her. "Stop worrying that the bottom will fall out. Besides, Train is head over heels for you. I see how he looks at you when you two are together."

I knew he liked me a lot, and the feeling was mutual. Maybe that was the reason for my nerves. I liked him too much.

"Let's get that dress," Mom said, "then grab a quick bite before you have to work."

My stomach settled, and the nerves were gone by the time we paid for the dress and found a restaurant that served good seafood. At fifteen minutes to five, Mom dropped me off at the art gallery. After we said our good-byes, she drove away. I was about to go in, when Train sauntered up with a huge grin on his face. He was dressed in a crisp white shirt and brown pants.

Whoa! The butterflies in my stomach took flight as I whistled. "Who are you? And what have you done with my boyfriend?" He looked good in nothing, in swim trunks, and in jeans and his wild-saying T-shirts. But dress pants and a dress shirt? Heat shot down my belly. His hair was even slicked back and tucked behind his ears, highlighting his clean-shaven jaw.

He grabbed my hand and ushered me around the building to a small alley that was surprisingly clean. Before I could say a word, his tongue was in my mouth. I melted into him, my hands sliding around his waist to his butt, which was tight and toned.

He broke the kiss, dragging his lips along my jaw to my ear. "I had to see you before dinner."

"Are you addicted to me?" I teased.

He eased back. "I'm crazy for these luscious and delicious lips." He pressed his fingers to my mouth. "I'm definitely addicted to these babies." He cupped one of my breasts. "And I would love to dive into this." His hand slid down to my lady parts. "My mom went up to my aunt's house in Myrtle Beach for the night." He pressed his body against mine.

"You mean you want to play with my jumanji?"

He shrugged. "Okay. But more than play."

Heat rose up to burn my cheeks. "Really?" Suddenly, a wild tap dance broke out in my stomach, a mix of nerves and excitement. I hadn't had sex in over a year, but it wasn't so much the thought of sex as it was the boy in front of me who brought out the butterflies. Taking our relationship to the next level could make me fall head over heels for Train, and that alone scared me. "I get off at eight."

He waggled his eyebrows. "Then again at nine, ten."

I rolled my eyes, and my belly rolled too. "Right now, I have to work."

He had a permanent grin on his face as he escorted me to the entrance of the art gallery. We made plans for him to pick me up later since my mom had the car. Then he gave me a chaste kiss good-bye.

By nine that night, I was walking into Train's bedroom at his house on the golf course. Unlike his room at the beach house, this one had more than a bed. A desk with a high-backed chair sat under a shutter-covered window. A dresser lined the wall opposite the bed, and the walls were covered with posters. One in particular caught my eye. The poster was of a girl wearing a parka with a furry hood, and her long blond hair was windblown around her face.

"Who's the girl?" *Please don't say you have another former girlfriend.* Otherwise, I was out.

He turned on the stereo that sat on top of his dresser. "Skylar Grey. She was at the Music Farm a few weeks back."

That was the weekend my mom dumped me. "I've never heard of her."

He sat on the edge of his bed. "She kind of looks like you, although she's older."

I studied the poster. I didn't see the resemblance, not in that one, but the poster next to it had another photo of her. She did have striking eyes, but I couldn't tell if they were blue or green. No matter. The girl was pretty with the way she had her braid draped down her chest.

"Montana," Train said in a soft, raspy voice.

I swung my attention to the bare-chested quarterback. "When did you take off your shirt?" I licked my lips, and Skylar became a distant memory.

He closed the distance between us. "Do I detect nervousness?" He tipped up my chin with his fingers. "You sure have different sides to you." He leaned down, his breath tickling my neck. "Rather sexy to see you a little apprehensive."

It wasn't that I was apprehensive. I also wasn't all talk, either. I wanted Train badly. We'd practiced enough foreplay that the *Guinness Book of World Records* would have been impressed. I knew myself. I knew going all the way would take our relationship to a deeper level, and I was afraid. I was afraid of him, of us, and of heartbreak, which was why I hadn't pushed to do more than just grope each other. Above all else, I had to make sure he didn't want to rekindle his relationship with Nina. Ninety-nine percent of me believed he had no desire to return to his ex, but that one percent shone brightly.

"Montana," he whispered in my ear. "Where are you?"

I blinked as I swallowed the dryness in my throat. "I need to ask you something." I shrugged away from him and went to sit on his messy bed.

"Since when do you have a serious face?"

I was probably about to screw up the night and the fun we were supposed to have, but I had to know. "We have a great time together. You're yin to my yang. You get me. You don't mind that I'm wacky or bold or say or do stupid things. And I think I know the answer to this, but I don't want to assume. Do you still have feelings for Nina?" I held my breath.

His brows furrowed. "For real?"

Silence thickened the air.

Train wrenched a hand through his brown locks as he squatted down in front of me. "I can't stop thinking about you. When I'm not with you. When I am with you. In the shower in the mornings." He plastered on an impish grin. "At dinner earlier tonight, I couldn't tell you what half the conversation was about. I hardly heard a word. All I kept thinking about was you."

"That's because you knew you would play with my jumanji tonight."

His hands coasted up my thighs. "Maybe that and I love spending time with you. But we don't have to bone if you don't want to. We can make out until our lips are red and raw and my balls are blue."

I busted out laughing.

He started to crawl up, causing me to lie back. "I have no feelings for my ex."

I believed him. And at some point in my life, I had to take a chance with my heart even if it meant letting him in in a tiny way.

I planted a hand on his super-sculpted chest. "Not so fast. I want you to do a striptease like you did at the beach house."

He chuckled. "Only if we replay that entire scene." He dragged my hand down to his hard-on.

Even though I'd had quite a bit to drink that night, I hadn't forgotten what I'd done or how I'd enjoyed having my mouth around his penis. "You've got to strip first."

He jumped off me and went over to his stereo behind me. Within a second, a slow and sexy song filled the room. "In case you haven't heard her music, this is 'Come up for Air,' by Skylar." He helped me off the bed. "Dance with me."

"Wait. I thought we were—"

He touched my lips with his finger. "Shh."

He wrapped one arm around me and put his hand on the small of my back, then he crooked his elbow so his other hand was in the air, waiting on mine.

I pressed my palm to his.

"We'll have to dance at the ball, so call this practice." He gently guided me to him as he rested his chin against the side of my head.

On the first day of school, he'd said he didn't dance, but he was quite the dancer. Then again, I guessed he had to be if he attended the debutante ball every year.

We swayed to the music, me following his lead. After a minute, he twirled me around, and I couldn't help but feel like Cinderella. Then he let go of me, and one side of his mouth ticked up as he started unbuckling his belt.

My heart kicked into gear. Hell, it was already sprinting. It *had* been since I'd walked into his room. One minute, I was shaking; the next, laughing; the next, falling for this boy who was making my heart soar.

I clapped and giggled as I watched in awe of how he was swaying his hips, slowly pushing his pants down. I went up to him and helped him wiggle out of his clothes. Then, as the song was hitting a crescendo, we began taking off my clothes. When the song ended, we were both completely naked, feeling each other. I traced dips and valleys on his chest and abs before I had my hand around his silky, warm erection. But I lost my grip when he bent over to suck one of my nipples into his mouth. I arched into him, running my hands through his soft locks. Then he kissed his way down my stomach, while his expert fingers coasted along my butt and my legs. When his mouth was oh so close to my lady parts, he peered up at me, his eyes full of arousal as they held me prisoner.

My breathing grew shallow, my stomach fluttering with anticipation. I nodded as I moistened my lips.

He continued kissing until his tongue snaked out and licked my clit. I opened my stance, and he licked again as I held on to his head. My legs shook as my belly twisted into a glorious knot. I moaned as he drew me to the edge until my moans became one loud scream. He kissed his way back up my body, while I tried to slow my breathing.

He stopped to tease and play with my nipples before he raised his head and sucked in my bottom lip. "Are you okay?"

"Don't let go of me, or I might collapse."

He shuffled us over to the bed. "Sit." Then he snatched a condom from the nightstand. Within seconds, he had the condom on and was hovering over me with his hands pressed into the mattress on either side of my head. Without warning, he pushed inside me. "Oh fuck." He froze, briefly closing his eyes. "Are you sure you're not a virgin?"

"It's been a while." I grasped his hips. "Hold one second." My body needed a second to accept him.

Pain etched his handsome features as his hair fell forward. "Put those long legs around me. That might help."

He began to rock into me, slow and steady. I matched every thrust as we spewed noises together. I'd never had an orgasm when a boy was inside me. But Train was hitting a spot that sent shivers through my body. The more we moved together, the wetter I got, and the more he groaned, the more my belly knotted.

He picked up his pace, both of us sweating. When he thrust into me again, I clamped down on his erection. He stiffened and grunted loudly before he said my name.

I blew out a breath before he gave me the most beautiful smile that melted me where I lay.

A drop of sweat hit my face as he lowered his head and kissed me. "Maybe I can go longer the second time around."

I did orgasm way too fast as well. "Longer, shorter, it doesn't matter, as long as we please each other. Besides, we can do it again and again." I was turned on, just seeing how I affected him.

"You are without a doubt my addiction. Sex or not, fast or slow, you're amazing."

"Ditto." I prayed, though, that coming down off an orgasm wasn't clouding his judgment.

Chapter 20

Train

FOR OCTOBER, THE WEATHER WAS perfect for hanging at the beach. Montana and I were surfing, or more like I was teaching her how. Her fear of not being able to see under the water had diminished since that first day I'd given her swimming lessons.

"Let's go in," she said. "My legs are tired."

"Get on my board. I'll pull you in."

She climbed on and lay on her stomach. "I can paddle in."

I held on to my board. "I know, but what if I want to take care of my girl?"

She gave me the sexiest smile as her big blues sparkled. "I would jump your bones right now if I weren't tired, hungry, and waterlogged."

"We could always have a quickie before we eat."

"You have to catch me first," she teased as she paddled in, the waves pushing her closer and faster toward the shore.

I swam in behind my beautiful girl. We'd become inseparable since we had sex two weeks ago. The first time with Montana had been fucking amazing. After our first round, we'd gone three more before she had to go home. I'd loosened up, and she had as well. We'd taken turns exploring each other, and each orgasm seemed more powerful than the last. I didn't know why or what that meant. All I knew was sex had turned into slow and mind-blowing lovemaking that I didn't want to end.

Montana was relaxing on my board at shore with her front facing the sun when I got to shore. I hovered over her, wanting nothing more than to get naked, but our friends were lounging up near my beach house. I'd invited Austin, Reagan, Elvira, and Lou out to spend the day.

"Should we give our friends a show?" I teased.

She held up her hand in front of her face to block the sun. "Ooh, I like shows."

I kissed her belly. "You wouldn't mind people watching?"

She sat up, squeezing water out of her hair. "That would be hot."

I shouldn't have been surprised. One thing I'd learned about Montana—she loved attention.

I helped her up, then I grabbed her butt, tugging her to me. "You're something else, and I can't get enough of you."

She flattened her palms on the sides of my face. "Are you falling for me, Train Everly?" she asked in a Southern drawl.

My pulse raced as I locked eyes with the gorgeous girl. "Something is happening, but I couldn't say what." I honestly couldn't. When I wasn't with her, I thought about her constantly. When I was with her, I couldn't take my eyes off her. She made me laugh. She made me do things I wouldn't even have dreamed about doing, like stripping and dancing. And most of all, sex was off the charts with her.

She ran her tongue along my bottom lip. "You just want my body."

It was more than her body, but I wasn't willing to say that out loud, not until I knew for sure that my lust wasn't clouding my true feelings.

I stuck my tongue in her mouth, exploring, tasting, and taking. She purred liked a kitty cat as my dick grew in size.

"Train," Austin called. "Burgers are ready."

"Fuck," I said.

"No, that's for later," she replied as she darted up to the house.

"You're so funny." Chicks had it easy. When they got aroused, no one could tell. But a dude? We were screwed.

I dove into the surf to let my body deflate, then I grabbed my board and joined the group.

Montana was downing a bottle of water. Reagan and Elvira were sitting in lounge chairs, clad in shorts and swim tops. Austin was flipping burgers onto a plate. And Lou was inside, glued to Sunday afternoon football.

I toweled off, snagged a soda out of the cooler, then sat down at the patio table, which had all the fixings for burgers.

Austin stuck his blond head inside the sliding door. "Lou, get your butt out here. Food's ready."

Everyone found a seat around the table. Lou removed his ball cap as he sat next to Elvira then pecked her on the lips. I'd learned recently that Lou and Elvira had thing for each other. Reagan and Austin were hot and heavy in their relationship. And I had my girl. I wasn't sure how I'd gotten so lucky, especially when I hadn't been sure if I would ever take a chance again on dating. And here I was, falling for a girl that gave relationships a whole new meaning—the kind that made my body sing and my life so much richer.

We dove into the food, talking about football. We had two games left in the season, and the team was enjoying a perfect record. Coach Holmes was happy. On the other hand, I couldn't say my old man was happy. My performance on the field had been good but not great. I had been sacked in the last game, and I'd thrown an interception in the last game. I had thought my dad would've nagged me about those two plays, but he hadn't said a word. I wondered if he hadn't because of the conversation we'd had on the football field a few weeks back when I told him how he fucked with my head.

"Montana," Austin said. "Has your mom heard from Joey Dennison?"

Coach had filled the team in on Joey Dennison and told them he hoped the former Naval Academy player would show up to give us some pointers.

"Honestly, I don't know," she said in between bites of her burger. "I'll have to check."

The sliding door whooshed open at my back.

"Hey, Mr. Everly," Reagan said.

Dad was decked out in shorts, a golf shirt, and a ball cap. "Guys. Gals."

I got that my dad owned the house, but he was rarely there. "What are you doing here?"

"I need a minute. Let's take a walk down the beach," he said to me.

Maybe he was ready to give me his two cents or complain about my performance on the field. Whatever the case, my pulse raced. I didn't want to fight with him in front of my friends. "Be right back," I said to the group.

They whispered as my dad and I ambled down to the water's edge. The afternoon breeze was picking up as high tide rolled in.

"Dad, if you're here to fight—"

He held up his hand. "The coach at USC called me today. You're in. You got your scholarship."

I would've smiled or even hugged him, but his tight features gave me reason to pause. "Then what's up? Are you mad at me for speaking my mind the other day?"

"I heard you. I didn't say a word when you threw that interception. I wanted to, but someone reminded me that I was once in your shoes. But you don't see me happy because I'm still concerned about your off-field performance."

I walked away from him then back. "I messed up one time, and you're still hanging that incident over my head?"

He moved his hands around as though he was conducting an orchestra. "Train. You broke someone's collarbone. And let's not forget he was the starting quarterback for Clemson. That kind of shit makes the news. That is also the kind of shit you don't need. Otherwise, they'll pull your scholarship."

"Is this about Montana? Have you moved on from football to tell me who I can fuck, date, or marry?" I balled my hands into fists. He came here to give me good news. Yet all he was doing was driving a wedge further into our father-son relationship.

He scratched his unshaven jaw. "Are things serious with her?"

I seriously wanted to punch my old man at that moment. "What's this about?"

"Are you also seeing Nina?"

"Fuck no."

"Then why was Nina in the neighborhood?"

"Come again? You mean outside this house?" I pointed up toward the street.

He nodded. "When I drove up, she and a red-haired boy were getting into a white truck that was parked in front of our house."

I paced. The last I'd seen Nina other than in the halls at school was when she caused trouble at my beach party weeks ago. "I've had nothing to do with Nina. She swears we're getting back together. She's jealous of Montana. She threatens trouble. But she hasn't followed through on any of her threats."

"Well, let's make sure she doesn't cause any trouble for you again. Or Montana, either."

I pinched my eyebrows. "Wait. Don't bring Montana into this."

"Train, did you or did you not get into a fight with a guy because you were jealous?"

"Montana is not Nina." Although I'd wanted to cream Ferris when he touched my girl, but that was before we were dating. She wouldn't cheat on me. I knew in my gut that Montana wasn't that type of girl.

My dad rubbed his temples. "Watch your back. And if Nina is as jealous as you say, then watch Montana's back. Jealousy wears many hats, and the worst is the one that threatens your safety. And I mean your safety and Montana's."

I glanced out at the whitecaps in the distance. My old man was talking out of both sides of his mouth. "I thought you were worried about my scholarship. Now it's my safety?"

"Son, I know we've had a strained relationship. I know I ride your ass about football. But I don't want anything happening to you, and not because of the scholarship. You're my son. I love you."

I was a little tongue-tied. That was the first time he'd put me before football.

I lowered my shoulders. "I'll be careful. I should get back."

On our way to my friends, I racked my brain, trying to figure out what the fuck Nina had been doing outside my house. It figured that she was ruining a perfectly good moment, and she wasn't even there.

When we reached the patio, my dad swung his arm around my shoulders as though he was a proud father. "Everyone, you're looking at the starting quarterback for USC."

"Shut up." Austin vaulted out of his chair and threw his arms around me. "Congrats, man."

Then the line hugs and congrats followed, starting with Lou, Elvira, Reagan, and finally, my girl.

Montana jumped into my arms, peppering kisses all over my face. "I'm so proud of you."

"I got to run," my dad said. "I'll talk to you later, son." Then he was gone.

Montana slid down my body until she was standing. "You two looked like you were in a heated discussion. Like not happy talking, either. What's going on?"

I didn't want to go into every detail, but they should know about Nina. "When my dad drove up, he saw Nina and Drew getting into a white truck."

Montana stiffened in my arms.

Austin dropped into a chair. "Maybe they were visiting someone else in the neighborhood."

Reagan sat in Austin's lap. "Jan has a house down the street, but she's not friends with Nina."

"They always say you have to watch out for the quiet ones," Lou said.

"Nina's not quiet," Elvira added.

Montana sighed. "No, but her actions have been as of late. She's made idle threats. But maybe she's calculating her time or planning something big."

"What could she possibly do?" Elvira asked. "I mean without physically hurting us?"

"The woman is evil," Reagan said.

Lou chomped on a chip. "That might be true, but she's not the type to physically harm anyone. Come on. With the exception of Montana, we've all known her for years."

"Let's just keep our eyes and ears open more," I said.

While Lou was right, he was talking about the old Nina. The new Nina was not nice at all.

Montana planted a hand on my stomach. "She wants Train back, which means she wants me out of the picture."

I squeezed Montana to me. "No one is breaking us up." I would do whatever it took not to let that happen.

Chapter 21

Montana

ELVIRA, REAGAN, AND I WERE hanging on the front lawn before school. The weather for October had been mild, a little humid, and definitely better than the cold winters of New York. Students mingled with their friends as the three of us found a spot near one of the shade trees that dotted the area around the school. Since yesterday, I'd been trying to wrap my head around Nina and her appearance at Train's beach house. Up until then, I'd assumed she was all talk with her threats. Even though she hadn't done anything, I was creeped out by knowing that she could've been spying on us. I did like to put on a show. I didn't like people who spied on that show.

"So, what are we going to do about Nina?" Reagan asked, leaning against the tree.

I flicked my chin at Drew, who I'd just noticed was talking to a group of guys by the cement benches in front of the school. "Maybe we can ask Drew."

Reagan darted over to Drew and pulled him back to our circle. "Tell us what you were doing outside Train's beach house yesterday." Reagan was feistier than me. Her tone could have quieted a forest of animals.

Fear coated Drew's freckled face. "How do you know that?"

"Answer us." I sounded as if I was ready to bite off his head, and I was.

"Drew." Elvira said his name in a motherly tone. "We just want to make sure that Nina doesn't get you into trouble. Because, you know, stalking can get you in trouble with the law."

His Adam's apple bobbed. "If you must know, I wanted to ask a girl to the debutante ball. She has a house next to Train's. Nina went with me for moral support."

I hadn't seen Nina with any friends other than her little interaction with Ferris that first week of school. Speaking of Ferris, I had fired him the previous week. I wasn't comfortable around him. I didn't think he would do anything bad to me, but he was nosy about Train and about me. My mom had always said to follow my intuition. I hadn't taken on another tutor, either. If I needed help, I would ask Train. He would help me work through my math problems.

"Who's the girl?" Reagan asked.

A hand settled on my lower back. His ocean scent gave him away before I could react. Train kissed me on the ear. "Morning, baby."

I lifted up on my toes and gave him a chaste kiss on his lips. "Hi. We were just asking Drew why he was at your house yesterday."

Train skirted around Elvira and me to stand next to Drew. "I'm all ears, dude."

Drew looked even more frightened with Train beside him. "I was visiting a girl."

"Who? Melanie Schneider? Is that the cheerleader you want to take to the ball?"

Drew nodded.

Elvira and I exchanged a surprised look. I was shocked that Train knew Drew wanted to ask a girl out. If he'd been talking to Drew, then he could've been talking to Nina. Maybe he had after I left last night. A shiver rolled through my spine. I shouldn't have been jealous. I knew he wasn't into her anymore. He would freeze into an ice sculpture whenever she was near. Regardless, doubt niggled in the back of my brain.

"Melanie?" Reagan parroted with a hitch in her voice as though Melanie would never go out with Drew.

"She lives two houses down from my beach house," Train said.

Elvira sighed loudly. "I guess we were worried for nothing."

I didn't know if I agreed with her. Still, if Drew had been there to ask a girl out, then I would relax too.

"Drew, did Melanie say yes?" I asked.

He gripped the straps of his backpack. "She said she would think about it. Can I go now?"

We'd all been so engrossed with Drew that no one saw Nina coming. She slid closer to Train, wearing a miniskirt and a tight-fitting blouse. "Leave my cousin alone."

Train went ramrod straight.

I shot daggers at Nina. If she so much as touched Train, I would use my fists. I'd never punched anyone before, but I was willing to today.

Train casually loped to my side. "Come on, baby," he said to me.

"Train, I thought we could talk." Nina's drawn-in eyebrows belied the sweetness in her tone.

Drew scurried away.

Elvira, Reagan, Train, and I headed for the school's entrance.

"I so want to punch her lights out," Reagan said.

"It's best not to engage her," Train added.

Nina giggled loudly behind us, but the sound was downright eerie.

Once inside the school, we were about to bank left, when I spied two boys admiring something on the wall in the hall that led to the admin wing. I untangled my hand from Train's and hurried over to the wall. My jaw slammed to the floor.

Train sidled up to me. "What the fuck?"

Elvira and Reagan both said, "Cool design."

I hadn't shown them my tagging signature. I'd only shown one person my Spunk design, and that person was standing next to me. Train would have never done something as crazy and stupid as painting my signature on the school's wall.

"You said that you painted the wall of the gym in your last school. Right, Montana?" Elvira asked.

"I didn't do this." My voice cracked. Principal Flynn would automatically think I was the one who did, though.

"Does anyone else know that this is your signature?" Train asked.

"Wait," Reagan said. "This is your signature?"

"No one," I said to Train. "And yes, Reagan, taggers always leave their signature on any graffiti they do. It's a way for us to brag without anyone other than taggers really knowing who did the cool artwork."

"If you ask me," Elvira said, "seems whoever did this sucks."

161

I was too shocked to see past the horrible way the person hadn't stayed in the lines when coloring in the block letters. Then my vision blurred for a second. The color was green. I'd lost my green paint can. I still hadn't found it.

I clenched my fists. "Someone is setting me up."

"You can't go to jail for this," Reagan said.

"This is vandalism," I said. "And if the school presses charges, then yes, I can."

Train kissed my head. "They don't have proof it was you."

He was right. I didn't see this on Friday when we were in school. And I was with Train all weekend except Saturday night when I was working.

"Let's go," Elvira said. "We need to get to class."

My stomach hurt as we ventured down to computer class. "The only person who doesn't want me here is Nina."

"True," Train said. "But maybe Ferris is mad at you for dropping him as your tutor. He asked you out. You said no. Then you fired him."

All of a sudden, it hit me. "Ferris saw my artwork in my notebook when I was working on a math problem."

Train let out a low growl. "I'll kill the fucker if he is trying to get you kicked out of school."

I might have to help him.

The four of us walked into computer class just as the bell rang. No sooner had I sat down than the speaker crackled. "Montana Smith, please report to the principal's office immediately," a female voice said.

I swallowed hard as I clutched my bag then gave Train an *I'm screwed* look. His pissed-off expression didn't help untie the knot in my stomach. I didn't have time to check on Reagan and Elvira as I hurried out. Once in the hall, I inhaled some deep breaths to calm my pulse. Before I made a move, Train came out.

"I'm going with," he said.

I smiled at my handsome boyfriend. "That's sweet. But I can handle myself. Go back to class. You're my partner, so you need to take notes."

He bit his lip, seemingly struggling with what to do. "I swear, if Ferris is behind this..."

"Train, you have your scholarship to think about. Don't do something

162

stupid. Besides, we don't have the facts. The principal probably wants to see me for something else." I highly doubted that. I pushed him. "Go."

"Montana, you need support, baby."

I wanted to cry at how caring and protective he was. "Thank you, but I got this. I'll text you when I know something."

"Promise?" he asked.

I nodded.

We locked lips for a quickie, then he went back to class.

My sandals slapped along the floor, the sound echoing in the deserted halls. I knew Principal Flynn wanted to talk to me about the graffiti on the wall. What I didn't know was who the guilty party was. I'd taken a different route to the admin wing. I didn't want to see that wall again. But when I rounded the corner, I also didn't expect or want to see my mom sitting in a chair just inside the admin office, reading something on her phone. I gulped down air. *Nothing to be afraid of. You're innocent.* Even so, I had work to do to convince my mom I didn't do anything wrong. After all, she knew I loved to tag, and she knew my signature.

The admin wing was an open floor plan of cubicles that sat in the middle with offices surrounding them on two sides. A counter headlined the wing with a sitting area for guests on the left and mailboxes on the right for teachers.

Mom lifted her gaze when I entered. I couldn't tell if she was surprised, angry, or indifferent. I nodded to Ms. Jones, one of the admin assistants, who was depositing mail into the teacher's slots.

She returned the gesture with a flick of her black hair. "Mr. Flynn will be with you in a moment." Then she resumed her task.

"Do you want to tell me what I'm doing here?" Mom asked in a low and hard tone. "Because I saw something on the wall on my way in here."

"That wasn't me," I said.

"That *is* your signature," she returned with her mean-mom face.

Before I had a chance to say another word, Principal Flynn stalked out of his corner office. He was a hard man to miss since he stood about six eight with his large belly poking out.

I tried to read his stony expression, but I was coming up empty.

My mom rose, securing her purse on her shoulder before she tucked a strand of hair behind her ear. "I swear, Montana."

I was swearing under my breath.

Principal Flynn fixated on my mom. I almost rolled my eyes. She had an effect on men that always made them do double takes. She was beautiful, but I didn't care to witness men drooling over her.

She smoothed a hand down her crisp black knee-length skirt.

Maybe the principal was into her long, tanned legs, or maybe he was into boobs. Like me, Mom certainly had a rack on her.

Principal Flynn extended his hand. "Mrs. Smith, I presume."

I had the urge to snap my fingers as if to say, "I'm over here."

"Please, call me Georgia," Mom said, not correcting him that she was a Ms. and not a Mrs.

Small talk between them ensued as we followed the principal into his office. I tuned them out as I texted Train that I was going into the principal's office now.

Principal Flynn waved his hand at the two chairs in front of his glass-topped desk. The office was rather cozy with bookcases, filing cabinets, and plants giving life to the room.

He folded his bulk into his chair as he combed a hand over his dark hair. "I called you both in because it has come to my attention, Montana, that you could be responsible for the graffiti on the boys' locker room door and also the recent artwork on the wall down the hall from the admin offices."

I straightened. "I already told you, sir. I didn't tag the locker room door."

Mom crossed one leg over the other and began wiggling her foot back and forth. She'd always had that tell when she was stewing or thinking.

He leaned his elbows on his desk. "Are you sure? Because graffiti can warrant legal action."

Mom whipped her head my way. "Tell him the truth."

I wasn't too surprised that my mom didn't believe me, given my past history with graffiti and considering my signature was plastered on the wall. So I had to find a way to prove I wasn't the guilty one.

I ground my teeth. "I didn't tag the school. I—"

"Then how do you explain this?" Principal Flynn opened a desk drawer and produced a green paint can.

Well, there was the green paint can I'd lost, or more like left on the floor outside the boys' locker room, although he couldn't prove the can was mine.

"Is that yours?" Mom asked, her foot jerking faster than before.

The air conditioner was blowing from a vent overhead. Yet the cool air did nothing to dry the sweat beading up on my forehead.

Principal Flynn handed the paint can to my mom. "According to the name on the can, I would say it is Montana's."

Holy shit. I never put my name on my art supplies.

"Montana," Mom said. "Start talking."

Principal Flynn sat back in his chair, interlacing his fingers and resting them on his belly. "Let's start with the locker room door."

I cleared the lump in my throat. "Fine." I had to at least tell the truth to try to clear my name, even if the truth did make me appear culpable. My mom had once dated a lawyer who threw the word culpable around in conversations he'd had with my mom. "The night of the first football game of the season, I wanted to tag the locker room door. I had my paint cans ready, but then I backed out. Mainly because of you, Mom. I promised you. And my reasons to tag weren't worth me getting into trouble. I also heard something in the hall that night, and I got spooked and ran. I left that paint can, or at least my paint can, on the floor. But I promise, I didn't do it. As far as the wall, that wasn't me. Whoever did the recent drawing was sloppy." I'd never seen the picture on the door. "I'm not sloppy. Besides, I was with Train all weekend."

"Mr. Flynn," Mom said. "Are the school doors open on the weekend?"

"They usually aren't, but the cafeteria staff was scheduled to come in yesterday to stock supplies. Aside from that, the janitor unlocks the doors at six in the morning on school days."

"I was with Train all day yesterday and in bed at six this morning," I said. "Someone is setting me up."

"Who?" Principal Flynn asked.

"I don't know. Nina Morris, maybe." I didn't add Ferris's name. I wasn't sure if he would have been so catty as to ruin his valedictorian status because I didn't want him as my tutor anymore. But I made a mental note to talk to him, especially considering Nina had been chummy with him.

Principal Flynn wrote her name down. "Why do you think Nina did this?"

"Because she's threatened me. She's Train's ex-girlfriend, and she doesn't like that I'm dating Train."

"Should I be worried about this Nina girl?" Mom asked Principal Flynn.

He steepled his fingers. "Nina has always been an exemplary student with a clean record." He picked up his desk phone. "Ms. Jones, please find Nina Morris and have her report to my office." He clicked off. "I will get to the bottom of this. I hope, Montana, you're telling the truth."

"Mr. Flynn, Montana has an alibi for the entire weekend. When she wasn't home, she was either working or with her friends."

"You believe me?" I asked Mom.

"We'll talk later." She didn't give me a warm and fuzzy.

"Can I go back to class?"

Principal Flynn nodded. "We'll talk soon."

Yippee. I was hanging by a thread from getting expelled. I swore I would find out who was setting me up and clear my name.

My mom rose. "Montana, walk me to my car."

"Sir," I said. "How did you get the paint can?"

He smoothed out his tie. "Someone left it on the floor outside the admin office. We found it when we came in this morning."

Mom and Principal Flynn exchanged a handshake and said their good-byes.

I texted Train. *Almost done.*

He responded, *Meet me down on the football field.*

"Thanks for your time," my mom said.

Principal Flynn beamed at Mom. "It was nice to meet you."

Then we sped past the painted wall and out the doors to her car.

A lawnmower whirred somewhere nearby.

"Why didn't you tell me about the locker room door?" she asked with her car keys in her hand.

"You wouldn't have believed me. When you found my paint can, you assumed I'd tagged. So what was the point? I'm not even sure Principal Flynn believes me."

"This has your name written all over it," she said.

"I know. And I'll get to the bottom of who did it." I just didn't know how yet.

She grabbed the bridge of her nose. "You can't afford to get expelled."

"Mom, I'm not taking the blame for something I didn't do."

"Tell me about Nina's threat."

I kissed her quickly on the cheek. "I will later. I need to get to class."

I left Mom and wound around the school, down to the football field. Computer class should have been ending at any moment. I sat on the top row of the bleachers, enjoying the morning sun and thinking. I had a study period next, so I was free, but Train had calculus. I wasn't in any of his other classes since he was taking all advanced subjects.

He jogged up with concern swimming in his eyes. "What happened?"

"Don't you have calculus next?"

He sat down beside me. "Don't worry about me. I'm getting straight As, anyway."

If it weren't for the eagerness on his face, wanting to know what had gone down, I would've teased him about his good grades.

"Remember I told you I lost a paint can? Well, it showed up in Principal Flynn's office with my name on it. I don't think the principal believes I tagged the wall, but he's not convinced I didn't tag the locker room door. I gave him Nina's name. He called her down to his office, but I didn't see her when my mom and I left."

"He called your mom in? Wow. Did you give him Ferris's name?"

"No. I truly believe it was Nina. Ferris might be mad at me, but he doesn't strike me as a guy who is that catty, especially when it could ruin his valedictorian status."

"If Nina painted the wall, how did she know what your signature looked like?"

I puffed out my cheeks. He brought up a good point. "Nina was chummy with Ferris. So maybe he told her. I plan to talk to Ferris."

"Not without me," he said.

I was cool with that. "But don't break his bones. You have a scholarship to worry about."

"Someone cares," he said in a sugary tone.

I cared what happened to him… maybe more than cared.

Chapter 22

Train

I WALKED OUT OF SCHOOL WITH Austin.

"Dude," Austin said. "I think I should be there when you talk to Ferris so you don't end up in the back of a police cruiser. "Seriously, we have two games left. Coach will have a fucking coronary if you get caught. You won't play in the game on Friday. And your old man will have your balls on a platter."

At lunch, I'd filled him in on everything that had happened with Montana that morning. "Someone is fucking with Montana, which means they're fucking with me. Nina isn't going to confess that she vandalized school property even if she did. And Ferris isn't, either. All evidence points to Montana."

We dodged kids hurrying to their cars.

"You've fallen for her, haven't you?" he asked.

I released a breath. There wasn't any reason to deny it. I had fought with every fiber in me not to date girls this year. But Montana wasn't just any girl. "Yeah. I guess I have." Confiding in my best friend felt as though a weight had been lifted.

He shoved his hands in his jeans pockets. "Does she know?"

Austin and I stopped at a shade tree, the same one I'd found Montana at that morning. She and I had agreed to meet in the same spot. I scanned the area. No Montana.

"Well?" he probed.

"Not yet. And only because I'm a little afraid. She's got the full package. She's loyal, caring, feisty, sweet, sexy, and when I'm not with her, I feel lost. But please don't tell Reagan. I want Montana to hear it from me."

"My lips are sealed, dude. You know I wouldn't share that info with anyone unless you wanted me to. So when do you plan on telling her?"

I shrugged. "I'm not sure." I didn't know if there was ever a right time.

"You know what I think? You should tell her at the debutante ball. Girls love to hear how you feel when the soft music is playing and you're slow dancing with them."

I busted out laughing. "Since when did you become the love guru? Oh wait. That's when you're planning on telling Reagan."

He looked away. "Back to Ferris."

"Man, don't get all shy on me." I thought I would have been the one to fight my feelings.

He swung his brown gaze my way. "I'm busted. Okay."

At that moment, I spotted Montana and grinned.

She tucked her hair behind her ear as she bounced up.

"You look happy," Austin said to Montana. "Is it because of this dude?" Austin pointed at me.

"Maybe," she teased as she batted her lashes.

I loved the shy, flirty vibe she was giving off.

"Okay, man," Austin said to me. "I'll cover for you with Coach. Don't be long. And definitely don't ruin those hands. Remember, we have two more games." He darted off.

"He's right," Montana said. "Don't hurt Ferris."

I was about to respond, when Ferris stalked out, his black spiked hair glistening in the sunlight. "You wanted to talk. So talk." His tone was a little too sharp for my taste.

I fisted my right hand. "Don't be a prick. Montana asked you to talk. You said yes. So don't make it sound like we're forcing you."

He held up his hands. "I have to work tonight. Let's get this over with."

"Tell me the truth about your friendship with Nina," Montana said. "Are you tutoring her? Or are you spying for her?"

"I don't know what you mean," Ferris said.

Montana jutted out her chin. "Let me be frank. You're the only person other than Train who knew of my artwork. You know, the one the school's been talking about today. The one that someone painted on the wall near the admin wing. Did you give her my artwork? Or were you the one to vandalize school property?"

He studied Montana. "I did no such thing. And how would I give her your artwork unless I stole your notebook?"

Montana's blue eyes grew as big as the sun.

"Ferris, you better not be lying," I said calmly even though he'd had guilt written all over him when Principal Flynn had confronted Montana that day outside the library.

Lines dented his high forehead. "Or what? You're going to break my collarbone? Try it. I'll press charges. Then you won't play for USC."

Motherfucker. I got nose to nose with Ferris. His breath smelled of onions. "Are you goading me?"

He didn't back down. "Stating a fact, fucker."

Montana gripped the arm I was ready to swing. "Train, don't. He isn't worth the hassle or your scholarship." Her light and airy voice penetrated the side of my brain that said she was right. But the urge to break his large nose was tempting.

Montana then pushed Ferris. "Get out of here. And if I find out you're lying, I'll let Principal Flynn know that you're an accomplice, which should bring into question your run for valedictorian."

Ferris rolled his eyes as he marched off without a word.

Sweat dripped down my face. "He's lying."

"Maybe," she said. "But let things settle for a day or so. I have to get to work, anyway." She seemed too calm for someone whose reputation was on the line and who was in danger of getting expelled.

"Why aren't you freaking out like you were this morning?"

She peered up at me. "Because Elvira told me that whoever is behind the tagging or trying to set me up will make a mistake. They always do. But right now, Principal Flynn isn't expelling me, which means that will only make the guilty person try again. And I firmly believe that person is Nina."

Part of me agreed, and the other half of me said Ferris was the asshole causing trouble. "Then we should confront her too."

"No," Montana said emphatically. "We wait and see what she does next. She's cunning. You should know that."

I wrapped my arms around her. "I do. But I want all this to be over with. I'm tired of her making idle threats. I'm tired of watching my back around every corner. But most of all, it pisses me the fuck off that you're involved and taking the heat for something you didn't do."

My phone rang. I released Montana and checked the screen. Austin's text was in all caps. *GET THE FUCK DOWN HERE NOW.*

I showed Montana.

"Go," she said.

After a quick kiss, I sprinted down to the locker room. I didn't want to leave Montana, but she and Austin were right. I couldn't fuck up football, but I had to help Montana clear her name even if that meant confronting Nina.

Chapter 23

Montana

AFTER DROPPING OFF MY COLLEGE applications to the guidance counselor, Ms. Shepard, I headed down to the football field. Mom and I had filled out the college paperwork the night before. We had also talked more about Nina and how I believed she was the person setting me up. Mom had said something similar to what Elvira had. It wasn't *if* Nina would get caught; it was *when*. I was hanging on that cliché, but I also had to work more on Ferris. I would bet my life that he knew something. Maybe if I confronted him without Train, he would be more open with me.

Speaking of my swoon-worthy boyfriend, he and I had spoken right before I went to bed. We'd chatted more about college than about Nina, Ferris, or what had happened that day. He was stoked that I'd applied to USC's art program.

I thought it would be cool to attend the same college as my boyfriend. I giggled at the word "boyfriend." Nikko had been the last steady guy I'd dated, and that was over two years ago. But I was high on Train. My heart was on board too, although at the moment, I was worried.

Train hadn't shown up for school. I'd called with no luck. I'd also sent several texts but received no response. Reagan and Elvira had no clue. My stomach was in a ball of knots. I hadn't eaten. I was on the verge of freaking out. In history class, I asked Austin where Train was. He didn't know and couldn't get ahold of Train, either.

The odd thing was I hadn't seen Nina at all in school, which also made me think that Train and Nina were together. He'd wanted to talk to her, but if he was with her, she wouldn't have let him talk. Instead, she would have stripped him naked.

He wouldn't let her do that. I didn't know Nina that well, but she'd shown me enough of her personality that I knew she would do whatever she needed to do to get Train. And since he wasn't the type of guy to hurt a girl, he might not have a way to stop her.

I navigated the halls down to the locker room. Since school had let out about thirty minutes ago, the guys were probably changing. Before I checked the locker room, I stuck my head into Coach's office. Mom had heard back from Joey Dennison.

I knocked.

He lifted his head from his computer.

"I came down to tell you that Joey Dennison is in Europe. I'm sorry." Mom had gotten an email yesterday, explaining that he was on vacation.

Coach frowned. "Thanks anyway."

"Maybe he can help out next season." I didn't know that for sure, but I felt bad for Coach. His face had brightened when he found out that my mom had dated Joey.

"Sounds good." He resumed reading his computer screen.

I bounced down the hall, and as I approached the locker room, my stomach tightened. Maybe Train was having second thoughts about us, considering I attracted trouble, and he couldn't let anything jeopardize his USC scholarship. *Stop thinking the bad thoughts.* The voice in my head was having a jolly time, leading me to believe the worst.

I rolled my shoulders back as I entered the stinky room, my gaze searching every boy who was either stripped down to his skivvies or shirtless. The voices hummed but died when the guys laid eyes on me. Derek jumped off the bench and blocked me with his hulking physique.

I peeked around him to no avail. "I'm looking for Train."

He folded muscled arms over his equally sculpted chest. "He's not here." His tone was curt.

"Bull." I stepped around him.

He blocked me again. "Do yourself a favor and wait until after practice."

Sweet Lou, Elvira's new beefy boyfriend, sidled up to Derek. "Train is in the weight room, Montana." His voice was friendly as he glared at Derek. "Please remember that things are not always what they seem."

I pushed Derek out of my way, although he let me. "Nina's in there, isn't she?"

I kept my gaze ahead until Austin emerged from in between a bank of lockers, dressed in his football pants and no shirt. His blond hair was pulled back with a black bandana. "Montana, he's only trying to get answers."

Nina wouldn't give Train any answers, not ones that were true.

"Austin," I warned.

He slid out of my way, clearing my path to the door that seemed ominous ahead. When I glanced through the window, a knife went through my heart, and I lost my breath.

Train had Nina pinned against the punching bag like he'd done to me. I saw stars, bright and blinding, and flattened my hand on the wall to keep me upright. It sure didn't look as if Train was trying to get any answers.

Nina was touching Train's face as she batted her eyelashes up at him. If that wasn't painful to see, then her hand on his ass was enough to make me vomit. Scratch that. Bile rose quickly into my throat when I finally absorbed Train in nothing but his boxer briefs.

With my pulse beating loudly in my ears, I pictured ripping out Nina's thin hair, strand by strand. I didn't know what I wanted to do with Train. Whether he was talking to her or not, he was too fucking close to her, and that closeness was driving that knife further through my heart.

I puffed out my chest, pulled open the door with so much force that it banged against the wall, and stormed in.

Nina scrunched her face with a *ha-ha* grin.

Bitch!

Austin rushed to my side as though he would protect me. He cleared his throat.

"I told you guys to leave us alone," Train barked, not looking over his shoulder. His hands were fisted at his sides.

"I'm not one of your guys. I thought I was your girlfriend." I sounded as though someone was shaking me. "But I see I was wrong."

He flew backward, zeroing in on me with panic swimming in his eyes. "It's not what you think."

I swept my gaze over him from head to toe, relieved that at least he didn't have an erection like he'd had with me. "What is it, then? Is shoving your body against your ex your way of getting answers? What's next? You rescue Nina from drowning then take her to bed to make her talk?"

I wanted to erase the satisfied smirk on Nina's face. *Bitch!*

Austin rushed over to hop on a treadmill, which seemed odd until Coach Holmes's voice rang loudly in my ears.

"What's going on?" Coach asked from behind me. "And Everly, why the fuck are you practically naked with two girls in here? Don't answer that. I'll deal with you in a minute. First"—he wagged a gnarly finger at me then Nina—"get out. If I see either of you in here again, I'll have you suspended."

I swallowed hard, wanting nothing more than to scream bloody murder at Train, Nina, and myself. I wasn't about to get suspended over a boy. I would rather get kicked out of school for anything else. I had so many conflicting emotions barreling through me. I believed Train wanted to help clear my name. I believed he didn't want anything to do with Nina. But I was deeply hurt by the way he was trying to get Nina to talk. Giving into her desires wasn't a way to get answers. *You did the same to him when you brought him over your house and used your sexuality to get answers.* But neither of us was in a relationship with anyone else.

Shut up! I screamed at my conscience. Then I laughed to myself. I was halfway to crazy. I glared at Train hard, trying to keep my sanity, my dignity, and from bawling my eyes out. I straightened my spine and walked out. As soon as I crossed the threshold, several pairs of eyes were on me. Some guys looked as though they wanted to console me, while others were shaking their heads.

"I'm sorry," Derek said as I passed him.

Once I made it out to the bright sunshine, I shuddered, trying to hold back tears. But my tears dried up when heels prodded behind me.

"Train doesn't want you." Nina's voice was sure and so flipping loud. "Train and I got too much history to throw away."

Her cousin Drew might have been shy, but Nina shopped at a different mall.

I whirled around. "You threw away any chances with Train when you cheated. Also, I know you're behind all the graffiti in school, and you wrote my name on the paint can that you found. An orange jumpsuit will look good on you."

She held her head high, although a hint of fear shot out of her murky gray eyes. "You can't prove a thing."

"Watch me. And stay away from Train."

"He wants me. You saw him all over me." Her voice held so much pride.

I met her, nose to nose, with my fists ready to punch. "He was using you to get answers." I wasn't sure about that. "So again, stay the fuck away from him and me." I turned on my heel to leave.

"Bitch," she said.

Don't engage. Keep walking. I did one better. I ran home, my mind a jumbled mess. The image of Train's body almost flush with Nina's made me want to bawl my eyes out. I'd never wanted a boy to affect me like Nikko had, but my emotions were on overdrive. The act of pounding my feet into the pavement kept my tears at bay until I reached the house.

Mom was removing bags of groceries from her car. When she saw me, she froze, almost losing a bag. "What happened?"

I huffed out breath after breath. "Nothing." I took one of the bags from her then slammed the trunk, the act reverberating through me.

"Did Mr. Flynn find out more about the vandal? Or did something happen with you and Train?"

The minute she said his name, my tear ducts flew open. I stomped into the house and into the kitchen then set the grocery bag on the counter.

Mom came in a second later. When her hands were free, she pulled me in for a hug. "I'm going to assume it's Train since if your name was cleared, you'd be happy. Unless the principal is suspending you."

"It's Train!" I cried.

"Aw, honey." Her sweet motherly tone made me cry harder. She eased back and lifted my chin. "Tell me what happened."

I snagged a tissue off the desk next to the fridge. "I found Train with

Nina, like their bodies were almost flush together. She had her hands all over him. I know he's trying to help me clear my name, but he didn't have to be so close to her."

She started putting the ice cream and other frozen foods into the freezer. "Did you talk to him?"

"I didn't get a chance to." Even if Coach hadn't come in and Train and I had talked, I wouldn't have listened. He could've told me he loved me, and I wouldn't have heard him. Well, maybe I would've heard that, but I might not have believed him.

"Do you love him?"

I wiped the snot from my nose. "I don't know. Maybe." My stomach felt as though someone had taken a filet knife and carved out the lining. "It gutted me to see them together."

"Was he touching her? Did you see them kissing?"

I shook my head. "He had his arms at his sides."

"Honey, maybe it's not what you think. You even said that he's trying to help clear your name. And if Nina wants him back, it sounds to me like she'll do anything. Women have their ways of luring men back into their seductive web."

She had seemed to be doing a bang-up job, although Train had been tense, as though he'd wanted to punch her. Still, he didn't have to talk to her in his underwear or be so close for her to get the point. *That girl will never get the message that Train doesn't want her.*

I sniffled. "I hate feeling like my insides are being ripped to shreds. Why does love hurt? It's not supposed to."

She smoothed a hand over my hair. "Love will be worth all the pain with the right boy."

"Train isn't the right boy." *Yes, he is. He's handsome, sexy, he likes all my flaws, he can dance, he saved my life, he's a good kisser, and when he looks at me, I feel like I'm the only one he wants, or at least I hope I am.*

She gave me a weak smile. "Don't give up on him, Montana. Your emotions are tender right now. Let things die down."

Maybe she was right. "I should get ready for work. Thank you, Mom."

She kissed me on the forehead. "I love you."

"Ditto," I said as I went up to my room.

After I dried my tears, freshened up, and changed into a red sundress and black sandals, I went down to the kitchen, where Mom was finishing unpacking groceries. "I'm off to work. Do I look okay?" My eyes were puffy.

"Beautiful," she said. "Work will take your mind off things. Now, be careful. Oh, and Montana, I know when you get upset, you tend to do things that get you in trouble." Her tone held a warning. "Promise me you won't tag or do something stupid."

I hadn't even considered tagging, although she was right. "I promised you I wouldn't." But maybe it was time to break some rules. Then we would move again, and all the high school drama, including Train, would be a speck on a map.

Ten minutes later, I parked my car downtown and headed up the street to the art gallery. Dusk crawled through the streets of Charleston, and people strolled along as if they didn't have a care in the world. I wished I didn't have anything to care about, but sadly, I couldn't get my mind off of Train and my mom's question. Did I love Train? He did make my stomach flutter. One look into his sea-green eyes, and I was a pile of mush. Not only that, but he made me want to punch him and kiss him at the same time. I didn't know if love was any of those things.

I was a block from the gallery when my phone rang. I fumbled for it in my bag. When I got my hands on my cell, the ringing ended. A moment later, a message on the screen showed I had missed a call from Train. I waited a second to see if he would leave a message. When one didn't register, I shoved the phone back in my bag. I didn't have time to talk anyway, and I wasn't in the mood, either.

Carol, my manager, greeted me with a nod over her reading glasses when I breezed in. A sip-and-paint session wasn't on the schedule. So I set to work, helping customers with any questions they had about the various paintings and pictures that peppered the walls around the gallery. My two-hour shift actually flew by. I was thankful for the distraction from school, Nina, and Train, although, if I were being honest, I wanted to call Train. I wanted to ask him all sorts of questions. *Why weren't you in school? Why didn't you answer your phone?*

When my shift finally ended, Carol came out of her office. "Montana, I'll see you tomorrow night for the sip-and-draw event."

If I'm not dead from heartbreak. "Sure," I said before heading into the humid night.

On the way to my car, I passed by an alley and heard two people arguing. Normally, I didn't venture into alleys, but the guy's voice sounded scarily familiar, as did that of the girl he was arguing with.

As I padded down the dead-end path, a muted light from the building on my right illuminated the area, and the faint smell of garbage tickled my nose. The deeper I got, the more my eyes opened, not only at the sound of their voices, but at the fact that the guy was tagging the building on my left.

I stopped midway to admire his work until I realized he was painting my flipping signature—Spunk. Only the artwork was ten times better than the one at school. I tore my gaze away to find Nina standing close by.

"Are you following me?" Nina asked.

I glanced past her to the guy with dark spiked hair. "Ferris?"

I was too frozen to do anything, when Nina pushed me. I fell backward on my ass as fury coursed through me like an angry cat who'd lost a mouse.

Ferris caught Nina's arm just as she was about to punch me.

I hopped to my feet, listing to one side before I steadied myself.

With Nina in his grasp, Ferris asked, "What are you doing here, Montana?"

I let out a nervous laugh. "Me?" The puzzle pieces were slowly falling into place. "You *both* are out to get me? I can see why Nina would, but you, Ferris? That's where I'm lost. Are you mad because I ditched you as my tutor? Or are you mad because I won't go out with you? And why this building?" When I walked past them to get a closer look at the graffiti, I spotted a paint can on the pebbled ground and wondered if they had written my name on the can. I picked it up and inspected it in the dim light, but I didn't see my name. I pivoted on my heel to face them. "I'm waiting."

Ferris's chest heaved as though he was ready to talk. Nina, on the other hand, pulled free from him and launched herself at me.

I sidestepped her, and she fell on her hands and knees, growling like a rabid dog.

Hmm. I was holding paint in my hand.

Nina jumped to her feet.

I pointed the nozzle at the side of her head. "Talk, or I'll spray your hair blue."

Her eyebrows shot up to her scalp. "You wouldn't."

Ferris walked over to her. "Tell her," he said to Nina in a gruff tone. "It's over. And I'm out."

"No," Nina whined. "She doesn't belong in this town. She doesn't deserve Train."

"Ferris," I said. "Do you honestly want to go to jail? Vandalizing school and now private property? Do you want to ruin your chances for making valedictorian?" I hoped one of those options would hit home with him.

He packed up his paint cans with the exception of the one I held. "This building is owned by Train's dad."

I gulped down air. "So you thought spraying my signature artwork would make me the guilty one? Like you did in school? And what? You think Train will find out and not want me anymore?"

Nina's body was stiff as a board. "Don't talk, Ferris."

I still had the paint can pointed at her.

Ferris tipped his chin at Nina. "I didn't do the one in school. She did."

"Argh!" she squealed. "Stupid boy."

I understood Nina's motives but not his. "What is she holding over your head?"

Nina moved an inch. I pressed down on the nozzle, letting the paint fly, coloring her hair bright blue.

She hunched her shoulders, stomping her feet. "I will end you."

I lowered the can but kept it directed at her. "Move again, and I'll paint your body."

Ferris glowered at Nina. "I needed the money. And you owe me my other half."

"I'm not paying you crap. You didn't even follow through on the school wall. I had to do that."

"Oh, so you did vandalize the school." I eyed both of them. "And the locker room door?"

Ferris threw his bag over his shoulder. "Her. Not me. All I did was tutor you, try to get you to go out with me so your attention wouldn't be on Train, and I shared your artwork with Nina."

At that moment, something occurred to me. "Did Ms. Shepard ask you to tutor me?" After hearing his confession, I got the feeling I had been duped from the very beginning.

He nodded. "Ms. Shepard did."

I didn't know whether to be relieved or not. Regardless, a smart guy like Ferris had fallen under the spell of a woman who'd probably ruined him and his chance at being valedictorian. Sure, the prestigious honor of graduating as the smartest person among the senior class was based on grades, but other factors also played a part, like not getting into trouble—at least that was the way my last school had handled valedictorian.

"You're such a loser, Ferris," Nina said with disgust.

I had to decide how to clear my name. Ferris's confession was great, but Principal Flynn needed to hear it, and I wasn't sure what to do about Mr. Everly's building. One thing I needed to do was somehow get rid of my signature that was splattered on the brick. I could paint over it. But my mind went blank when Nina kicked me in the stomach.

I bent over, clutching my waist, as Nina ran, screaming that she was being attacked.

Ferris started to run as well. "Sorry, Montana, but a girl screaming rape doesn't bode well for me."

I stilled for a second until I could get air back in my lungs.

"Hold on, young lady," a man's voice said from the mouth of the alley.

My heart raced. *Please don't let it be the cops.*

In New York when we'd gotten caught, we ran, but in that alley, the only way out was the street. "Never tag in alleys," the leader of my crew had said. "No way to run."

I didn't have to run, though. I *was* innocent, and I had to take my chances that the man would believe me. So I puffed out my chest and headed for the street. As I got closer, the man's tall stature became clearer and clearer. Train's look-alike, dressed in an expensive suit, materialized. Mr. Everly had Nina and Ferris blocked.

"She did it," Nina cried as she stabbed a finger at me.

The lights of the city streets sprayed a brighter light on Nina's blue hair. I snickered quietly. This type of paint wasn't water-based, so she would have a rough time washing the color out.

Shock and disappointment coated Mr. Everly's face when he laid eyes on me. I didn't know why I felt small under his scrutiny. He wasn't my father. *But he is your boyfriend's.* That was up for debate.

Mr. Everly glanced at the paint can in my hand. "Montana, did you paint my building?"

"Yes, she did." The words rushed out of Nina's mouth.

"No, she didn't," Ferris said.

I gave Ferris a quick nod as my muscles loosened for the first time since that morning.

Mr. Everly rubbed his jaw. "Let's go into my office."

Whether or not I was innocent, my mom was going to throw a royal fit. She'd warned me before I left the house that night not to tag or do something stupid. I hadn't tagged the building, but painting Nina might be considered stupid in her eyes.

I trailed behind Mr. Everly and the other two. When I rounded the corner, I came to an abrupt halt while several cuss words went off in my head. I blinked to orient my vision and determine whether the woman in the black cocktail dress with her blond hair on top of her head and her stunning face made up was my mom. I couldn't decide if I was more shocked to see Mom or to see her dressed as if she was going on a date.

An imaginary set of brakes screeched to a halt more at the idea that she was on a date with Mr. Everly, and certainly not at the fury shooting out of her eyes.

"Montana Smith." Mom's harsh tone brought me out of my stupor. "I'm very disappointed in you. You promised me."

"That's your mom?" Ferris asked in a very low tone. "Hot."

With the paint can in my hand, I appeared guilty. So her tone and words weren't a surprise. However, I couldn't shake the idea of her and Mr. Everly. "Are you and Mr. Everly dating?" She'd never told me she had a thing for him, at least not that I could remember. No, I would've remembered that.

Mr. Everly cupped her elbow in a gentlemanly sort of way. "Georgia,

I'm sorry about our dinner, but this will take a few minutes." Mr. Everly ushered us into the building, holding open the glass door.

My mom pursed her lips. I knew she was trying to keep from shouting at me.

"It's not what you think," I said as I passed her on my way in.

Once we were all inside, Mr. Everly flicked on a switch. Lights sprayed down from the high rafters above. Architecture-style desks dotted the room with a glass-enclosed office in the back.

Nina shuffled to a leather chair in a small waiting area adjacent to the door. Ferris did as well. Now that I could see much better, Nina's knees had a little blood on them, and paint not only covered her hair, but specs of blue dotted her face. Ferris, on the other hand, was wearing a pissed-off expression that could have scared a bear. As for me, I stood not far from the entrance, still trying to wrap my head around my mom and Mr. Everly.

My mom, smelling like Christian Dior, came up beside me. "Is this Nina?"

"Yes," I said. "And this is Ferris, my old tutor."

Mr. Everly unbuttoned his suit jacket as he leaned against a reception desk. "Someone start talking, or I'm calling the cops."

The squeak of the front door announced a visitor. Train sauntered in along with a gust of warm air. He honed in on me. His gaze was probing, deep, soft, and apologetic, until he took inventory of the room. Then confusion washed over him. "What's going on?"

"How did you know we were here?" I pushed down the butterflies in my stomach. The guy got me all mushy even when I was mad at him.

He flanked my right side. "I came down to see if I could catch you at work. But then as I was driving by, I saw you come in here." His eyebrows squished together. "Blue is a good color on you, Nina."

I stifled a laugh.

"Son," his dad warned before he stuck a glare at Nina, Ferris, then me. "The charges for vandalizing in this historic city can be quite steep. So I would suggest someone start talking."

Ferris cleared his throat, the sound echoing in the swanky office. "Montana is innocent." Defeat and regret swam in his dark eyes.

Again, he was absolving me of any wrongdoing, which was great, and I wasn't complaining. But if he'd conspired with Nina to hurt me, then I was curious why he didn't start by saying that Nina had paid him off.

"Then why do you have a paint can in your hand?" Mom asked. "And why were you in that alley?" Her voice held steady.

"I was walking to my car when I heard them arguing. And the paint is Ferris's. I picked it up to make sure my name wasn't on it." She didn't need to know that I'd wanted to spray over what Ferris had done.

Train chuckled. Nina gave him the middle finger.

"Watch yourself, young lady," Mr. Everly said.

"So you didn't tag private property?" Mom asked.

"I've been telling you I haven't," I said.

"She attacked me," Nina whined. "See? I'm bleeding." She touched her knees. "And for that, I'm going to press charges."

Ferris rose, hiking his bag over his shoulder. "I tagged your building. Nina tagged the school's locker room door and the wall. We used Montana's artwork, wanting people to believe it was her who was vandalizing property. Nina paid me a thousand dollars to get information on Montana while I was tutoring her. Then she doubled the money if I helped her tag your building. The money helped, but frankly, your son pisses me off. So I was glad to do it."

Train lunged, but his father pushed off the counter and caught him. "No you don't."

Train struggled for a second until I snagged his hand. I might have still been angry with him, but I didn't want him to ruin his college career, and Ferris could have done just that by pressing charges for assault.

Train spun around, his sea-green eyes riveted on me. "We need to talk." His voice was strangled.

"Later," I said.

"If all that is true," Mom said, "then I suggest both of you get your butts into Mr. Flynn's office first thing in the morning and confess."

"Yes, ma'am," Ferris said.

"Can I go?" Nina asked.

Mr. Everly wagged his finger at Nina. "Answer, Ms. Smith."

Her face reddened. "Fine."

"Both of you will do as Ms. Smith asked," Mr. Everly said. "You will also meet me here on Saturday morning and paint that entire side of the building. In the meantime, I will decide if I'm going to press charges. Is that understood?"

"Yes, sir," Ferris blurted out.

Nina didn't answer. Instead, she grimaced at me.

A muscle jumped along Train's strong jaw. "Nina, answer my father."

The girl was downright stubborn.

She flattened her painted blue lips together. "Fine."

"Good," Mr. Everly said. "Both of you may go."

They both rushed out as though the building were on fire.

A collective sigh bounced between Mr. Everly and my mom.

Then, as though nothing had happened, Train asked, "Are you two dating?"

Mr. Everly checked his watch. "We were going to have dinner."

"Can I take a rain check?" Mom asked. "I would like to take Montana home."

"Sure," Mr. Everly said. "Train, let's grab a bite."

Train gave me a weak smile. "I want to talk to Montana first."

"You'll have plenty of time tomorrow," Mom answered for me.

I wondered if she was reading my mind. I wanted some time to think. I'd been through a lot today. Hell, I'd been through more than my fair share of drama in the last seven weeks of school than I had all of last year. Sure, I'd gotten into trouble, but graffiti wasn't drama. I'd kept mostly to myself, and no one had ever tried to accuse me of something I didn't do.

Train pleaded with me, a puppy dog expression on his face.

I almost jumped into his arms, but my mom was nudging me. "Let's go, honey. Lawrence, call me tomorrow?"

Mr. Everly escorted us to the door. I barely glimpsed at Train as Mom and I walked out and into the balmy October night.

Mom hooked her arm in mine. "You had me worried for a minute. And while I'm proud that you stuck to your promise to me, I am disappointed that you ventured down that alley. You could've gotten hurt. And I don't care if you know them. People in this country die more by the hands of people they know. You need to make better decisions, Montana. Not only that, spraying Nina wasn't the answer, either. Bullying someone who is bullying you isn't how to deal with the situation."

"But she needed to be taken down a notch," I said.

"Montana"—her voice morphed into mom mode—"if Mr. Everly didn't hear Nina scream, then what would've happened? Things could've gotten way out of control. And that is my point. You got lucky that no one was hurt badly and that paint and a few scrapes were the worst of it."

"Mom, do you think that Mr. Everly will press charges against Nina and Ferris?"

"If I were in his shoes, I would."

The tables had turned. Seeing Nina and Ferris going through a similar situation like I had at my last school when I'd gotten caught tagging made me realize how bad I'd really been.

Chapter 24

Train

I SAT IN MY DAD'S OFFICE with my head in a daze. The day had been fucked up from the beginning. That morning on my way to school, I had taken a detour to my beach house. I wanted to confirm Drew's story that he'd been in the neighborhood the previous Sunday to ask Melanie to the debutante ball. She confirmed that he had. When I got back into my car, I was ready to call Montana to tell her I was running late, but I couldn't find my phone. So I retraced my steps, returning home. When I entered, I heard my mom crying. I bolted into the kitchen and found her on the floor. My phone and everything else became the least of my worries.

After a long trip to the emergency room, we discovered she'd sprained her arm. By the time we got back to the house, it was time for football practice. I'd planned to skip practice to take care of my mom, but she insisted I go.

No sooner had I undressed in the locker room than Nina stormed in. I lost my shit. I wanted nothing more than to tell her to fuck off. The problem was she'd never taken no for an answer and would have made a scene. She always had an uncanny way of disrupting the team's mojo, and mine, for that matter. More importantly, she'd given me the perfect opportunity to confront her about the graffiti.

Dad snapped his fingers. "Son, I've been calling you all day. How come you haven't answered? We need to sign the scholarship papers."

"I lost my phone." I still couldn't find the sucker. "And Mom sprained her arm, in case you want to know. She fell out of her wheelchair as she was trying to get out of it this morning, but she's fine."

They had a good relationship for two people who were divorced.

"Is she not taking her arthritis medicine?" he asked.

"She is. She was having a tough morning, I guess." My mom had more trouble in the mornings with her rheumatoid arthritis.

My dad shrugged out of his suit jacket then folded his bulk into the leather chair beside me.

We sat in silence for a good minute or two.

"Train." He said my name in his fatherly voice.

I fisted my hands in my lap. "If you so much as tell me who I can and cannot date, I seriously will freak out."

He leaned forward and put his elbows on his knees. "Chill. I like Montana."

"And her mom," I said. "What's up with that? Are you dating her?" It was weird to see them both dressed up, and the thought of him dating my girlfriend's mom was even weirder.

"We were going to have dinner. Nothing else. Son, I got a glimpse of your rage when you wanted to punch Ferris's lights out. That cannot happen, son. You can't throw down every time a guy you don't like pisses you off. And before you get all worked up, hear me out." He scrubbed a hand over the stubble on his jaw. "I'm not telling you this because of your football scholarship. I'm telling you this because I don't want to see you get hurt. I'm sure Montana doesn't, either. Please think before you lash out at anyone."

Cracking my knuckles, I blew out a breath. "I know you worry about me and my future. But let me find my own way. If I get hurt or screw up, then it's on me to deal with the consequences."

"That might be hard to do as your father. Something you might not understand until you have kids of your own."

"True, but I'll promise to not use my fists to settle things if you promise to cut me some slack." I wouldn't mind having a relationship with my father that included conversations other than football.

"Deal," he said as he let out a sigh. "Let's go check on your mom." He collected his suit jacket. "Oh, and we have a meeting this weekend with the coach at USC."

After he locked up and we were walking to our cars, he asked, "Do you love Montana?"

"Montana is different," I said. "She's talented, she's beautiful, and she makes my heart race every time I think about her or when she walks into a room. She makes me laugh, and she makes me do things I never thought I would do, and not illegal things, either. So if you call that love, then yes."

He grinned. "Glad to hear that."

I gave him a sidelong glance. "Really?"

He draped an arm over my shoulders. "Yes, son. I just want you to be happy. And I can tell she does it for you by the way your face lit up when you looked at Montana earlier."

I crossed my fingers that I could fix things with her.

The next morning, I leaned against my truck outside Montana's house. The air had a slight chill to it, which helped keep the sweat at bay, unlike last night when I'd tossed and turned and couldn't get Montana off my brain, waking up every minute in a heap of sweat. I prayed she would hear my side of things.

The front door opened.

I lifted my head and locked eyes with the girl who'd stolen my breath on the first day of school. Her beautiful face was blank, as if she didn't even see me. Suddenly, I didn't know what to say. I'd planned a whole speech last night.

Montana, I am an idiot. What you witnessed yesterday wasn't what it looked like.

But as I watched her long bare legs eat up the distance between us, I again lost my breath—not only because of her legs, or the waves and waves of blond hair that felt soft between my fingers, or those pinkish lips that had turned blue when I saved her in the ocean, or the way her body felt against mine when we'd danced in my room. I lost my breath because I knew without a doubt that she had my heart in the palm of her hand. Sure, I'd told my dad and Austin I loved her, but at that moment, the realization became even clearer.

"You're a little early," she said. "The trash man doesn't come until next week." She hiked her bag higher on her shoulder and breezed past me in cute shorts and wedge sandals.

I hurried up to her. "I deserved that. But can we talk?"

She kept her head down. "Nah. You showed me enough yesterday."

"Yeah, about that..."

She stopped and peered up at me. "I'm mad at you."

Man, I wanted to kiss the pout off her face. "I'm a moron. What you saw yesterday was me trying to control a bad situation. When Nina came into the locker room, I saw red. She wouldn't get out, and she wouldn't leave me alone, and she was making a scene. So I brought her into the weight room to talk to her. And I thought it was a perfect opportunity to try to get her to confess." I had threatened her by telling her the school could press charges for vandalizing. That part had gone over her head. "But all she tried to do was kiss me and get me to touch her. I tried every angle I could without hurting her. The only thing I could do was corner her to make her listen. I know what you saw looked bad, but I promise on my grandfather's grave that I did not engage in any physical actions with her other than breathing on her."

Montana let out a wild laugh. "Looked to me like you were trying to hump her. And why were you in your underwear?"

"I wasn't thinking. You've got to believe me." I would have gotten down on my knees and begged if Montana wanted me to.

She puckered her plump lips. "Why weren't you in school yesterday? And how come you didn't answer your phone?"

I backed away slightly, when all I wanted to do was pull her to me and hold her. "Things got crazy yesterday. I went over to Melanie's house because I wanted to confirm Drew's story, but then I lost my phone, and my mom fell. I had to take her to the emergency room."

Several emotions flickered across Montana's rosy cheeks. The one that resonated the most was regret. "I'm sorry about your mom. Is she okay?" Her voice was soft, but that hard glint in her eyes hadn't gone away.

"In pain but okay."

She lowered her shoulders. "A lot happened yesterday, and I haven't gotten my brain around all of it. Oh wait, I haven't gotten the image of you in your briefs almost plastered against Nina out of my head." She huffed as she put one foot in front of the other.

"Montana, please. Hear me out."

She pivoted on her wedge heel and stomped back to me. Then she poked me in the chest with her finger. "I'm not ready to listen to how Nina had her hands on you. You could've backed off. And you only did that when I walked in. What if I hadn't shown up? Huh? What would've happened then?" Her little nostrils flared.

"I was about to leave when you came in. I swear."

"Seems to me you only added fuel to her fire. Plus, she'll probably try to grope you again now that you gave her an opening."

"Montana, baby."

She stuck her nose up in the air and turned to leave.

"I can give you a ride." I would have done anything to keep us talking.

She didn't look back, wave, or anything.

Her neighbor across the street chuckled. "Women, right?" the middle-aged businessman said.

Okay, she didn't say we were through or that she didn't want to see me anymore. So I had hope, and I wasn't giving up.

As I trekked back to my Hummer, I had a thought.

Chapter 25

Montana

SPRINKLERS HISSED AS I PASSED house after house. The sound reminded me of the day Train and I had wandered down the golf path behind his house. That was the first time we'd started to loosen up around each other. Since then, our relationship had grown so much until yesterday. I expected him to roll by me or stop to offer me a ride again, but the closer I got to school, I realized that wasn't going to happen. My path to school wasn't the only way.

On the way home with Mom last night, she'd counseled me that today would be a better day and that I would see things with Train in a whole new light. But when I'd found him outside my house, looking all sexy and apologetic, it had triggered the image of him in his underwear while Nina had her hands all over him. And no matter how sorry he was or how much I believed he was sorry, I couldn't flip a switch on my emotions. I needed more than ten hours to process things.

Elvira and Reagan chatted as I approached our usual spot on the front lawn. Reagan had her hair up in a ponytail, while Elvira was sporting a headband that pulled back her short brown bob.

"Oh my God," Reagan said, biting on a nail. "I heard what happened yesterday."

"Which part?" I asked.

"Austin told me about Nina in the weight room and how Train was trying to convince her to confess her guilt over framing you when you showed up."

As I listened to Reagan, I debated whether to go back home. Rumors would be all over the school, and I was completely over rumors and whispers and all the other drama. I almost wished I were back at my last school, where I got lost in the thousands of students.

When the bell rang, I sighed. "Let's go in."

Elvira hooked her arm in mine. "Are you okay? You're mad at Train, aren't you?"

Since they were my best friends and I would eventually tell them about last night, I figured I would get that over with while we walked to computer class.

By the time we entered class, Reagan and Elvira were speechless.

"So I hope Nina and Ferris go to the principal's office today and confess," I said.

"Blue hair," Elvira said. "That's got to suck."

As I sat down, my heart hammered, knowing Train would walk in at any second behind us. Yeah, I should've stayed home. Maybe two days of not seeing Train would do the trick to get over what had happened.

The warning bell shrilled through the halls. Mr. Salvatore closed the door.

I glanced at Train's empty seat. Surely he wouldn't miss school two days in a row. Maybe he was mad at me for walking away.

Mr. Salvatore opened his mouth to speak, when the speaker crackled. Then a male voice cleared his throat. "Um…"

Reagan glanced at me. My gaze darted to the speaker above the whiteboard.

"Okay." Train's voice blared into the classroom. "Can I have your attention? Principal Flynn has given me the green light to steal a few minutes of your time to talk football. As everyone knows, we have a perfect record of wins going into the last two games of the season. We want to keep that record, but we have a tough matchup against Charleston High on Friday. We beat their asses in our first game, but by the skin of our teeth. They'll want revenge. So I'm asking everyone to come out and support us, not only this week, but next week as well. Make sure you bring your rowdiness and voices."

His Southern drawl sent warmth directly south.

"Oh," Train said. "One more thing. Montana Smith, if you're listening, I'm sorry. I swear I was only trying to clear your name. I went about it all wrong. Please forgive me. My life would suck without you. You're the only girl I want."

All eyes swung to me. My cheeks burned, and I'd never been one to get embarrassed easily.

Reagan clapped, as did Elvira.

"Mr. Everly," Principal Flynn said in the background. "That has nothing to do with football. Now get to class."

"Wait," Train said. "I just need to say one more thing."

Silence filled the room, while tears filled my eyes.

"Montana, I love you," Train said.

I became a statue in my seat.

Reagan tapped her hand on my desk. "Did you hear that? Wow! That was a cool way to declare his feelings."

Everyone in class began whispering with the kids next to them.

"Hey, are you crying happy tears?" Reagan asked. "Please say yes."

My tongue was glued to the roof of my mouth. My palms were sweating, and my throat was swollen.

Mr. Salvatore tried to lecture, when the speaker crackled once again. "Montana Smith, please report to the principal's office immediately," a female voice said.

Great. Train had declared his feelings, and I was the one to take the rap. I collected my bag and gave Reagan and Elvira a weak wave.

As I headed to the admin wing, I decided to take the hall in which my art signature had been painted. When I reached the end of the hall and made the turn, I ran into my mom.

She was dressed in shorts and a cotton top with her hair up in a bun. "Why are you crying?"

I beamed from ear to ear. "Train just declared his love for me over the school's PA system."

"That's great. So you're not mad at him anymore?"

"Maybe a tiny bit. What are you doing here?" She'd said she would call Principal Flynn, but I hadn't expected to see her.

"When I talked to Mr. Flynn earlier, he asked me to come in. He wants to have a group meeting with you, me, Nina and her parents, and Ferris and his parents."

Relieved wasn't even the word to describe how I felt about my name getting cleared. Now I was eager to see if Nina would get suspended or expelled. I wasn't sure if Principal Flynn had anything to hold over Ferris's head since he hadn't defaced school property.

Anyway, Mom and I passed the wall in question. It had been cleaned and had a new coat of paint. But the wall became a dot in my vision when I spied Train standing outside the admin office, chewing on the inside of his cheek.

He was cute when he was nervous.

"Hey, Ms. Smith." He nodded at my mom.

"I'll be inside," Mom said as she went in.

He shoved his hands in his jeans pockets. "Did you hear my message?"

"Maybe," I teased.

"Montana, you're killing me. I'm in love with you. And I said I was sorry."

"I know. Yesterday, I was so angry I couldn't see straight. Last night, I was in shock when I found Nina and Ferris in that alley. Then when I saw you outside my house this morning, I wanted to kick you and kiss you at the same time." Tears burned. "I'm just overwhelmed."

He picked at a strand of my hair that was stuck to my mouth. "You're the only girl for me."

"Why did you use the speaker system to tell me you loved me?" Not that I was complaining. I wasn't. And standing before him with his delicious scent and love in his eyes, I knew he was serious about his feelings. "You could've started with that earlier outside my house."

"Actually, I didn't know when the right time to tell you was. Austin said girls like to hear those words on a dance floor at the ball. But when you wouldn't listen to me, I had to find another way to say I was sorry. And as I was talking on the PA system, the mood felt right to tell you I love you."

Mom knocked on the floor-to-ceiling window, motioning me to hurry.

"I better get in there," I said.

"Can I kiss you?" he asked.

I blinked.

He flattened his palms on my face as his lips ghosted over mine. "I

196

don't ever want to do anything to screw us up again." Then his tongue was in my mouth, and I was melting into a pile of mush.

An hour later, I left Principal Flynn's office with a permanent smile on my face. He'd suspended Nina for two weeks. Ferris hadn't received any punishment from Mr. Flynn. Mr. Everly, on the other hand, hadn't weighed in on if he would take legal action against Nina and Ferris. Regardless, I didn't have to see Nina for two weeks unless she made an appearance at the debutante ball, which I would bet she would. Nevertheless, my life was looking up. My current mission was to show Train Everly how he had my heart in the palm of his hand.

Chapter 26

Train

I STOOD IN THE DOORWAY OF the Palmetto Country Club, the venue for the debutante ball. I was waiting with bated breath for my girl. I'd planned to pick up Montana, but I was running late. My mom needed my help with some last-minute details in setting up since her arm was in a sling. Montana had called to inform me that she was on her way with her mom. It was probably best that I didn't pick her up. Otherwise, we wouldn't have made it to the dance. I would've taken a detour to the beach house and locked us in my room for the evening. I couldn't disappoint my mom, though. I'd promised her I would at least stay a couple of hours before I snuck out.

Ten days had passed since I told Montana that I loved her. After that, life had gotten better. With Nina's suspension, Montana and I were able to breathe. Sadly, though, I'd barely gotten to see my girl outside of school. I'd had football practice every day after school, and last weekend, my dad and I had traveled up to USC to sign my scholarship papers.

Needless to say, I'd only gotten a quick feel of her curvy body during lunch or in between classes, but I wanted—no, needed—more. Lots more. I wanted to strip her naked and do things to her that I'd read in her mom's books. Yep, I was a reading fool. All of Ms. Smith's books had some great sex scenes that I wanted to try on the girl I was in love with. I wanted to experience them with Montana.

Austin and Reagan emerged from his truck curbside, where the parking attendants were helping guests out of their cars. They both waltzed up with Reagan's arm around Austin's. My best friend looked as if he had just stepped off the cover of *GQ*. His white-blond hair was slicked back, his body was dressed in a black tuxedo like the one I was wearing, and he had his everyday cheeky grin plastered on his face.

My gaze flicked to Reagan, who had a lovestruck expression on her face as she lifted her flowing soft-yellow gown to walk.

Austin snapped his fingers. "Stop checking out my girl."

"She's beautiful," I said. Austin and I had known Reagan since the eighth grade, and up until that moment, I'd never really noticed how pretty she was. Or maybe my attention to detail of a woman's body was in direct correlation to all those books I'd been reading by Casey Stewart, aka Georgia Smith. Montana's mom was a master at stringing together words and scenes. She described characters in detail and opened my eyes to the way people carried themselves and to their body language, their expressions, and certainly to the sexier attributes of a character.

Reagan blushed. "Thank you, Train." Then she ribbed Austin. "He can look but can't touch."

"Not planning on touching anyone but my girl if she ever gets here." I searched the other cars waiting in line for a parking attendant. I'd spoken to Montana about thirty minutes ago, but it felt like hours. I'd chewed about every nail on my fingers.

Reagan kissed Austin on the cheek. "I'm going in to find Elvira. I'll let you two guys talk about hot girls."

Austin and I shuffled out of the doorway and down onto to the wraparound porch, where I had a better view of the cars pulling in.

Austin removed a small flask he had inside of his jacket, when I spotted Ms. Smith's Lexus pulling up. I yanked the flask from him and took a swig of whiskey. The expensive liquor barely burned as it slid down to warm my chest. We could always count on Austin's father for his eclectic taste in whiskey.

Austin snatched the flask from me, when one of the parking attendants helped Montana out of the car. I lost my fucking vision and the ability to stand. Not only that, but my heart galloped so fast, I seriously thought it would jump out of my chest.

Austin rested a hand on my back as he wolf-whistled. "You're not going to make it. Are you?"

Shaking my head, I gripped the railing. "Not one minute."

Montana smiled at the attendant as she waited for her mom, and my heart soared to new heights. That fucking smile was enough to make my knees shake, not to mention the off-the-shoulder gown she was wearing that exposed her creamy skin from the neck all the way down to the swell of her breasts.

"Go, man. Don't let the attendant garner all her attention."

Adjusting my bow tie, I clomped off the porch and down the steps. When I did, her gaze darted my way, and her smile got even bigger. I kept walking until I almost ripped the attendant's hand out of hers. As soon as her hand was in mine, my pulse slowed a tiny fraction, and everyone around us blurred.

She gazed up at me with strikingly big blue eyes that oozed all kinds of love and lust. Yeah, tonight would be a night to remember for sure, and the icing on the cake would be Montana and me alone for the entire night at my beach house, provided her mom would give her the thumbs-up. If not, then I would have to kidnap Montana. But I dismissed that idea because before Montana and I snuck out of the ball, I would have a chat with Ms. Smith. After all, I would like to think I was a Southern gentleman.

Montana lifted up on her toes and pecked me on the lips. "Train." Her voice was breathy. "Where are you?"

I blinked. "I'm having a hard time breathing." I had to be honest. "You are so fucking beautiful. How did I get so lucky?"

"Well, you're not lucky yet." She winked, her long, long lashes sweeping her perfectly pink cheeks.

Her mom cleared her throat. "Shall we go in?"

I hadn't even seen her mom and still didn't since I couldn't take my eyes off my girl. But before I had a chance to escort Montana into the ball, Elvira's voice popped the bubble around Montana and me.

"Oh my God! I love that dress!" Elvira practically screeched.

Montana said something to Elvira, and the two started chatting like a record on high speed. I was left with Ms. Smith, who I now noticed looked very elegant in her dress. Like her daughter, she had her blond hair twisted up on her head, exposing a long neckline. I could see why my dad had eyes for her. Hell, I couldn't blame him in the least. I wasn't sure how my mom felt about my dad dating, but I would bet it didn't bother her since they were divorced and had been for quite some time. I, on the other hand, hadn't wrapped my head around my dad dating my girlfriend's mom.

I extended my elbow to Ms. Smith, while Montana and Elvira locked arms as they went into the ball.

She hooked her arm in mine. "Thank you, Train."

"Is my dad showing up tonight?" I hadn't had a chance to talk to my dad about the ball. He and I had football on the brain, especially since we were going to the playoffs.

"I don't think an event like this is his thing," she said. "He did mention he donated quite a bit to the cause, though."

I chuckled. "Not quite my thing, either."

Back when I was in the ninth grade and my mom had explained to me the basis of the debutante ball and how important it was to status at that time, I'd protested. I didn't want any part of parading around in front of the rich to say, *Hey, I'm a man now, and I can get laid.* She argued that the ball wasn't like that. But my dad and I agreed that the ball served no purpose. So my mom had decided to change things up, adding charities to the program while keeping the tradition of what a debutante ball had been for many years.

Montana's mom and I strolled into the party behind Elvira and Montana. The room was buzzing with soft music from speakers overhead, kids talking in groups, chatting parents with drinks, and the band tuning their instruments in front of the wall of windows that overlooked the eighteenth hole of the golf course.

Ms. Smith and I settled near a bar adjacent to the door, while Montana and Elvira vanished into the crowd of about two hundred.

"I understand that you're in love with my daughter," Ms. Smith said in an even tone.

My stomach did a somersault. "Yes, ma'am."

I'd said those three little but powerful words to Montana, yet she hadn't said them to me. Granted, she'd been super mad at me the day I'd told her, and we hadn't been together since except for school. I suspected she was struggling with how or when to say she loved me. I shouldn't have been so presumptuous to think she would say "I love you," but there was no doubt in my mind that she had feelings for me.

"So, Ms. Smith, can I steal your daughter for the evening?"

She gave me a sidelong glance. "You mean sleep with my daughter."

I pulled on my bow tie. The damn thing was about to strangle me. "I wasn't born yesterday. And let's not forget I write about hookups."

"I'll be honest, then. I'm asking your permission to spend the night with Montana. And it's not just a hookup."

She studied me, partly with curiosity and partly with motherly concern. "You have my permission, but break her heart, and I will do my best to cast you as a creep in one of my books. Oh, and I will make sure readers know who the creepy character is based on."

I grinned like an ass, when I should've been shaking like a fucking leaf. "I have every intention of making sure her heart never gets broken."

"Then show Montana how much you love her." She gave me a cheeky smile, when my mom popped out of nowhere.

My mom adjusted her sling over her black knee-length dress. "Georgia, is my son talking your ear off?"

Nah. Ms. Smith is giving me ample warning not to hurt her daughter, or else she will have my balls splattered all over the pages of her novels.

"Train, please fix your tie," my mom said as she set her brown gaze on me.

I adjusted the noose, or what felt like a noose, then kissed her on the cheek. "I'm going to find Montana." I weaved through the guests as a soft beat of music began playing from the band.

I found Montana, Austin, and Reagan standing at a table near the dance floor. Montana cuddled up to my side, threading her fingers with mine. With my thumb, I traced circles on Montana's hand. Then Derek and his girl, Jan, joined us. Like the rest of us, Derek donned a tux and had his brown locks combed behind his ears, while Jan wore a simple short black dress with her blond hair in an updo similar to Montana's. The only ones in our gang not present were Elvira and Lou. I spied them dancing. I chuckled as I watched Lou, big and wide, trying to wiggle his hips to the upbeat song. Everyone in the circle followed my line of sight.

"That's just wrong," Derek said. "Lou is not meant to dance."

All of us chuckled.

"I guess that girl Melanie said yes to Drew after all," Montana said. Next to Lou and Elvira, carrottopped Drew looked awkward as he held onto Melanie's hips as though he was afraid to get too close. The petite girl appeared equally uncomfortable. I was happy for Drew, though, that Melanie had said yes to him. He might have been related to Nina, but he didn't have any of her cunning ways.

I was about to kiss my girl, when Ferris's spiked head of hair bobbed up to us. He hadn't gotten suspended like Nina had, but my dad had pressed charges against both of them. He'd felt that Nina and Ferris needed to learn that every action has a consequence.

"I still can't believe your dad pressed charges against them," Montana said.

I wasn't surprised at all. My dad had worked hard to build his contracting business, and he couldn't allow anyone to get away with something they'd done to not only take money out of his pocket but to break the law in the process.

Ferris gave all of us a tentative smile. "Train, is your dad here? I need to talk to him."

"No. What's up?" I asked.

"My dad wants to settle my case before it goes before a judge," Ferris said.

I wasn't getting involved. "Well, you'll have to call him."

"Montana," Ferris said. "Again, I'm sorry for conspiring with Nina to make it look like you were the one to spray graffiti at school and on Mr. Everly's building. If you do need some help with math, I'll be glad to help."

Montana leaned into me. "I accepted your apology in the principal's office the other day. So you don't need to keep apologizing. And as far as a tutor, I'm good. Train helps me when I have a question."

I glanced past Ferris and tensed.

"What is it?" Austin asked.

Nina weaved through the crowd, beelining toward us. She wore a proud smile as though she had some great news she was dying to share.

Montana swore under her breath. "We should consider a restraining order."

Reagan giggled. "Or I could sew her mouth shut."

Ferris even swore. "I'm out of here." He got lost among the swarm of people.

Not a bad idea, but before I could whisk Montana away, Nina was standing in our group.

The song ended, and Elvira and Lou came over. Another song started, but none of us moved as we stared at the girl who reminded me of a Smurf with her blue hair.

"Are you here to cause trouble?" Elvira asked.

Nina fixated on me, while Montana held steady in my embrace. "Train, can I talk to you alone?"

Montana snorted. "For real? When are you going to get it through your thick head that Train doesn't want anything to do with you?"

Nina's nostrils flared.

"Whatever it is, Nina, you can say it in front of the group." If she thought she was going to get me alone, she was smoking some powerful weed.

She pressed her red lips into a thin line. "Fine. It's not like all of you won't hear it anyway." She folded her arms over her chest. "Train, since I cheated on you last year, my life has gone to hell. I regret what I did to you." Her tone softened. "And I thought you loved me enough to take me back. But I was wrong, and I wanted to apologize to you." She sounded sincere.

Maybe I was the one smoking the weed. "Why now?" She'd made Montana's life hell as well as mine.

Nina lowered her gaze to the floor. "Because my parents have decided that I would do better to finish my senior year at a boarding school. And before I leave on Monday, I wanted you to know. So do you accept my apology?"

"Is that your only apology?" I asked. She wasn't getting away without acknowledging that what she'd done to Montana was wrong.

Nina studied me, scanning my face. I didn't have to look in the mirror to know that I had to be wearing a hard, mean mask.

Nina focused on Montana. "I only wanted Train back. And I would've done anything to get him back. But I can't have someone who doesn't want me. So I'm sorry to you too." Again, her tone was mostly genuine. After all, I'd known the many sides of Nina.

Montana straightened in my arms. "I wish you the best at boarding school. And thank you for apologizing."

There wasn't much else to say, and I wanted Nina gone. Apology or not, she wasn't hanging with us. I had other plans, anyway. "Thanks, Nina." Then I tugged Montana onto the dance floor, and even though the song was upbeat, I pressed my body against Montana's and swayed to my own music.

"That was awkward as hell," Montana said.

Understatement of the year. "But she apologized, and we won't have to deal with her in school anymore." That last statement loosened my muscles.

The night was looking up. Suddenly, Montana's body was flush against mine. The music, Nina, and our friends became history. My body sprinted to life as we barely moved, gazing into each other's eyes.

"Kiss me," she said.

"If I do, I'm not responsible for what happens next." I brought our joined hands down to rest on her chest as I lightly traced a finger over her cleavage. "You're exquisite," I said as I dipped down to kiss her.

She let out a soft moan.

That was it. We had to get out of there. "I want to be alone with you," I said in her ear.

The song ended, and we headed off the dance floor.

"Give me a minute," she said. "I need to do something. I'll be right back." She disappeared before I could tell her that I'd gotten her mom's approval.

Chapter 27

Montana

I PONIED UP TO THE LEAD singer. "Can I steal the mic for a minute?"

"We were about to take a break," he said as he bowed. "The floor is yours."

My stomach did a few flips as I held the mic stand, facing hundreds of people. One of my duties tonight was to introduce my mom. Lucy had spoken to my mom earlier that week to ask her if she would be interested in an author signing for her many fans in the area with the caveat that all proceeds from her books sold at the signing would be donated to the Feed The Hungry charity. With that in mind, Lucy thought it would be good for me to announce the details of the book signing at the ball and say a little about my mom.

"Your excitement about how proud you are of your mom will energize the crowd," Lucy had said.

"Can I have your attention?" My voice shook.

Conversations ceased as people drew their attention to me. I had no fear when it came to most things in life, but public speaking wasn't on that list.

I searched the crowd and found Mom. She and Lucy were sitting at a table to my left. Mom smiled, her pretty face lighting up.

I took in a quiet breath, hoping to calm the nervous nellies in my stomach. "My name is Montana Smith."

Mom sat up straighter as she placed her hand in front of her stomach then swiped up as though she was trying to tell me to take a breath. So I rolled my shoulders back and inhaled.

Then I slowly scanned the room before I locked eyes with Train. My stomach went haywire. He winked and gave me a wolfish grin.

I licked my dry lips. "I'm excited to announce, for those booklovers in the room, my awesome mom. Mom, will you join me?"

She smoothed her hands down her dress as she came up on the makeshift stage.

Someone whistled.

"I would like you to meet Georgia Smith, aka Casey Stewart." As I talked, I kept my sights on her. "She's a *New York Times* best-selling author and a best-selling mom. I'm proud of you, Mom."

Her eyes filled with tears.

"I know I've been a rebellious brat since I started junior high. And over the years, I acted out more than most teenagers."

"That's what we do," Derek teased from somewhere on my right.

Some people laughed. Parents shook their heads.

I'd had time to think over the last several days. The bubble I'd had around me for so long burst the night I caught Nina and Ferris in that alley. In some ways, I owed them a thank you. I'd always had an *I don't care* attitude even when I made my mom angry. I'd always felt that she deserved to be hurt for ignoring me. And whether it was Nina, Ferris, the warm year-round weather, Train, my new friends, or spending quality time with Mom, I suddenly saw things in a new light.

I grabbed her hand. "So, Mom, I'm sorry for putting you through years of stress. I've always known the difference between right and wrong. It's just taken me until now to admit it. And even though I've kept my promise to you since we moved here, I've never truly apologized to you."

She patted her eyes.

"Anyway, I'm getting offtrack." I faced the crowd. "Lucy Everly and I wanted to let you know that my mom will be signing books next Saturday afternoon right here at this golf club. The proceeds from that signing will go to benefit the same charity, Feed The Hungry, and Lucy will have more to say about the charity in a bit."

The room erupted in applause.

"Also," I said, finding Train, "I owe my boyfriend, Train, an apology."

His eyes were wide.

"Lou told me that things are not always what they seem. And he was right."

"Hell yeah." Lou pumped his fist in the air next to Train.

My gaze was unwavering from the boy who'd snagged my attention the first day of school. "I should've trusted that you were only trying to find answers to clear my name."

"Just tell him you love him already," Austin shouted.

Elvira and Reagan giggled.

My knees were trembling. "Train Everly, you're the only boy I want, and I do love you."

Our group of friends hooted and whistled.

Train stalked up, but before he could get to me, Mom gave me a hug.

"Honey, that was a wonderful speech." She eased back. "Thank you. I love you."

"I *am* sorry for all those times I got into trouble," I said.

Mom patted the area underneath her eyes. Then she flicked her head at Train, who was waiting at my side. "Go. You have my permission to spend the night with him."

An hour later, after our good-byes to his mom, my mom, and our friends, Train and I were parading through the dimly lit beach house and into his bedroom, where he closed the door. I made myself comfortable on the edge of the bed as he flipped on a light that sat on his dresser. He shucked his shirt before he turned on some music.

I swore that if Skylar Grey weren't belting out one of her songs, Train would have been able to hear my heart pitter-pattering against my ribs.

He pulled me to stand, then we started slow dancing to the music. It was the same song we'd danced to the night we had sex for the first time. The song might have been the same, but the look in Train's eyes was far from the same—soft, not desperate or scared, and full of love rather than lust.

He let go of me to unfasten the pins that held up my blond locks. My hair tumbled down. His chest rose as his gaze skated over me, while mine did a whirly loop around his upper torso then down to the strip of hair that disappeared into his tuxedo pants.

He gave me a sexy grin. "I thought my heart stopped the day you walked into computer class, but I was wrong." His eyes became hooded. "I love every inch of you, inside and out. "And I want to show you." Then his mouth was on mine, his tongue begging for access.

I opened without protest. When our tongues met, my heart opened up so wide that tears pricked my eyes. I wanted him as much as he wanted me. He moaned as he peppered kisses along my jawline then down my neck. I dipped my fingers into his soft locks as his lips wandered leisurely all over my face and neck.

I arched into him, dragging my nails up and down his back, feeling his taut muscles and soft skin. His arms went around to my back, where he unzipped my dress. I unbuckled his belt as my dress lithely fell to my feet. The cool air made me shiver but didn't stop me from undressing him. When he was completely naked, his penis standing at attention, I slid down his tall body until my mouth was face-to-face with his erection. Then I glanced up at him as his chest heaved. His eyes were hooded as he bit down on his lip.

I slowly licked the head. He flinched, grabbing hold of my hair. Then I lost all control as I grabbed ahold of his shaft, hard and silky, and closed my mouth around his erection.

He groaned loudly, causing my nipples to harden and the butterflies in my stomach to take flight. I loved hearing him moan and breathe heavily each time I licked then sucked. So I upped my pace and stroked the velvety skin along his shaft.

When I took a breath, he pulled me to my feet. "My turn." Then he slowly removed my thong, which was the only piece of clothing I was wearing since I hadn't worn a bra underneath my dress.

I shimmied out of the barely there fabric and stood before him, completely naked with my hair spilling down to cover my breasts. But he wasn't ready for nipple action. Instead, he teased and played with my clit with the tips of his fingers until he knelt in front of me and replaced his magical hand with his equally magical tongue. I gripped his head, mainly so I wouldn't collapse or fall backward. The faster he circled my clit, the faster the raging storm inside me swirled in delight. Stars floated in front of me. I spewed little noises, my breathing growing shallow. I opened my stance wider to give him better access. When I did, he slipped two fingers inside me. The combination of his tongue and fingers sent me over the edge. I screamed his name as my body shook.

Before I had a chance to register anything, I was on my back on the bed, and he was pumping inside me. He sucked on my nipples, one then the other, and with each thrust, I became dizzier and dizzier.

"That's it, baby. Moan for me," he said in a husky voice. "How does it feel with me inside you?"

"Amazing," I answered in a voice that sounded foreign to me.

Suddenly, he pulled out. "Roll over," he commanded. The firmness in his voice sent a wave of pleasure down to settle in between my legs.

I obeyed. Then, with his help, I was on all fours, a position that was new for us. He pushed inside me. He reached around me to pinch my nipple as he shaped my hip with his other hand. The sensations and feelings were too much, yet not enough.

"Harder," I said as I did something I'd never done before with a guy—I began to play with myself while Train moved in and out, his breathing getting heavier by the second.

I let out soft moans as I pleasured myself while he pleasured us both. I had almost reached a state of orgasm when, once again, I was on my back.

Sweat slid down Train's forehead. "I have to have those long, beautiful legs around me."

When I granted his wish, he thrust into me. As we got into a rhythm, his gaze locked on mine. "God, you're beautiful." His voice was strangled as though he was trying to hold back.

I slipped my hand between us and worked myself until we both reached that jumping-off-the-cliff feeling of flying into nothingness. When I arched into him, he grunted my name then stilled.

I giggled then kissed him profusely as though I couldn't get enough of him.

He lifted up on his elbows. "What's so funny?"

"You took several plays out of one of my mom's books. Didn't you?"

He grinned, his sea-green eyes lighting up. "Maybe the one where you were on all fours."

"Well, keep reading, then. Because I want more of what we just did."

He smoothed strands of sweaty hair from my forehead before he rolled off me and pulled me to him so we were facing each other. "You're not weirded out that we did a move or two out of your mom's book?"

I giggled. "Not at all. But you said at one point you had been."

He traced a finger over my cheek. "Yeah. But tonight, I wasn't thinking about anything but you and me. What we just did was natural and fucking awesome."

"I haven't asked you how you found my mom's book." I knew my mom's books were in bookstores, but it had been odd that Train showed up in computer class that morning with her book.

"I had to get CliffsNotes for English, and I spotted your mom's picture on a book in a store in the city. But enough talk. You're all mine tonight, and the only thing I want to hear is you moaning."

Every part of my body warmed as my heart swelled to huge proportions, knowing that I was one of the luckiest girls alive.

Epilogue

Montana

MAY IN SOUTH CAROLINA WAS as hot as the middle of summer. Then again, I did live in the South. The winter had had several days of cold weather, but I'd always laughed at those kids that came into school dressed as though a blizzard whipped around outside. A winter in New York would've been killer compared to the forty-degree temperatures that South Carolina experienced.

I ran to school, knowing that I would be soaked in sweat. I couldn't wait to share the good news with Train. I'd texted him to meet me on the front lawn. I'd wanted to tell him my big news on the phone last night, but then I wouldn't have gotten to see his face.

Cars of all shapes and sizes pulled into the lot, while kids loitered on the front lawn of the school, taking in the morning sun as they chatted and texted. We had one month left before graduation, and I was itching to get on with my life. I'd been the model student. My grades were better than ever. I hadn't had the urge to tag, nor did I have anyone trying to get me expelled. School had been easy and great without Nina around.

Elvira held her notebook in her arms and raked her brown gaze over me as I approached the shade tree we'd dubbed our hangout spot.

"What's with the happy face? Did you get laid again? God, Montana, you and Train are like glued together."

I stuck out my tongue at her. "So? You shouldn't sound jealous. You got your main squeeze in Lou." They'd been inseparable since the fall.

I adored Lou, who was always the voice of reason, especially when the football team had lost in the playoffs back in early November. He'd been the one to crack jokes at the after-party, helping all the players to release some tensed mojo from losing.

Train had been bummed even after the party, but his USC scholarship had overshadowed the loss.

Elvira blushed. "Tell me what's going on."

"Not until I tell Train," I said.

"Please tell me you're not pregnant." Her voice resonated with worry.

I snorted. "Hell no."

Her shoulders visibly lowered as Reagan bounced up. "Who's pregnant?"

I rolled my eyes hard. If she'd heard before she reached Elvira and me, then the rest of the crowd had to have heard as well. By the end of the day, the rumor would be in full force.

I checked the kids hanging out around us, glancing past Reagan's wide hazel eyes. No one seemed to be lurking in our direction. I grabbed Reagan's tanned arm. "Hush. I'm not. And it wouldn't be cool to start that rumor." I could envision Train going ballistic over a rumor like that.

"You two would make great babies," Reagan said, losing the freaked-out expression.

With my blond hair and blue eyes and his sea-green eyes and brown hair that lightened in the sun, I agreed that our children would be knockouts. But we had a long way to go before we crossed that part of our relationship.

"All right, Montana," Elvira said. "Are you and Train ready to submit your computer project?"

I let out an audible sigh, relieved that we were on to a new topic. "It's all wrapped and ready to go." Train and I had worked tirelessly on the author app that we designed for my mom. Her fans had been downloading the app left and right. In today's class, we were scheduled to present the statistics on the app and how it was working out for my mom's business.

"We should get inside," Reagan said.

"You guys go ahead. I'm waiting on Train," I said.

As they went in, I made my way to the edge of the lawn, where it met the parking lot. I was about to send Train another text when Ferris stalked toward me. He had kept to himself after Train's dad settled with him out of court. Ferris, or more like his parents, ended up paying a hefty fine into the thousands of dollars. Nina had done so as well.

"Are you ready for graduation?" Ferris asked, still sporting spiked hair minus the sideburns.

"I am," I said as muscled arms came around me from behind.

Train kissed my ear. "What's going on?"

Train and Ferris would never be friends, but Train didn't tense anymore when Ferris was around.

"We were talking about graduation," Ferris said. "But I do want to invite you both to a party I'm having this weekend. I know we're not friends, but I do owe your father a ton of thanks for not taking me to court. I was able to keep my academic scholarship with North Carolina State."

"Congrats on valedictorian," I said.

Ferris started for the building. "Hope to see you at the party."

Other students ran by as the bell rang.

I checked out my buff boyfriend. "We're going to be late."

His hair was damp. He wore his "Funk You" T-shirt, which hung over jeans that rode low on his hips.

I planted two hands on his chest. "I do love this T-shirt, although the 'Puck This' one is also my favorite."

He waggled his eyebrows. "What say we puck this school and head to the beach?"

"We have to present in computer class," I said.

He threaded his fingers through mine. "What did you want to tell me?"

Oh yeah. I dipped into my bag and removed an envelope then held it up with two hands so that the return address faced him.

He quickly scanned the envelope as his eyes went wide. "Seriously?"

I nodded. "I got accepted to USC." I'd also gotten accepted to the local college, but it was time that I spread my wings. My mom was happy and sad. She wanted me closer but understood that I had to start the next chapter of my life as an adult without her. Besides, she had Mr. Everly to keep her company. They were hot and heavy. And she'd written three books since we moved to South Carolina, so she had several publicity tours planned for next year.

Train lifted me by the waist. "Fuck. We do need to celebrate."

I giggled. "After school. We can go surfing." Train had been teaching me how to surf. I was also a much better swimmer, thanks to him.

"Baby, I have other plans to celebrate this awesome news. It involves you and me naked. Then we can go surfing."

We walked into school at the same time the last bell rang.

I didn't care how we celebrated as long as I was with him.

Dear Reader:

Thank you from the bottom of my heart for taking the time to read Breaking Rules. This book was a blast to write, and I hope you fell in love with Train and Montana like I did. If you would like to see more of the cast of characters in Breaking Rules or you just want to drop me a line, my email is susan@sbalexander.com.

Also, when you have a moment, a short review would be greatly appreciated. Your help in sharing this wonderful story would mean the world to me.

With love
Susan

Sign up for my NEWSLETTER:
http://sbalexander.com/newsletter

Come join my fan group, Maxwell Mania, on Facebook:
https://www.facebook.com/groups/maxwellmania/

You can connect with me:

Website:	https://www.sbalexander.com
Facebook:	https://www.facebook.com/sablexander.authorpage
Twitter:	https://www.twitter.com/sbalex_author
Instagram:	https://www.instagram.com/sbalexanderauthor/
Goodreads:	https://www.goodreads.com/sbalexander

ACKNOWLEDGEMENTS

First and foremost, I want to thank my fans, readers and bloggers. Without you guys I wouldn't be writing. You motivate me, you support me, and you encourage me. I'm humbled by all the reviews and messages I've received along the way. Hugs and kisses to each and every one of you for taking the time to take this journey with me and sharing your excitement.

To everyone in Maxwell Mania, I love the crap out of you. Thank you for loving my books and spreading the word.

The team at Red Adept Publishing is without a doubt the best editing team in the industry. Lynn, Alyssa, and Neila, thank you.

I can't say enough about Streetlight Graphics and for my amazing covers. Love you guys.

The publishing industry changes constantly, and without Katey Coffing's inspiration and coaching I wouldn't have come this far without her.

Kylie Sharp, Amy Korbel, and Jennifer Lowe thank you for all your support, feedback and advice. Love you ladies.

Tracy Hope, you are my super fan. You've read my drafts and every line I've ever written, even when it was rewritten fifteen times. You're honest in your feedback when something isn't working. You kick me in the butt when I need it. And you've brought my books to life with your creative vision and superb producing skills of my book trailers. Love and hugs!

Finally, to my main squeeze, Bill, you have my heart! Love, love, love you.

More titles by S.B. Alexander

To read samples and find out where to purchase all books visit:
http://sbalexander.com/books

-

The Maxwell Series:

Dare to Kiss – Book 1

Dare to Dream – Book 2

Dare to Love – Book 3

Dare to Dance – Book 4

The Maxwell Series Boxed Set – Books 1-3

Dare to Kiss Coloring Book Companion

The Vampire SEAL Series:

On the Edge of Humanity – Book 1

On the Edge of Eternity – Book 2

On the Edge of Destiny – Book 3

On the Edge of Misery – Book 4

CPSIA information can be obtained
at www.ICGtesting.com
Printed in the USA
LVOW08s0859230517
535498LV00002B/319/P

9 780998 915708